Christmas
Secrets
in the
Scottish
Highlands

BOOKS BY DONNA ASHCROFT

Donna Ashcroft

Christmas Secrets
in the
Scottish Highlands

bookouture

Published by Bookouture in 2023

An imprint of Storyfire Ltd.
Carmelite House
50 Victoria Embankment
London EC4Y 0DZ

www.bookouture.com

ISBN: 978-1-83790-694-9
eBook ISBN: 978-1-83790-693-2

To Chris
Without you none of my books would exist xx

1

HOLLIDAY

Holliday Harrison stood at the window of Christmas Lodge watching tiny flakes of snow flutter and settle onto the long track that joined the road leading to Christmas Village high street – the direction their visitor would arrive from. The three cabins that lined the edges of Christmas Resort's driveway were in darkness, aside from the sparkly red, green and gold lights twinkling around the windows and doors in the failing light. She'd visited the closest cabin – Reindeer Retreat – earlier in the afternoon to have it ready for their unexpected guest, refreshing the Christmas decorations and making sure the space was especially festive and welcoming.

Holliday heaved out a sigh as foreboding stirred in the pit of her stomach. 'I've got this awful feeling about our visitor,' she confided.

'Don't fret. It'll be okay, hen,' Bonnibell Baker, one half of the resort's management team, said in her soft Scottish lilt, coming up to stand beside Holliday and patting her shoulder. The older woman's curvaceous frame was wrapped in one of her trademark long red dresses. The outfit had earned her the moniker 'Mrs Santa' years before and the name had stuck.

'This place is so special. I can't bear the idea of anything changing...' Holliday flinched when she spotted the glint of car lights in the far distance, wondering if they signalled that the life she adored was about to end.

'I understand – and I'm sure nothing will,' Bonnibell said gently. 'We'll wow our potential new owner and he'll buy the business and help us to get it shipshape again. No one with any sense would change something that's been working so well for over twenty years. This will just be an investment opportunity for him, I'm sure – we probably won't see him again after this week. You'll see.'

Holliday mashed her lips together before brushing away a dark-brown curl that had fallen into her eyes. As the car's head-lights grew larger, she adjusted her velvet hat and smoothed down the edges of her red skirt before fiddling with the pom-poms, scissors and tubes of glue she carried like talismans in her white apron. As the resort's 'Art and Entertainment Manager', they were essential tools for Holliday's job and she rarely went anywhere without them.

'I didn't think Christmas Resort was supposed to be up for sale,' she said uneasily, squeezing a pom-pom between her fingertips as she watched a shiny black Jeep finally pull to a stop in front of the lodge. Her fluffy white cat, Frosty, darted from between the trees, the bells on his red collar jangling, and leapt onto the car's warm bonnet.

'Mr Gray has been hinting that he wanted to put the resort on the market for a while now. He wants to retire and buy a house closer to his children and the offer's too good to refuse, apparently. We both know the business needs a big influx of cash. It's popular but there's always something in need of repair, especially recently because we've had so many guests,' Bonni-bell said quietly.

'What if we say we don't want him to sell?' Holliday gulped. 'What if this buyer is all wrong for the place?'

Bonnibell frowned. 'That's not really up to us, is it, hen? Besides, there's no reason for us to stand in the way of the deal. We need to give the investor a chance. Who knows, he might be good for the resort, especially if he has deep pockets. It's not just the maintenance work, I've got lots of ideas for additional things we could offer guests, maybe even a new cabin or two...'

Holliday watched as the door of the Jeep flew open and a tall figure leapt out and started to shoo Frosty off the car with an impatient wave.

'You can't read anything into that, I'm sure he adores animals...' murmured Bonnibell. The older woman then sighed as Holliday sucked in a breath before walking to the entrance of the lodge and swinging the front door wide open.

Frosty scampered into the warmth, immediately disappearing into the sitting room to the right of the hallway where the resort's guests often congregated around the open fire and piano in the evenings.

Holliday watched the stranger swipe snowflakes from his hair and stride to the back of the Jeep before he pulled out a small grey suitcase and matching laptop bag from the boot. He stomped up the wide wooden steps onto the decking that was adorned with almost every imaginable shape and size of Christmas decoration. Holliday swore the man recoiled as he took in the festive scene before his expression smoothed and he turned to give her his full attention.

'Mrs Baker?' the man asked.

His low, sexy voice reverberated right through to Holliday's bones. A shiver ran down her spine and she shoved her hands into her apron again so she could squeeze another pom-pom, determined to ignore the sudden frisson she felt. He was beautiful. It was the only word she could think of to describe him, perhaps because her brain was now the consistency of a toasted marshmallow. His thick, brown hair had been swept back from his forehead and tousled, probably a result of him dislodging the snowflakes moments before. His mouth was full and there were creases around his cheeks and the corners of his eyes, suggesting he smiled a lot, or at least used to. He certainly wasn't smiling now. His jaw was angular and faintly square and he had a tiny cleft in the centre of his chin that Holliday's granny – when she was alive – would have attributed to something fanciful like an angel's kiss.

Holliday opened her mouth as her boss came to stand beside her. 'That's me actually. Please call me Bonnibell.' She held out a hand for his bags, which the man didn't hand over. 'Season's greetings with extra greetings because it's the first of December. Come in. This is Holliday Harrison, she's in charge of guest entertainment and craft at Christmas Resort. I've asked her to show you around and to get you properly acquainted with everything while you're staying.'

The man's eyes flickered slowly over Holliday's face and her red, velvet outfit and his eyes widened. 'Damon MacAndrew,' he said gruffly before abruptly turning his attention back to Bonnibell.

'Your cabin's ready but I've made hot chocolate and mince pies so you can have a quick bite before you move in,' Bonnibell said excitedly. 'I expect you're feeling peckish after the long drive up from London?' She winked when he began to shake his head. 'They're a speciality of Christmas Lodge.'

'Ahhh... I should probably take my things into my room first.' He looked uncomfortable. 'I've got a few things to do.'

'You really can't say no until you've tried them,' Bonnibell insisted in her most compelling tone. From fretful parents to tired children and grumpy grandparents, guests rarely refused Mrs Santa.

Damon paused, looking reluctant, before slowly nodding and walking inside. 'Well that's... certainly festive.' His mouth pinched as he took in the large hallway which had been swathed in thick garlands of holly and mistletoe, interspersed with multicoloured lights that twinkled through the greenery. Two huge Christmas trees stood like sentries on either side of the large staircase at the far end of the hallway which led up to the staff living quarters.

'Isn't it? Our guests absolutely adore it. We grow the foliage ourselves in greenhouses and refresh it regularly. Doesn't it smell so Christmassy?' Bonnibell exclaimed, before stopping to study him. 'This is going to sound strange, Mr MacAndrew, but have we met? There's something very familiar about your eyes...' She narrowed hers, looking perplexed.

Damon shook his head as he dipped his chin and carefully lowered his bags onto the shiny oak floorboards. He cleared his throat. 'I've got one of those faces, people say it all the time.'

Bonnibell chuckled. 'I'll expect it's those Hollywood good looks. You've got the kind of face we're used to seeing on the big screen.'

Damon flushed and glanced around, frowning. 'Is it usually this quiet? I'd be very surprised if you cover your operating costs. I might have to reduce my offer...'

'We only have guests staying for three and a half weeks of every month,' Holliday explained, waving him across the hallway and past the staircase, towards the kitchen located at the back of the lodge. 'This is supposed to be what we call our fallow period – it gives us time to restock, repair and have the odd day off. We're fully booked right through to the end of February – that's why we asked you to time your visit now. We understood it was quite urgent.'

Holliday's tone must have betrayed her unhappiness because she heard Bonnibell quietly tut and saw the edge of Damon's mouth curl downwards, and she instantly felt guilty. The man might be being critical about the business, but she wasn't really giving him a chance.

'I'll try not to be any trouble,' Damon said dryly, following Holliday into the kitchen.

It was huge and took up most of the back of the lodge, with high ceilings that had been decorated with garlands of poinsettia leaves, sparkly lights and tinsel. It always seemed to smell of freshly baked biscuits. The kitchen cabinets were forest green and the large stainless steel counter in the centre of the room offered plenty of space for food preparation. There were novelty cutting boards in the shape of snowmen and matching place mats scattered across the flat surfaces, adding splashes of colour and festive fun. Bonnibell grabbed three Father Christmas-shaped mugs from one of the cupboards and poured the hot chocolate, layering it with marshmallows and sprinkles, before doling out the drinks and offering Damon the plate of mince pies first. She indicated that he should sit on one of the wooden barstools closest to the counter.

'Dig in and then Holliday can show you to your cabin. I've got a special feast planned for later this evening, which I've invited the rest of the team to join us for. We're like a family here so you'll want to meet them all.'

Damon raised an eyebrow as he picked up a mince pie, his nose wrinkling before he bit into it. Then his expression transformed into one of pleasure and surprise.

'We usually sing carols in the sitting room after dinner, everyone joins in,' continued Bonnibell.

'Oh, I don't sing...' The man started to cough loudly and Bonnibell walked around the counter to thump him on the back before pushing his mug of hot chocolate closer.

'It's okay. It's not compulsory,' Holliday said brightly.

'You really don't need to go to so much trouble. I'm perfectly happy to look around the resort on my own,' Damon ground out, looking around the kitchen with barely disguised disdain.

'Oh, it's no trouble. I'm sure after you unpack and refresh you'll be ready to join in – it'll give you a feel for what we offer our guests. Holliday's going to give you the full resort experience while you're staying,' Bonnibell said. 'That's why you're here, after all. To really get a sense of what you're buying into. I heard you've had your heart set on owning Christmas Resort for years now.' She beamed and leaned forwards, her gaze intense. 'Can I ask what in particular appealed to you?'

'Oh I don't know.' Damon lowered his eyes to his half-eaten mince pie and Holliday saw his hands flex. 'I read something about it in the Sunday papers once.' He glanced around the room, looking unimpressed. 'It seemed like it might be a good investment. I suppose I couldn't get it out of my mind. I've got room for something different in my portfolio,' Damon continued, although his voice had grown more distant.

'Really?' Holliday asked, her tone sceptical.

'You knew the journalist who wrote that article, didn't you, hen?' Bonnibell asked Holliday.

She nodded without looking at either of them. She reached into her pocket and squeezed a pom-pom.

'We had zillions of bookings after it was published.' Bonnibell grinned, seemingly oblivious to the odd atmosphere. 'What we offer *is* unique. There's nowhere else in the whole of Scotland quite like it. Just look...' She swept an arm, taking in the hoard of decorations in the kitchen. Almost every surface shone, twinkled or glittered.

Holliday steeled herself and took over, watching Damon carefully for some flicker of connection. If the man was serious about buying the resort, surely he'd start to look enthusiastic any moment now? 'There's nowhere in the world that offers the full Christmas experience all year round. We've got families who return year after year.'

Bonnibell smiled. 'It's proved a very popular concept.'

'Um...' Damon sighed. 'Where did you get the idea from?'

The question felt like it was more the result of their eagerness to share than any genuine interest. All of Holliday's senses were now jingling like musical goosebumps were dancing across the back of her neck.

'My husband, Connell, and I got the notion years ago. You'll meet him at dinner later,' Bonnibell explained. 'It was when I couldn't see my brother over Christmas because he was working in the States and the air fares home at that time of year were astronomical.'

Damon nodded, but his expression remained blank. Holliday felt another twist in the hollow of her stomach. Something felt off. She knew from experience how fragile life could be, how things could get ripped out from under your feet with no warning. Was her anxiety due to this man? Or was it just that he was a stranger, a catalyst for change and a threat to everything she held dear?

'We realised how hard it can be to see loved ones in December,' Bonnibell continued. 'It's not just the cost, there are so many pulls on people's time. But book a break and you can have your Christmas anytime of the year. Families stay in cosy cabins bursting with beautiful decorations – we spare no expense. They can help to dress the tree, build snowmen, dance, sing carols, bake mince pies' – her pink cheeks glowed as she nodded at the plate in front of him – 'do all the traditional things together that they might not normally have the opportunity to do.'

'Even in summer,' Holliday interjected, still watching Damon's face for signs of enchantment. 'We've got all sorts of ways of simulating the true Christmas experience. Our guests are never disappointed, you'll be able to see that from the spectacular Trustpilot reviews.'

'It's true.' Bonnibell nodded proudly. 'Thanks to Holliday's help over the last two years, our guests have been able to make each other gifts and the week always ends with stockings in the morning, then a full Christmas day including roast turkey with all the trimmings—'

'Or nut roast,' Holliday filled in. 'We offer vegan alternatives to all our meals.'

Damon blinked.

The older woman nodded again and hesitated as if waiting for him to comment, looking a little perturbed when he remained silent. She picked up another mince pie. 'So that's how this whole thing started.'

'Right,' Damon said, looking longingly towards the hallway. 'Well...' He started to rise.

'As to how we made it happen,' Bonnibell continued and he lowered himself back down. 'Connell and I put together a business plan, and then looked for someone who'd be able to purchase the resort. Someone who had faith in what we were doing. It took a while but we eventually found Mr Gray, who was willing to be our financial investor.' She fluttered a hand. 'We've been running the resort for him for almost twenty years now and we're always booked for months in advance.' She gave Damon an assessing look. 'But I'm sure you're aware of that too? I expect you've done plenty of research or you wouldn't be here. Holliday will share the accounts with you whenever you want and she'll be able to answer any questions. I thought since you were a similar age that she'd be the best person to show you around.' She blinked innocently.

Damon cleared his throat and shook his head. 'That's not necessary.' His tone was clipped. 'I'm already sure this is going to be the perfect opportunity to add to my portfolio. I would have bought the resort without coming at all.' He looked irritated, which just added to his mystery. 'But Mr Gray thought it was important I got a proper overview of what you did here first. I told him it wasn't necessary but...' He glanced around the kitchen again with a peculiar expression.

'Well we're happy you came. I've a feeling you're going to love it here,' the older woman cooed.

'And you really don't want to see the accounts?' Holliday

checked as the jingles at the back of her neck started to jangle too.

Bonnibell gave her a silent look of disapproval.

Damon shook his head. 'It's really not necessary. I know everything I need to.'

'But...' Holliday began. What kind of person bought a business without checking it was profitable? They could be hiding all kinds of things, he could be buying into a money pit. Either the man was an idiot, or there was something strange going on.

'Don't mind Holliday, she's very protective of Christmas Resort.' Bonnibell winked. 'I value that about her, but I also understand sometimes we make our decisions based on our gut feelings.' She tapped her chest. 'I'm guessing you want to buy it because you love Christmas so much?' Bonnibell surmised, her smile spreading. 'Do you have lots of memories from the season?'

'Um... yes, a fair few.' Damon cleared his throat and then took a large bite of his mince pie, which made it impossible for them to ask him any more questions. He nodded and hummed his approval, taking an inordinate amount of time to chew before finally washing it down with the last of his hot chocolate. 'Well, this has been... charming. But I really should move into my cabin now.' He started to hop down from his chair.

'But we haven't had time to show you around the lodge,' Bonnibell protested.

'We can do that later. I'm sorry but I really have to make some urgent calls,' Damon said, looking meaningfully towards the door where Frosty was now standing staring at him. 'Ahh,' he groaned nervously as the cat started to saunter into the kitchen, making a beeline for him. Damon immediately climbed back onto the stool and frowned at the cat. 'I'm allergic,' he said, glancing at Holliday. 'To cats. They make me sneeze.' He pinched his nose and pointed to Frosty, who was now slowly winding himself around the bottom of the chair.

'He probably knows that, he can be quite contrary,' she said, staring at Damon, wishing she knew what the man was thinking, wondering if her cat was trying to tell her something.

'Perhaps you could put him in the sitting room, hen?' Bonnibell asked.

'Of course,' Holliday said, scooping up her pet and heading towards the hall just as Damon made a loud *achoo* sound. She paused at the doorway and spent a few seconds watching Damon as Bonnibell handed him a festive tissue and continued to chatter about the resort's many facilities and activities. But he just didn't seem... invested. There was something about the way he held himself, all rigid shoulders and stiff limbs, like he was holding something behind a wall, something he didn't want them to see. She'd felt the same when he'd arrived – instead of the usual gasps of delighted surprise when he'd seen the festive entrance, he'd looked... almost nauseated.

Holliday put the cat on the floor of the sitting room and squeezed a pom-pom between her fingers again as she gazed around. This place had saved her two years ago and she wasn't about to let it fall into the wrong hands. Which meant she was going to have to do everything in her power to persuade Damon MacAndrew that he didn't want to buy Christmas Resort after all.

2

DAMON

'That's really not necessary.' Damon hovered in the doorway of Reindeer Retreat as the woman dressed as a cross between Santa and a sexy art teacher unlocked it and wandered inside, motioning that he should follow. He stood on the threshold, watching as she paced the room, turning down the red and green sparkly duvet and plumping the cushions on the king-sized bed, checking the various multicoloured lights were flickering at the correct angles. Her hair was dark brown and she'd tied it into a knot and he wondered briefly what it would look like if she let it hang loose before shutting down the thought. He'd been up early this morning and was obviously suffering from some kind of brain meltdown due to tiredness.

'Aren't you going to come in?' Holliday asked, narrowing her large eyes as she studied him.

If Damon had to guess, he'd have said they were blue, although he hadn't got close enough to know for sure because she kept firing quick, suspicious glances in his direction and hadn't held his gaze in a while.

'Sure.' Icy tentacles of dread froze the pit of Damon's stomach and he had to steel himself before forcing his feet to finally step over the threshold. Then he dumped his two bags onto one of the fluffy snowflake-shaped rugs on the wooden floor, feeling faintly nauseous. He'd never expected to see this room again, aside from in a bad dream.

His stomach twisted as he had a sudden memory flash of his ex-wife, Willow, answering a message on her mobile four years earlier – flushing at the response as she sat on one of the sumptuous red velvet chairs that edged the open fireplace. Her silky black tights had been hugging her long, long legs and he remembered marvelling at her perfection and at how she'd ever agreed to marry him at all. He'd been so in love, so... stupid. Blinded by a shiny bauble of a woman who'd hidden disloyalty and faithlessness behind a gorgeous facade.

'The heating is on, but it's a little temperamental, so do you want me to light the fire too?' Holliday asked brightly, turning towards him as the lights that were draped across the ceiling illuminated her face.

She was pretty – not Willow stunning, but oddly appealing. She couldn't have been more than five foot two, but the set of her shoulders warned Damon she wasn't someone he should trifle with, that she'd perhaps sensed something about his story didn't add up. Her suspicious vibe had been ramping up since he'd sat in the kitchen in Christmas Lodge and he wished he could convince her that he'd rather be left alone before he gave something away. He didn't need her approval, but Mr Gray would get suspicious if Damon didn't at least get the full rundown of the place, so he'd have to play the game. He needed to acquire Christmas Resort. It was the only way he could move on with his life.

'It's fine.' He looked around, taking in the familiar decorations, the tree bloated with glittery ornaments, and the door at the back of the room that Damon already knew led to a bathroom. His mobile began to complain, indicating its battery was about to die. 'Sorry, give me a minute,' he muttered, pulling the phone from his pocket and grabbing a charger from his laptop bag before seeking out the socket hidden to the left of the bulging oak bookshelf. Damon quickly plugged it in and when he turned, Holliday was frowning at him.

'How did you know there was a socket there?' Her forehead creased, prettily.

Damon cleared his throat. 'Lucky guess,' he said, cursing himself for being so careless as she shoved her hands into the wide pocket of her apron and continued to stare. Had she sensed something was off about his response? He let a breath out when she nodded slowly.

'There are towels in the bathroom, toiletries, a hair dryer, dressing gown, slippers – everything you're likely to need for your stay.' Holliday wandered to the wardrobe and opened it. 'You've got your own fridge, which is stocked daily with soft drinks, Christmas cocktails and various nibbles, although I'd recommend you don't snack so much you spoil your appetite,' she advised sternly. 'Bonnibell is an excellent cook and you won't want to miss out. Also, if you don't eat everything on your plate she gets offended.'

'Thanks,' Damon said, remembering how he'd put on four pounds during his last visit to the resort, and vowed to forget the fridge existed. He glanced back towards the front door, which he'd left open, hoping Holliday would take the hint because it was freezing. When she didn't move, he made a point of rubbing his forearms.

'Dinner will be served at seven,' she finally sniffed. Her eyes dipped back to the plug socket and the ridge in her forehead deepened. Then she waved towards the open fire. 'Be careful, if you don't light it correctly it can really spit. One of our guests almost went up in flames a few years ago.' Her eyes glittered. 'We had a horrible time with insurance. Just something you might want to be aware of in case it didn't come up in your research. It certainly wasn't mentioned in the article.' She offered him a grim smile.

'I'll bear that in mind,' Damon said, stepping aside as Holliday made her way towards the door just as the white cat with the red sparkly collar trotted onto the Christmas tree-shaped welcome mat and let out a high-pitched miaow. 'Could you take that' – Damon wagged a finger as the creature blinked at him – 'with you, please?' His nose started to itch and he pinched it.

Holliday gazed at him thoughtfully before scooping the cat into her arms. 'No problem,' she said lightly, although her face betrayed the barest hint of impatience.

Damon watched as she stepped into the snow, waiting by the door until she and the cat were safely back in Christmas Lodge. Then he closed his door and leaned on the solid wood, thinking he was going to have to be very careful around Holliday Harrison while he was staying here.

Damon's mobile went off three times before he bothered to read the screen and saw the missed calls were all from Scarlett. His big sister had been trying to talk him out of coming to Christmas Resort for weeks and he had no intention of speaking to her now he was here. He switched off the mobile before tugging the soft dressing gown he'd put on after his bath tight around his chest. Then he draped the hood over his hair because the heating didn't seem to be working properly and he'd waited too long to light the fire after Holliday had left so the room had already got chilly. He wandered to the cabinet on the right of the room, peered into the rectangular mirror and pulled a horrified face when he realised the dressing gown doubled as a reindeer costume, complete with matching antlers which poked from either side of his skull.

'This place is ridiculous,' he complained, shoving off the hood and turning his back as a memory of Willow applying makeup using the same mirror assaulted his senses. Christmas music began to play from the corner of the room and he strode towards it, desperate to switch off the noise. That was when he spotted the snowman-shaped phone which was now flashing and wriggling its squidgy hips. He picked up the white receiver and guessed it was his sister before she even spoke.

'You're ignoring me,' Scarlett said dryly. 'You should know by now that won't work.'

'How did you get this number?' Damon sighed, slumping onto the edge of the bed and gazing into the fire, which was beginning to catch, throwing a soft orange glow across the floorboards and bed.

'Google. Then I spoke to a lovely woman called Bonnibell who told me you arrived a few hours ago – she was delighted to put my call through to your room,' his sister said brightly. 'How do you feel about being back at Christmas Resort?' Voices abruptly began to shout in the background and then Damon heard a clatter and a loud scream. 'Is there blood?' his sister screeched and he heard a young voice shout something, then a door slam. 'Your nephews are fighting again,' Scarlett said. 'Everyone's alive so I'm going to ignore them for a while.'

'It's fine, everything's fine.' Damon scraped a hand though his hair. 'They put me in the same accommodation.' He glanced around, the twist inside his chest palpable.

'Tough break,' Scarlett said, her tone distinctly clipped. 'Then again, perhaps this is an opportunity for you to finally face up to what happened with Willow, rather than just digging a new virtual hole and throwing soil over it so you don't have to deal with what's inside...'

'That's not what I'm doing,' Damon said tightly, getting up to stride around the space, still clutching the receiver to his ear. Everything was so sparkly, so beautiful. He remembered when he'd carried his wife over the threshold four years earlier because they'd been celebrating their third wedding anniversary and Willow had insisted. How full of love and hope he'd been, and what an absolute fool she'd taken him for. 'I'm just...'

'Eradicating Willow from your life.' Scarlett sighed. 'I get that. I did the same when *he-who-must-not-be-named* left me in the hospital with new-born twins, remember?' She swallowed. 'Which is why I understand how you feel. But I went to see a counsellor, got a new career and a boyfriend—'

'Husband,' Damon interjected, smiling when he thought of his patient new brother-in-law. 'I'm not looking to replace Willow and I definitely don't need to talk about her. I just can't move on while these memories are still...' He wafted a hand around his head. 'Out there festering in the world.'

'So you're going to destroy or change every special place you ever went with her, force them out of existence because you think somehow that'll make those memories disappear. Do you know how crazy that sounds?' Scarlett squeaked.

'Destroy is the wrong word for what I'm doing. I prefer repurpose. It's not that bad...' Damon stopped by one of the large square windows and peered into the darkness. Snow was falling again, huge flakes that had already added a couple of inches of white to the top of his car.

'It's the same thing,' Scarlett scoffed.

Damon ignored her. 'I bought the gallery where Willow and I first met and turned it into a beauty salon.' Now the gallery was gone it was harder for him to remember the moment when he'd first caught his ex's eye, the visceral reaction he'd had when she'd smiled. That memory had disappeared along with the expensive artwork. He swallowed. 'And the restaurant I proposed in,' he added quietly. 'I turned that into a deli. Now when I walk past it on my way to my office, I remember that evening but it's less tangible, less real... The waiters aren't hovering over the table where we sat, there's no one in the kitchen cooking the same meal we ate, or sharing the brand of champagne we toasted our good news with. I know you don't understand, but it works for me.'

'And the people who worked in that art gallery, or the restaurant?' Scarlett asked, her voice dripping with disapproval. 'What about them?'

Damon shrugged. 'I paid over the odds, offered them all jobs in the new business. Most of them stayed, the others I helped to get work elsewhere. The salon has a four-week waiting list and the deli's more successful than the restaurant ever was.' He leaned his head against the glass and shut his eyes.

'I wonder where all the artists who used to display their work in that gallery go now?' Scarlett sighed. 'And I heard the new deli is a little soulless.' Her voice was flat. 'That something important was lost when you shut the restaurant. I know you have the money and can do what you like – you've invested well over the years and it's paid off – but being able to do something isn't the same as doing what's right. You're playing with people's lives, Damon,' she scolded. 'Taking away their memories too. Putting your needs above theirs. It's not a good look.' She hesitated. 'I know about Christmas Resort. I looked it up. It's been running for over twenty years and it's beautiful.'

Damon screwed up his nose. 'Willow was cheating on me the whole time we were here, did I tell you that?'

Scarlett sighed.

'All I can think about is her sitting in this room texting with her latest lover while I was getting ready for dinner and congratulating myself on my perfect wife.' His throat felt dry and he opened the wardrobe and grabbed a bottle of cold water from the fridge before swallowing the whole thing down. The memory of sharing this same wardrobe suddenly ambushed him.

'What you're doing is wrong, Damon,' Scarlett said. 'What about the people who work there? This Bonnibell and her husband, Connell, sound like they love their jobs and you're going to take them away.'

He shook his head. 'I'm going to build a hotel in its place. It'll be bigger and better. The resort is getting tired.' He looked around. The room was clean but there were signs of wear and tear. Mr Gray had told him the resort needed an influx of cash and Damon had assured him he was ready to invest. He just hadn't mentioned that he planned to knock it down first.

'The new hotel will be stunning – I already have people willing to partner with me. An architect has drawn up rough plans which I'll be able to walk through while I'm here. I'm sure all the staff will be happy to stay. I'll give them new positions, pay rises. They'll be better off. I'll make sure of it.'

Damon blinked and his mind drifted to Holliday, to the way she'd glared at him. Would she be better off? Something underneath the layers of ice clamped around his heart shifted. *Guilt?* He shook his head, spun around and tramped back to the fire, turning away when he remembered kissing Willow in front of it. He glanced up, suddenly recalling the bunch of mistletoe that had been hanging there, and saw a fresh sprig. He reached up and pulled it down, threw it into the fireplace and watched it catch.

'You're stuck in the past,' Scarlett complained. 'That's why you can't let go. You need to build new memories, that's the only way to truly get over what happened. I've watched you wrestle with this for four years and nothing's changed. You're thirty-three, Damon. You need to start living in the present and dealing with your feelings. Willow's getting married again, she's moved on...'

'I know – and I bet she's already cheating on fiancé number two.' Damon took in a long, cleansing breath and let it out, exorcizing the memory of his ex. 'This is the last place, Scarlett, I promise. It's where we spent our final anniversary together. A few months before I found out what Willow had been up to the whole time we were together.'

He glanced at the bed, trying not to let the resentment overwhelm him. His ex had texted her latest lover from that spot when she'd been lying naked between the sheets and he'd been dozing beside her after they'd made love. He wouldn't be able to forget that until the cabin, Christmas Lodge – the whole damn place – had been razed.

The fire spat and Damon turned so he could watch the mistletoe twist then shrivel to ash in a crescendo of snaps and cracks, taking the memory of their kiss along with it. 'I'm doing the right thing,' he murmured. 'You'll see. I'll talk to you soon,' he added quickly before striding back to the snowman and replacing the receiver. Then, he unplugged the phone from the wall. All he had to do was get through the next few days, then he'd finally be able to put Willow behind him once and for all.

3

HOLLIDAY

Holliday inhaled the cold crisp air as she strode along the pathway that circled most of the resort's cabins and lodges. It was her daily evening walk, intended to clear her head, but all Holliday could think about was Damon MacAndrew and what she could do to put him off buying the resort.

Her mobile began to chime 'Last Christmas' from her pocket, and she fished it out.

'Holliday!' a rusty male voice boomed when she answered.

'Mr Hornbuckle.' Holliday smiled, shifting the receiver away from her ear. He'd always been a little hard of hearing and inclined to shout. 'Everything okay?'

'You're supposed to call me Charlie, dear, remember? We were neighbours for over five years, still are since you own the house next door. That practically makes us family,' the older man said kindly. 'And don't worry, I'm just calling to let you know that everything in The Ambles is shipshape. I've decorated the windows, hung the Christmas lights on the porch, front door and around the garden – in all the places they usually go.'

'Thank you.'

'The tree's been delivered and decorated and it's in the front room—' he added.

'To the right of the fireplace?' Holliday asked.

'In the exact spot I've put it for the last two years,' Charlie promised. 'The same place you and Adrian always positioned it.'

'Thank you again.' Holliday sighed, then said, 'Sorry for being fussy, but is the blue spruce exactly six foot?' She patted a palm against her racing heart when he rumbled an affirmative. Since her fiancé – Adrian Robinson – had died in a train crash and left her The Ambles, she'd been determined to keep the house exactly as it was when they'd both lived there. 'And you've used *all* the decorations?' She could picture each one. Probably because she'd lovingly crafted most of them. 'And the fairy lights will switch on at four thirty?'

'Of course, dear, and then they'll go off again at eleven o'clock just like always. Don't worry, it's under control. I'll send you some photos later. Are you planning on coming back to Cambridge to see it this year?' he asked hopefully.

Holliday stopped abruptly on the snowy pathway and closed her eyes, acknowledging the ache in her chest. She conjured up the pretty double-fronted Edwardian house on the leafy street just outside of Cambridge town centre, its high ceilings and airy rooms, and the farmhouse-style kitchen Adrian had spent hours cooking in for them both. 'I'm sorry. Not this year,' she murmured. 'Not yet.' Not ever, probably.

'You do know everything's exactly as it was with Adrian, same as every year.' Charlie's voice sounded far away and Holliday forced herself back into the present.

'I know, but I'm just not...' She swallowed, thinking about her fiancé, how happy they'd been, how much she loved imagining him still living in The Ambles. It was why she was finding it difficult to part with it.

The mortgage had been paid off when Adrian had died and

the house was hers free and clear, but running it from afar incurred a lot of expenses. There were just so many bills – electric, gas, water rates and council tax, not to mention quarterly cleaners and a gardener in the summer – but she couldn't bear the idea of calling a halt to any of it. It was as if by keeping the house going she was keeping Adrian alive in the world. She could imagine him living there, pottering around the kitchen, reading one of his biographies in front of the open fire. It was why, every year, her neighbour would hang the Christmas decorations on the first of December, the same day they always had. It was why if she ever thought about renting it out to help with the costs, her whole body immediately rejected the idea.

'I'm not ready.' She opened her eyes and looked around, trying to centre herself. Her gaze hooked onto one of the barns and the three sparkly reindeer ornaments sitting outside. In the evenings you could see those lights from miles away. She kept her eyes fixed on them, taking comfort from the familiarity of their shape and size. Adrian had proposed to her beside those ornaments when they'd been staying in the resort – and in the time Holliday had been working here they hadn't dimmed, moved or altered at all. If she had her way, nothing here ever would.

'You haven't been back for two years,' Charlie said as Holliday swallowed.

'Not since the funeral,' she agreed, almost choking on the word. It had been an awful day. Holliday's parents had passed when she was seven and she had no siblings. She'd lived with her gran for nine wonderful years until a stroke had taken her too, so she'd attended Adrian's service alone.

She remembered a funeral parlour usher had helped her into the church but had no recollection of the service or how she'd got home. She didn't remember packing her belongings either, or of closing the front door of The Ambles for the last time. The following few months were a blur too. In fact, Holliday could barely recall anything of that time before she'd arrived in Christmas Village, except that she'd been on a pilgrimage, visiting all the places she'd been with Adrian. Perhaps because it had helped her to feel closer to him. Holliday wasn't even sure if she knew. She did recall seeing a job advertisement in The Corner Shop on Christmas Village's main street for someone to run the entertainment and craft sessions at Christmas Resort and it had felt like a sign. After her visit with Adrian, she knew she'd feel at home here. So she'd applied, got the job and that had been the start of a new chapter of her life.

'Well, dear, until you *are* ready,' Charlie said gently, 'I'm more than happy to take care of the house as agreed. I have to tell you one of the gutters at the back of the building is hanging down, due to the recent winds I think. I'd fix it myself but I can't do ladders anymore, not with my knees...'

'I'll call someone and get it sorted,' Holliday said quickly. 'You don't need to worry, you already do far too much for me.' She thought about her dwindling finances and her shoulders tensed. She'd get paid next week and she barely had to spend anything living in Christmas Resort. It would be tight but she'd manage it.

'Thank you, dear.' Charlie sighed. 'I've bundled up and posted this month's mail just like always. Some of it looked important and there are a few Christmas cards in there, including one from me. I thought you'd like to have them...' He paused. 'Are you sure you're okay, Holliday? You know if you ever need anything, I'm here?'

'Thank you, and don't worry, I'm absolutely fine,' she said, reaching into one of her pockets to fiddle with a pom-pom. 'Please send me some photos of the decorations when you can.' Holliday smiled, imagining how the house would look when the lights flicked on. Then her smile faded when she remembered it would be empty inside.

· · ·

'She's a monster!' Innes Gibson flew into the large kitchen at Christmas Lodge, her long blonde plait swinging like an out-of-control pendulum, almost knocking one of the pretty glass mugs off the silver tray Holliday was carrying.

'She's my mother.' Leo Gibson let out a long-suffering sigh as he followed his wife from the hallway. He was still wearing his coat, weighty toolbelt and aged leather gloves, and the expression on his young face was resigned.

'She told me any woman who doesn't want to cook haggis wasn't good enough for her son. She *knows* I'm a vegetarian.' Innes swung around, waggling one of her delicate fingers.

Holliday put the tray on a counter safely out of the way. She knew better than to get close to her friend while she was mid-tirade.

'I'm sick and tired of being told you shouldn't have married me.' The housekeeper's eyes, which were the colour of aged bourbon, narrowed in her husband's direction.

Holliday had a sudden urge to intervene but held herself back. The newlyweds' relationship was fiery but the arguments always burned themselves out.

Leo scrubbed a hand through his surfer-blonde hair and shook his head. 'Mam's always been overprotective...' His eyes grew huge when Innes let out a shriek.

'I can't live with her anymore, Leo. I know we said we would stay with her when we got married—'

'It's only been five months,' he interrupted wearily.

'But it's going to take us years and years to save for our own place. I can't put up with her for that long. Especially when you *always* take her side.' Innes's eyes glistened.

Holliday suspected she was on the verge of an emotional meltdown so reached out and squeezed her hand.

'There, there, hen,' Bonnibell soothed, appearing from the doorway which led to the lodge's formal dining room. 'What's going on?' She took in the scene and opened the gingerbread man-shaped biscuit tin she'd left out on the serving counter, which she reserved for staff emergencies. 'Have some sugar, calm down. I made these this morning.' She waved the tin in front of Innes and Leo, studying their unhappy faces. 'Has my old friend Mairi been up to her tricks again?' she guessed.

'I've tried so hard with her but she hates me.' A tear escaped and rolled down Innes's cheek as she pulled up one of the bar stools, grabbed two shortbread biscuits and nodded before biting into them both at the same time.

Leo tore off his coat and gloves and grabbed a biscuit too. 'Mam's just...' He huffed. 'She's never been good about sharing me.' He cleared his throat. 'I don't want to upset her so I'm working on a way to get us our own place.' He tentatively stroked a hand over his wife's back. 'I told you that already.'

Innes swirled her arms. 'Doing what?' she pleaded.

Leo sighed and grabbed another biscuit from the tin. 'I've already said, it's better if you don't know.' His cheeks lit as he avoided her eyes. 'I promise that if you're patient we should be able to move out in a few months.'

Innes's shoulders deflated. 'Okay, I'm sorry.' She brushed a hand over her delicate features – squeezing the narrow bridge of her nose. 'She just upset me today. Normally I ignore her. But it wasn't just the haggis comment: apparently my hair gets every-where, I don't know how to stack the dishwasher properly and my perfume makes her feel sick.' She shrugged. 'I know I should try and be more patient but—'

Bonnibell walked up and clamped a hand on the younger woman's shoulder. 'It can be difficult. I had the same with Connell's mam, she hated me for ages. I won her round in the end, of course. No one can resist my mince pies.' She chuckled, her bulb-like cheeks glowing as a door slammed at the front of the house and then a pure-white husky with a bright-red collar bounded into the kitchen.

'Claus!' Bonnibell exclaimed, reaching down to pet the dog

until he moved on, making his way around the room so he could greet everyone, his bushy tail flying back and forth. 'Connell Baker, where have you been?' Bonnibell teased as a huge bear of a man entered the kitchen. He was over six foot four with a burly frame and a stomach that had been designed to fill a Santa suit perfectly. He brushed snowflakes from his white hair and strode to his wife so he could peck her noisily on both cheeks.

'I've been admiring our festive kingdom,' he boomed, nodding at Holliday, Innes and Leo before grabbing a handful of biscuits from the tin and patting his belly. 'I need to get into shape for our new visitors.' He grinned. 'Or who else will be a convincing Santa for the little ones? Not you...' He pointed at Leo's flat stomach before shoving a biscuit into his mouth.

'Did you find the elusive Ross Ballentine?' Bonnibell asked, putting the kettle on. She was referring to the grounds manager and outdoor adventure specialist who worked for Christmas Resort. The quiet man had a reputation for going on walkabouts, often disappearing into the remote Scottish wilderness, sometimes camping for days in extreme weather. But they had no way of contacting him because Ross refused to carry a phone. 'He missed an appointment with a visitor today and I was hoping he'd make up for it and join us for dinner this evening.'

'Ach, no sign, I'm afraid, but he'll be hunkered down somewhere. The weather's supposed to be getting worse and he won't take any chances.' Connell looked unconcerned as he took the last biscuit. 'I'm not worried. He'll turn up when he's ready.' He grinned. 'The man's part reindeer, after all. Built for the snow.' He pointed at the raging weather out the window. 'You know he's not keen on socialising, but if we get any bookings for his trips I'll contact him on the walkie-talkie he keeps in his cabin.'

Bonnibell's attention was suddenly caught by the bright-red clock above the stove as the small hand – which had a robin perched on the tip – inched closer to the number seven. She groaned. 'Sorry, team, but we're going to have to discuss all this later. Our potential new owner is due for dinner in less than half an hour and we're not ready. Leo' – she pointed to the handsome young man, using her best sergeant major tone – 'you need to wash and change. Try the shower in Mr Gray's room. It's a bit temperamental but it should be fine. I know you keep spare clothes in your truck, I suggest you use them. Innes?' she barked.

The girl jerked her chin.

'Please can you help Holliday set the table? I need to check on our meal.' Bonnibell squeaked as Frosty began to ribbon back and forth between her legs. 'Hen, you scared me.' She leaned down to stroke the cat as Claus came up to greet the feline too. 'You're going to have to hide yourself away this evening.' She nodded at Holliday. 'Perhaps you could put him in your bedroom? We can't have our important guest sneezing all night. Frosty'll be okay with Mr Jingles, won't he?' she checked, refer-ring to Holliday's white mouse, which lived in a cage in her bedroom.

She nodded. 'He'll be fine, they're friends.'

Bonnibell swept around and pointed Innes in the direction of the cutlery drawer. 'Good. I want this evening to be perfect.' She clapped her hands, looking excited. 'Mr MacAndrew obvi-ously has his heart set on buying Christmas Resort and we need to show him exactly how wonderful it is.'

'What will happen if he decides not to buy?' Innes asked, fiddling with the end of her plait.

Bonnibell frowned as she considered the question. 'I've no idea.' She shook her head. 'But I can't imagine why he wouldn't, can you?' She grabbed some festive oven gloves and knelt so she could peer into the oven.

Holliday gazed thoughtfully at her pet.

'I recognise that look. What are you planning?' Innes asked

mildly, grabbing another biscuit from the tin before scooping up a handful of knives and forks, and adjusting the figure-hugging navy dress she wore when she was in housekeeping mode.

'Nothing,' Holliday said in her most innocent tone, bundling up the cat before heading upstairs. If she put Frosty in her room and forgot to close the door, it wouldn't be her fault if the cat decided to wander around, would it? She knew her pet would instantly seek her out if he managed to escape – and knowing Frosty, he'd then plot a direct route to the one person in Christmas Lodge who most wanted to avoid him. It was the way he always behaved, as if he were determined to make everyone adore him.

Smiling, she dressed Frosty in a special red-and-white Christmas cape before gently settling him on the bed where the cat circled a few times before snuggling down and falling asleep. Then she left the door ajar and crept out of her bedroom. She'd let fate decide what happened next.

4

HOLLIDAY

'Perfect timing,' Bonnibell boomed as Damon wandered into the main hallway of Christmas Lodge exactly one minute before seven o'clock. Connell immediately helped him with his thin coat, brushing off the snow and hanging it up, and Bonnibell introduced her husband, Innes and then Leo as the handyman trotted down the staircase fully freshened up. Then she guided their guest in the direction of the dining room.

'I brought you these,' Damon said gruffly, turning so he could hand over a bottle of red wine and a box of chocolates to the older woman.

'Those are my favourites,' Bonnibell said, flushing as she clutched the box to her chest. 'How did you know?'

'Mr Gray told me,' Damon admitted.

Holliday watched her boss melt over the gifts, which were obviously a bribe, and caught Damon's eye to ensure he knew she'd clocked exactly what he was doing, but he looked away when Connell patted him on the back so she didn't see his reaction.

'Holliday will show you where to sit while we get ready to

serve and she'll pour you a dram of whisky to have while you're waiting,' the older man said, pointing them both towards the dining-room entrance. 'You'll want to prepare your stomach properly before you dig into your Christmas feast.' He laughed heartily. 'We'll just be a wee minute.'

Holliday gave Damon one of her most innocent smiles as she led him into the room, which was overflowing with Christmas decorations, and turned so she could watch his expression as he joined her. His eyes skirted the space and he pursed his lips, looking as if he'd sniffed something unpleasant.

'This is where we normally serve meals, including the Christmas dinner we host each Sunday,' Holliday explained, walking to the counter on the right of the room, which served as a bar area. She poured Damon a shot of whisky, added ice and handed it to him, watching as he sipped and nodded. Then she pointed to the long oak table. 'We can extend it to seat up to thirty guests and there are spare tables in one of the sheds if more of our visitors want to join in. Some people prefer to dine in their cabins.'

She paused as her mind whirred. 'It can be a logistical nightmare if everyone wants to be here at the same time.' Holliday buried her hands in the apron she was still wearing and crossed her fingers. 'So we offer dinner in here on a first come, first served basis. Not all our guests are happy with that – but Mr Gray gets involved if any customers complain.'

'He didn't mention that.' Damon studied her carefully. 'How regularly does he have to deal with guest grievances?' He folded his arms.

Holliday looked at the ground. 'Well... more often than you'd expect,' she muttered as her cheeks began to tingle.

'Interesting. I suppose a larger dining room would help with that,' Damon said thoughtfully, looking around. 'Or perhaps a proper restaurant could be built with more seating. Would you

say that would be a good idea?' He gazed at Holliday intently
and she wondered if she was being tested.

'There's nowhere to put a restaurant,' she snapped. The
man was talking about changes already and he'd only been here
a few hours.

'Right.' Damon drew out the word slowly. 'And do you have
fewer issues in the summer?'

Holliday shrugged. 'Sometimes we stay in here, but if it's
really warm we'll go outside. We have a couple of barns permanently set up with tables that are already decorated. I mean,
they're great... but when it rains the barns leak.' Holliday pulled
a face and waited for Damon's reaction, hoping he'd ask more so
she could embellish the fib with worries about the roof caving
in, enormous insurance quotes. Maybe she'd tell him a plague of
mice had been running havoc in the barn recently? Perhaps she
could take him for a walk tomorrow and put Mr Jingles somewhere in his path?

Holliday hid a smile with her palm but Damon simply
nodded, looking undisturbed, and wandered closer to the dining
table. Innes had laid places for the six of them at the far end,
close to the fire, and she'd put out tall white candles, festive
napkins, Christmas plates and crackers. Polished silver cutlery
sparkled alongside round red placemats abutted by delicate
water and wine glasses. In the centre of the table she'd placed a
circular snow scene complete with ice skaters and mini
snowmen that Holliday had made in a craft class with a few of
the guests the week before.

Damon skimmed a finger over the display. 'This is pretty.'
He sounded surprised.

Holliday swallowed the unwelcome bolt of pleasure at the
compliment. 'I ran a class last week focusing on table centre-
pieces. It took a while because one of the children poured glue
all over his clothes. There was a complaint about that too.' She
watched his face for signs of a reaction. But there were none.

Damon shoved a hand into his pocket before striding to the fireplace. He sniffed the air and his shoulders tensed. 'What's that smell? I recognise it.'

'Cinnamon,' Holliday explained. 'Our housekeeper, Innes, puts sticks of it in with the logs each morning.' She tried to think of something negative to say about that too, but nothing sprang to mind. She loved the fragrance; it always put her in such a good mood. 'You'll probably notice the same scent in your cabin – Innes refreshes the sticks every day.'

'Yes of course, I remember now,' Damon muttered.

'Remember what?' Holliday asked.

'Nothing, the smell reminds me of Christmas, that's all.'

Damon sounded weary and Holliday studied him, fighting the slivers of concern. Why did he seem so unhappy? What had made those shoulders hunch?

He'd dressed up this evening in dark trousers and an expensive-looking blue shirt with sharp creases across the arms and down the back. His shoulders were broad and the cotton shirt skimmed them, giving little away aside from their breadth. The creases that had been ironed into the clothing followed the arc of Damon's back to the waistband of his trousers and Holliday's eyes chased the lines to the curve of his hips, then down his long legs to a pair of shiny black boots that looked a little soggy. Were his socks wet? Hadn't he thought to pack sensible shoes? She felt a little sorry for him, which was both inappropriate and annoying.

Damon turned and cocked his head, studying the rest of the dining room. He examined the seven-foot blue spruce beside the fireplace which had been decorated with an eclectic array of colourful baubles, pom-poms and hand-made ornaments – many created in Holliday's craft sessions. Then his attention caught on the bookshelves in the far corner and his eyebrows met. 'What are those?'

Holliday turned. 'Photo albums. Every guest who stays has

a picture taken at the resort,' she explained, ignoring the pinch of pain in her chest. 'They can either be taken individually, or we do photos of couples or family groups.' She smiled. 'We send out copies a few weeks after the holiday as a special memento from the resort. Bonnibell insists on keeping a copy here too.' She wandered over to run her hand across the multiple leather-bound albums lined up across two long white shelves. 'She says once you're in one of the resort albums you become a permanent member of our family. I've no idea how many people we've taken pictures of over the years.'

'That's...' Damon cleared his throat as his cheeks paled. 'I didn't remember that...' Her eyes caught his. 'From the article I mean,' he added quickly, stepping back and putting a hand on one of the dining chairs.

Holliday's mouth pinched. 'Surely you didn't expect the journalist to mention everything about this place?' she asked, feeling protective. Adrian had been the one to write that article. It was how she had first come to Christmas Resort. Her fiancé had been a talented writer – and the article had been informative and thorough.

Damon ground his jaw. 'And every client who's ever stayed here is in one of those?' he checked, pointing to the shelves. His expression was blank, but there was something in his eyes that told Holliday he didn't like what he'd just heard. Although that made no sense...

'That's right,' Holliday said. 'It's a point of pride for Bonnibell.'

'What about the gaps?' Damon asked, wandering closer so he could examine the spines of the albums and the small openings peppered in between some of them.

'I'm not sure about them all, but sometimes the staff borrow them,' Holliday said, thinking of the one beside her bed, and the one in her bedside drawer that contained a photo of her and Adrian.

'Why?' he asked, obviously bemused.

Holliday sniffed. 'I've no idea.' She had no desire to share her reasons with Damon. She didn't particularly want to help him at all.

'The albums aren't dated?' he asked, looking closely at the spines.

'Every photo has a name and date hand-written on the back. But we don't have a system for organising them. It's not really about when people come, it's not been necessary to classify them. This isn't a library.' Holliday knew she'd gone too far when Damon stiffened. 'Most of the time, they just sit here.' She watched his frown deepen. 'Don't you like the idea?'

'I wouldn't say that.' Damon cocked his head and his expression cleared. 'I was just surprised that's all.' He scrapped a hand through his hair, mussing it attractively. 'I've never heard of a business doing anything like it.' He waved at the shelves. 'Keeping pictures of all their guests, I mean. There are probably lots of traditions I'll find out about when I buy the resort.' The toothy smile Damon flashed Holliday didn't reach his eyes and he scanned the shelf again, looking unhappy. 'It's... a smart business strategy, I suppose, reminding people about how much they enjoyed coming. I'm sure it encourages repeat bookings. It's a good idea. Do you include a discount flyer when you send the photos?'

Holliday felt her chest tighten with annoyance and shoved her hands into her apron again, seeking out one of the larger pom-poms so she could mash it. 'Absolutely not. We don't do it for business reasons.' Oh, this man was so wrong for Christmas Resort. 'This is far more than a money-making exercise, Mr MacAndrew,' she said icily. 'Sending the photos is more about making the joy of coming here last, giving our visitors enduring memories, a small piece of the magic they can enjoy at home. This is a special holiday for our visitors, a slice of life they'll never forget.'

'*Ahhhhh...*' Damon nodded. 'So it has nothing to do with making a profit. Of course...'

Was he mocking her?

'You're welcome to borrow any of the albums whenever you like. It might help you understand. There's something very uplifting about seeing all those happy faces. I suspect even *you* would find it hard not to get caught up in it,' Holliday said stiffly, struggling to remain polite. She wrapped her arms around herself, remembering how many evenings she'd spent perusing the books since she'd moved here, staring at the families and couples, wishing things were different for her.

'Um, I'll... yes, I might do that.' Damon downed the shot of whisky in one. 'Perhaps I'll take one to my cabin tonight,' he muttered.

Holliday nodded, although she doubted he was serious. From their brief conversations she could tell Damon just didn't get it. He really had no idea how special Christmas Resort was. Sure, he was easy on the eye and he hadn't exactly criticised the way they did things, but he didn't understand – which meant he'd almost certainly want to change things.

She turned as Innes walked into the dining room carrying a tray filled with bowls of crisps, nibbles and glass mugs which were all steaming. Then Holliday stood back, watching as the rest of the team came up to greet Damon again, and Connell put on Christmas music.

'Sit down, sit down,' Bonnibell boomed, grabbing Damon's empty whisky glass and guiding him to the head of the table before placing a fresh drink in front of him. 'This is one of our specialities – mulled Christmas cider.'

'I discovered this particular brand a few months ago in one of our local shops,' Connell interjected. 'It's called Secret Cider. It's fermented locally and it's a *braw* drink.'

'He means good,' Leo explained in his strong Scottish lilt.

'Although if you're a MacAndrew, perhaps you knew that already?'

Damon shook his head as everyone turned to look at him. 'It's an old family name; I've only ever lived in London,' he said, dipping his head to sniff the liquid. 'It does smell *braw* though.' He sounded impressed.

'Is your family from around here then?' Connell asked, pulling out a chair.

Damon nodded. 'From years back. My parents died when I was in my twenties though and there's no one here now,' he admitted.

'So you're alone?' Bonnibell asked, her voice filled with sympathy.

'No. I've got a sister, brother-in-law and two nephews,' Damon said, his eyes skirting the room as if he were uncomfortable about sharing.

Bonnibell must have noticed because she nodded and pulled out a chair. 'Holliday, why don't you sit to Damon's left?' She indicated to the rest of the party that they should take their places too. 'I've made appetisers and I've got a big festive feast planned, so I hope you're hungry. I love cooking, it's an important part of the experience here.'

'So I've heard,' Damon said, glancing at Holliday.

Connell sat and leaned closer to Damon. 'Anything you want to ask us, lad? I'll expect you've got plenty of questions.' He waggled his bushy eyebrows. 'Don't be shy.' The older man picked up his mulled cider and sipped, groaning appreciatively.

Damon glanced at the faces now staring at him and cleared his throat. 'There's nothing I can think of at the moment, thank you. I'll just take the time to digest your day-to-day routine and the overall set-up of the business. I'll be very happy to wander around on my own, I *really* don't want to bother anyone.'

'Oh it's no bother, Holliday's got lots of plans for you tomorrow, she's looking forward to it,' Bonnibell insisted, beaming at Holliday, who kept her expression blank. 'We thought you'd enjoy a walk around our Christmas Maze first thing.'

Damon blinked. 'It's really not necessary,' he said stiffly. 'I know you've all got jobs to do. I don't want to interfere with anything.'

His eyes skimmed Holliday's face and she could see reluctance burning in his eyes. Why was that?

'Oh, you really won't,' Holliday muttered. 'It'll be my pleasure to introduce you to Christmas Resort properly. I'm sure you're going to *love* everything about it.' Or just the opposite if she had her way. She already had plenty of ideas for ways to persuade Damon it wasn't the investment for him.

'Aye, this place is really quite something.' Connell patted Damon's arm. 'I can tell you're falling for it already.'

The younger man jerked his chin before grabbing a crisp and stuffing it into his mouth. He made a few affirmative noises as he chewed, but there was something about the way he looked that set off more jingles along the back of Holliday's neck. She sipped her mulled cider, studying him, looking away when his eyes tracked to hers. Then she caught a flash of red cape at the far edge of the doorway that led from the hall and she held her breath as Frosty padded across the threshold.

The cat took his time, slowly stretching his limbs as he surveyed the room before heading for Claus, who was sleeping in his favourite spot close to the bar. The cat nuzzled the dog, then he spotted Damon and his ears pricked and he started to creep towards the table.

A part of Holliday – a very small part – wanted to get up so she could put her pet back upstairs, but she stayed where she was. If Damon bought Christmas Resort, he'd change everything and she couldn't bear the idea. It was too special to just be an investment for someone who clearly didn't get it. There was too much at stake.

She watched as the cat tracked under the table and guessed he was probably now winding himself between everyone's legs, following the shortest route to his target. Bonnibell fidgeted in her seat and Holliday stilled, but then the older woman simply adjusted her dress and picked up her mulled cider.

Then Holliday saw Damon's mouth tense and his forehead crease in confusion. He put down his glass and pinched the bridge of his nose, wincing before letting out a loud *achoo*.

'Is everything alright, hen?' Bonnibell asked as the young man's eyes began to stream and he jerkily searched the room.

'I'm fine, I don't – *achoo*! – understand.' He shoved back his chair, stood and let out another loud sneeze. 'There must be a cat in here somewhere.'

'I don't think so, lad.' Bonnibell's attention darted to Holliday. 'You did lock Frosty in your room?'

'Of course.'

Holliday widened her eyes as her pet peered out from under the table and trotted up to Damon, who immediately backed up towards the fireplace. He sneezed again and Leo sprang to his feet and grabbed the cat, before sweeping him into the hallway. Then all eyes turned to Holliday.

'I'm so sorry,' she gasped theatrically. 'I've no idea how he escaped. I shut the door and he was sleeping on my bed when I left.'

'Ach, lass, he's always been sneaky,' Bonnibell said as Damon let out another loud sneeze. 'What can we do to help? Do you need an antihistamine? I've got some in the kitchen,' she fussed, waving her arms. 'You're not the first guest we've had staying with a cat allergy.'

Damon sneezed once more and nodded enthusiastically, before glancing at Holliday just as she hid her grin.

He narrowed his eyes, which were still streaming. 'Don't worry, I'll be back,' he murmured. He sneezed again and turned when he reached the exit, then he took a moment to silently stare at Holliday.

She felt her stomach twist. There was something in that chilly expression that told her he'd guessed exactly what she was up to. Which meant she'd have to up her game if she was going to save the resort.

5

DAMON

Damon was still half asleep when the doorbell chimed at the front of Reindeer Retreat. He took another long sip from his mug of excellent coffee. Innes had delivered a tray with a large steaming flask at seven o'clock this morning, complete with a Father Christmas mug and snacks. She'd invited him to the lodge for breakfast but he'd reluctantly declined – his stomach was still full from the feast the evening before and he suspected he wouldn't be hungry for at least another twenty-four hours. Although that hadn't stopped him from eating the platter of delicious cinnamon buns she'd brought with her.

Damon opened the door of his cabin expecting to see the young housekeeper again, and instead found Holliday. She was holding a pair of green wellington boots in one hand and a matching coat in the other. She looked pretty and he had to fight an inconvenient wave of attraction, instead filling his mind with the expression of guilt he'd seen on her face the evening before. He *knew* she'd allowed the cat to escape into the dining room, and had guessed it had something to do with his plans to buy the resort – he just wasn't sure why she was so against it. Had he inadvertently given something away?

'Morning,' Holliday said brightly, looking suspiciously happy to see him. 'Is it okay if I come in?'

Damon stood to one side, but shut the door as soon as Holliday crossed the threshold in case her pet was poised outside.

'As Bonnibell mentioned last night, we thought you might enjoy a walk around Christmas Maze this morning,' Holliday explained without meeting his eyes. 'I noticed at dinner your shoes were a little wet. We keep spare footwear and coats for guests – I guessed your sizes. There are gloves in the pockets of the coat and I've got a pair of warm socks if you need those.' She put the wellingtons and coat on the bed before reaching into the pocket of her apron and tugging out a dark woollen bundle scattered with multicoloured pom-poms which she held out. 'I run a weekly knitting club and, well... sometimes we make things for people. I thought they might fit.' She looked embarrassed.

Damon cleared his throat, wondering if Holliday had filled the pom-poms with itching powder or pine needles. If not, why would she be giving them to him? 'I really can't accept presents,' he said stiffly and immediately felt bad. 'I mean, thanks, but I've got everything I need.'

Holliday's smile dimmed. 'I'll put the socks on the tree – consider them a festive gift from the staff. I'm not trying to bribe you. If you decide to invest in the resort it should be because you've fallen in love with it. Otherwise you really shouldn't buy it at all.' She turned and gave him a look that would have withered a lesser man, but still managed to make him feel churlish, then propped the bundle between the branches of the small Christmas tree set to the right of the fire.

'The wellingtons are a good idea, thank you,' Damon found himself conceding, then he wandered to the window before he did something stupid like offer to wear the socks too. Something odd was happening to him. He didn't usually feel things like guilt. His heart was as dead as his marriage and he prided himself on that – he couldn't do what needed to be done in business otherwise. Perhaps he was coming down with something? He pressed a palm to his forehead but his temperature felt normal. Maybe he'd pop a paracetamol when Holliday left just in case.

'Everything okay?' she asked, sounding genuinely worried.

'Of course,' Damon snapped because he didn't want her concern. 'The weather's getting worse – should we postpone our walk?' He pointed to his car which was now blanketed in a thick layer of snow.

'It's been blizzarding all night so I'm not surprised,' Holliday said. 'It's what happens in the Highlands. If you don't like snow, it's probably not the right place for you. Have you considered investing in a resort somewhere hotter?' She smiled sweetly. 'I hear Thailand's quite lovely this time of year...'

'Not really,' Damon muttered. 'And you're right, I'm sure the weather will just make everything even *more* festive.' He kept his expression deadpan but knew he'd annoyed her because she frowned.

'Only if you wrap up properly.' Holliday patted her arms as if to emphasise the pillowy blue coat she was wearing. It was so thick it dwarfed her small frame but still somehow managed to hint at the curvy figure under it. 'We're expecting more snow later this morning,' she continued. 'So if you want to go out, you might want to consider wearing the coat – you're welcome to check the pockets for bribes, but you're more likely to find stray pom-poms than wads of cash.'

Damon reluctantly chuckled. Holliday was feisty and she obviously didn't like him. Years ago that might have bothered him, but now he appreciated her honesty, or at least that he could read her so clearly. It would make winning this battle of wills easier.

He watched as her attention meandered around the room

before stopping on the photo album resting on the table beside his bed. 'So you *did* borrow one...' Her voice was ridiculously pleased.

'Yep.' Damon nodded. He'd brought the album back after dinner, and had spent a quiet hour skimming through the pages, hoping he'd find the picture of him and his ex. He'd forgotten about it being taken until he'd seen the photo albums and Holliday had explained their significance. That's when the memory had hit him – of Willow dressed in a sparkly black skirt with a slit that travelled from ankle to mid-thigh. She'd put her phone away for long enough to pose for the camera, draping herself over him and devotedly staring into his eyes.

Damon's body went cold at the memory. When he eventually found the picture in one of the albums he'd rip it into tiny pieces, then burn it – and if he couldn't find it then once he owned the resort he'd simply arrange for every book on those shelves to be destroyed. He had no idea where the copy the lodge had supposedly posted to them had gone. Hopefully straight into a shredder. Damon had probably moved out by then. Just a couple of months after their time here, his marriage had ended when one of Willow's spurned lovers had told him about her many affairs, proving his story with a folder of photos and receipts. Devastated, Damon had arranged for the house they'd shared to be emptied and demolished. He'd made a fortune when he'd sold the four flats he'd had built in their place.

'So...' Holliday said. 'Did you look through it?'

Damon nodded.

'It's quite magical, isn't it?' Her voice was at least twenty degrees warmer.

He tried to read her expression. Was she aiming to put him at ease before she did something to sabotage him again, or was he being paranoid? He honestly couldn't tell.

'It gave me a useful insight into the type of clients who stay here,' Damon said blandly, keeping his expression poker straight.

Holliday's face fell and she swallowed before nodding. 'We should get going,' she said sharply, pointing to the wellingtons and coat she'd laid on the bed. 'I'll see you outside.'

Holliday barely said a word during the ten-minute walk towards Christmas Maze, even when they passed a huge Christmas tree bursting with decorations. In a moment of weakness, Damon commented on how attractive it looked. A few metres on, he spotted a golden sleigh parked outside a large barn. He stopped and ran a hand over the wooden frame, reluctantly impressed by the intricate workmanship. He'd definitely use it somewhere in the new hotel – maybe he could add it to the children's play area.

'Does this get used?' he asked, grudgingly picturing it filled with people and presents. He couldn't remember seeing a sleigh here when he'd stayed, certainly hadn't ridden on one with Willow, which meant it held no memories of his ex, at least.

Holliday's lips narrowed and for a moment Damon wondered if she'd respond, then her shoulders slumped and she nodded. 'Depends on the weather. In the winter if there's enough snow – like today – there's a small tractor that can be attached to the base and Connell uses that to pull it along. We've also got snowmobiles for the more adventurous.' She frowned. 'They require lots of maintenance and insurance though.' She sucked air between her teeth, reminding him of a plumber who was about to deliver an exorbitant estimate. 'It's expensive keeping them working all year round.'

'Is that so?' Damon said, yanking up the hood of the coat Holliday had loaned him before pulling it over his freezing ears.

Flakes of snow settled on his cheeks and one of Holliday's eyebrows winged up, silently signalling that she'd been right to suggest he dressed warmer. Score one for Holliday. Damon sighed and blew on his chilly fingers, then he shoved his hands in his pockets, immediately discovering the gloves, which he pulled out and tugged on too. Might as well let Holliday score two and stay warm – he had the whole day to even things up.

'What happens with the sleigh in summer?' he asked, because he had to give the appearance of being interested.

'We've got wheels we can attach and the same tractor to pull it along. It looks good, very convincing.' Holliday skimmed a hand lovingly over one of the red plastic seats on the sleigh. 'It's one of my favourite parts of the week. We take our visitors out on the evening before we celebrate Christmas. It's really quite something when you ride it across the hills at night.' She let out a soft sigh and shut her eyes.

Damon studied her long dark lashes, reluctantly transfixed by their contrast with her pale skin. Had she grown prettier since yesterday? Something in his gut protested as Holliday opened her eyes and frowned when she realised he was staring, and he had to look away.

'What?' she asked swiping at her face.

'Nothing,' he mumbled, embarrassed that she'd caught him, that looking at her had affected him. There was a ball of heat in his belly now and he didn't know what to do with it.

Holliday's attention slid back to the sleigh. 'Perhaps you might like to go out for a ride this evening. I can ask Leo or Connell to take you. We've got blankets to keep you warm.'

Holliday sounded so hopeful Damon almost said yes, but he forced himself to shake his head. 'I'm fine – I can picture the ride perfectly well.' He wasn't going to let himself be seduced by this place, or her, which meant he'd do well to avoid anything he might enjoy. Besides, it could be all part of a wicked plan to lose him in the grounds...

'That's really not the same,' Holliday said gruffly, before signalling up a small incline framed by fir trees layered in thick blankets of snow. 'Shall we get on?'

Damon followed and stopped beside Holliday as she paused to take in the view.

'Beautiful, isn't it?' she breathed.

He nodded as his eyes skimmed the landscape and he emptied his mind of Holliday and filled it with the plans he'd asked his architect to draw up. He'd check them over again when he was alone, then take a walk so he could see if there was anything he might want to change or add once the resort had been razed. 'Has anyone ever thought of putting a golf course here?' he asked. He'd included one in his wish list.

Holliday gasped, looking horrified. 'Why would they? Golf isn't exactly festive.'

Damon shrugged. 'Some people like to escape, not everyone's into Christmas...' He certainly wasn't after his experiences here.

'If they aren't, they really shouldn't be staying at the resort. That's our USP,' she said icily, stomping ahead.

Damon followed Holliday to the top of the incline and stopped again, taking in the fields of white. His toes were starting to chill and he stamped his feet, wishing he'd relented on the socks. From here he could see deep into the valley – there was a large patch of forest to its left and what looked like a small lochan beside it. 'Does this all belong to the resort?' He hadn't fully realised the scale of it until now, or how stunning the scenery was.

Holliday nodded. 'I don't know how many acres it is exactly, I'm sure Mr Gray has given you that information, but it goes on for miles.'

'How many lodges do you have?' Damon asked, stamping his feet again. He knew, but wanted to keep Holliday talking. Had to at least pretend to be taking an interest. If she suspected he only wanted to buy the resort so he could knock it down, she might share her fears with everyone else. Once Damon owned the place he could do whatever he liked with it – but until then, there was always a chance Mr Gray would refuse to sell if he got wind of his intentions.

'There are ten. They all need a fair amount of renovation and Bonnibell wants to expand and add more,' Holliday explained. 'I'm sure she'll speak to you about her plans. She's been talking about adding six yurts and she's got her heart set on a heated swimming pool.' Holliday hesitated. 'I don't want to be rude, but you should know there are lots of opportunities here but they're going to require significant investment. Lots of people would think it's not worth the trouble.'

Damon turned and looked into her clear blue eyes. 'I understand exactly what needs to be done.' He turned away when her expression softened and he felt a stab of guilt. 'I can see an outbuilding, but I understand there's no accommodation down there. Is that correct?' He pointed to what looked like a wooden shed set into the valley. 'What do you use all that land for?' Perhaps he could make the golf course larger, or add some luxury cottages in the wilderness. He'd speak to the architect about that tomorrow.

Holliday shrugged. 'Nothing much. The shed's used for general storage – Leo keeps his tools and equipment inside. In the summer guests go wild swimming in the lochan and we've got inflatable snowmen and Father Christmases that they race around stowed there too.'

Damon shuddered.

'Yep. It's a bit too cold for that this time of year,' Holliday agreed. 'Although if you do fancy a swim…?'

He shook his head. 'And the rest?' He circled an arm to take in the fields and forest. He'd walked some of the grounds with Willow when they'd stayed, although his wife hadn't been that interested in being outdoors. Still, there were enough memories here for him to want to change it.

'We offer festive wilderness hikes and experience days for those who want to enjoy the outdoors,' Holliday explained. 'I'm sure Ross Ballentine – our grounds manager and outdoor adventure specialist – would be happy to take you out. He runs organised tours for our guests, in between looking after the landscape and working on a rewilding project for Connell – I'm not sure about the exact details of that. You'll want to catch up with him while you're staying, but be aware he's very rarely around. There's a lot to keep on top of.' Her meaning was obvious.

'I'll make sure I book a meeting with him,' Damon lied, stamping the wellingtons on the ground again and shuddering because his feet were absolutely glacial. The cold had travelled from them to his thighs, and even his knees were aching.

'I'm sorry, are you cold?' Holliday asked innocently, glancing down at her thick silver snow boots.

Was it odd that the resort only provided guests with wellingtons…? Surely they were more suited to rain? When he built the hotel, he'd ensure everyone had access to warm footwear.

'We can go back to your room if you're struggling?' Holliday suggested, looking guilty – even though the temperature and lack of proper clothing were hardly her fault.

'I'm fine,' Damon said, thumping his feet on the ground again. How long did it take to get frostbite? 'Nothing a brisk walk around a maze won't fix.' He offered her a bright smile, masking the fact that his teeth were about to start chattering.

Holliday nodded, then fell silent as they followed the snowy path left through the trees, and Damon finally saw a sign pointing them in the direction of Christmas Maze. He almost cheered.

'Are you married?' she suddenly asked.

Damon found himself temporarily lost for words.

'I'm only asking because I was thinking your wife might like to see the resort before you decide to invest. Being out in the middle of nowhere is not for everyone. Although I suppose it depends on how hands-on you're planning to be.'

'No wife,' Damon said sharply, ignoring the way his stomach contracted at the mere thought of Willow. 'No pets, no one special at all.'

'I'm sorry,' Holliday said after a short pause.

'Don't be,' Damon grumbled. 'I'm much happier that way.'

'Lucky you.'

Holliday nodded before she breezed past him, but he didn't miss the tears in her eyes. Had to stop himself from asking what was wrong – what he'd said to upset her.

'There's the entrance to the maze,' she said, her voice clipped, pointing ahead to a snowy white arch flanked by inflatable snowmen. 'Start here and I'll meet you at the centre. Bonnibell asked Leo to leave us a picnic box with cakes and a flask of hot chocolate so we can celebrate when you find it.'

'Aren't you coming inside too?' Damon asked, turning back so he could check the narrow corridor crafted from tall fir trees that lined either side. It was dim in the maze but the trees were decorated with multicoloured fairy lights that illuminated the way.

Holliday shook her head. 'I know the maze really well, it'll be much more enjoyable if you work out where to go by yourself. There's an entrance around the other side, I'll access from there and that way I won't spoil your fun. Don't worry, I'm sure you won't get lost, we had a couple of ten year olds solve it on their own last week.' Holliday fluttered her blue eyes and then dipped her gaze to his feet.

'What's wrong?' Damon asked. The weather was definitely taking a turn for the worse. They needed to get this done so they could get back into the warm.

'Nothing,' she said brightly, swiping fresh snowflakes from her cheeks. 'I was just thinking you might want to get moving before you get any colder. I'll switch on the Christmas music in a minute so you can get the full experience. And, just to warn you, Frosty likes to sleep in here sometimes. Ignore him if he sees you.'

He grimaced.

'Also, there are giant inflatables at the ends of some of the pathways. Snowmen, a Father Christmas and a huge chimney – don't let them scare you if they catch you unawares.'

'Does the maze frighten a lot of your visitors?' Damon chuckled.

'Not *everyone*.' Holliday drew out the last word. 'But it's always worth warning people about surprises...'

Her expression remained blank, but Damon suspected Holliday was trying to spook him. The woman was easy to read. Why was that? He'd been with Willow for over three years and he'd never known what was going on in her head.

'We usually do safety briefings so I should tell you we've had a couple of guests slip on ice recently.' Her expression turned grave. 'Don't worry, Leo's added salt to the pathways this morning, but make sure you tread carefully anyway.' Holliday started to walk away, but must have thought better of it because she turned. 'Oh, and if you hear any growling...' She widened her eyes. 'Find somewhere to hide.'

'Why?' Damon asked.

She grimaced. 'Occasionally wild animals wander down from the mountains looking for food. It's nothing to worry about – unless they're hungry because the weather's been particularly bad.' She glanced up at the sky and frowned when a snowflake settled on her nose.

'What kinds of animals?' Damon tried not to grin.

Holliday's voice lowered. 'Wild boar, wildcats, we've had a couple of stray cows wander in too. Don't worry too much, no one's been injured *that* badly. Good luck,' she sang, before striding away.

'Wild boar…' Damon shook his head and chuckled before heading into the maze. He was going to have to watch himself. He was starting to like Holliday Harrison and that wouldn't do at all…

6

HOLLIDAY

Holliday peered through the bushy leaves of one of the blue spruce's that lined the maze and watched Damon stop when he reached the end of the path he was on before looking left and then right, obviously pondering which direction to choose. Her warnings of wild beasts clearly hadn't spooked him at all because he looked completely at ease and had barely glanced over his shoulder since she'd been spying on him. She shook her head and forcefully rustled the branches in front of her, making sure he'd be able to hear the noise over Michael Bublé's 'Holly Jolly Christmas', and ducked behind them again to ensure Damon didn't spot her and grow suspicious. But when she looked back moments later he was glancing around, looking mildly amused.

'So you think it's funny, do you?' she grumbled, then let out an ear-splitting *yowl*, doing her best imitation of a wildcat. It had impressed many of the children who'd visited the resort over the years – and Holliday was pleased with the way her voice carried over the song. 'Take that, *Demon*,' she whispered into the tree branches before carefully peering through them

again. Any person who'd even consider adding a golf course to
Christmas Resort was one she had to see off.

Holliday watched the man glance over his shoulder, then he
let out a loud chuckle, and stamped his feet, still grinning,
before turning right and walking slowly away.

'Seriously?' Holliday complained. He'd reach the centre of
the maze soon so she didn't have much time left to scare him.
She trotted along the pathway parallel to the one Damon was
on to keep up with him, and arrived just in time to see him
stride past the giant inflatable Father Christmas without stopping to admire it, his eyes firmly on the ground. Perhaps he was
concerned about slipping? Or more likely he didn't want to be
distracted by the festive fare. What was it with this man and
Christmas?

Holliday felt her temper flare when Damon passed the fairy
lights she'd spent hours arranging, then ignored the pretty
multicoloured baubles filled with festive jokes and messages.
He even snubbed the tiny snowflakes she'd crafted from tin foil
and the bunting the knitting club had spent weeks making.
'What's wrong with you?' Holliday grumbled as Damon disappeared around another corner. She began to run, determined to
arrive in the middle of the maze first, and that was when her
foot slipped out from under her.

'*Jingle Balls*,' she yelped, grabbing at a branch of a tree
lining the maze, dislodging big chucks of snow as she tried to
hold on but still went flying. Then her bottom hit the ground
with a loud thump, winding her as she landed on her back.
Holliday lay prone, looking skywards as snowflakes slowly
drifted from the clouds and settled on her face. She puffed and
eased herself onto her elbow, unable to stop the loud 'ouch' from
escaping.

'Are you okay?' The thunder of footsteps made Holliday
wish the ground would swallow her.

'I'm fine,' she spluttered, trying to get up as Damon knelt

beside her. 'I might have pulled a muscle.' She tried to move her right leg and winced. 'It's nothing. I tried to walk too fast and slipped.'

Damon took Holliday's hand and eased her to her feet. 'Well you did say it was slippery.'

He hadn't let go of her elbow and Holliday found herself leaning into him as she tried to put weight onto her leg, immediately stopping when pain shot through her calf.

'Shall we get you back to the lodge?' Damon asked, all signs of his previous humour gone.

'We didn't get to the middle,' she complained. 'I was going to beat you there and Leo's left us hot chocolate and some of Bonnibell's cake.'

'Which I can come back for later,' Damon said, stamping his feet again. 'I'm cold and I'd like to warm up.'

Holliday swallowed a fresh wave of guilt and nodded as Damon helped turn her so they could retrace her steps around the outside of the maze. 'This really isn't necessary. I'm sure I can make it on my own,' she grumbled as he encouraged her to put an arm around his shoulder and wrapped his own around her waist. His closeness had her body reacting unhelpfully.

'It is for me. The quicker we get back to the lodge, the faster I'll get these wellingtons off. My feet are freezing,' he said gruffly, helping her take a few tentative steps.

They fell silent as they slowly exited the maze, with Holliday hopping on one leg and Damon holding tightly onto her.

'It doesn't hurt as much now I'm moving.' Holliday flinched as they joined the path that led back towards the lodge. It was steep and despite the layers of grit Leo had sprinkled, slippery. Holliday's leg was throbbing but she was determined to do the walk unaided. She didn't need this man's assistance – you didn't accept help from enemies, it blurred the lines, lines she was already having trouble sticking to. Holliday tried to shake Damon off, unlatching her arm from around his shoulder, but she began to lose balance and her foot started to slide. She gasped as Damon suddenly scooped her into his arms, lifting her until she was staring into his face, which made her stomach go jittery. He held her gaze, and heat flooded through her, from her scalp to the tips of her toes.

'You don't need to carry me,' she said roughly, even as she hooked an arm around his shoulder and neck to stop herself from falling. She could smell him now they were closer – a mixture of linen and bergamot – and the scent was surprisingly sexy. Although it was probably just the borrowed coat, nothing to do with him. Or was she just trying to convince herself of that?

'It'll be quicker this way,' Damon said, breaking eye contact and striding down the pathway, picking up the pace, bouncing Holliday in his arms. 'You did warn me about hypothermia and I wasn't joking about my feet. I can't feel my toes anymore and if I don't get back to the lodge soon, I might not be able to walk at all. Then we'll be in trouble. Unless you're prepared to carry me?' His words were clipped.

Holliday decided it would be better not to respond. She might be accepting help from this man, but that didn't mean she was agreeing to a truce. He was all wrong for Christmas Resort and she wasn't about to forget it. Even if he was a whole lot kinder than she'd first thought.

'What happened, hen?' Bonnibell squeaked as she met them at the entrance of Christmas Lodge and signalled them both inside. The older woman had always had a sixth sense about staff or guests being injured, so Holliday wasn't surprised, but her boss witnessing Damon carrying her across the threshold set her teeth on edge.

'There was an incident in the maze,' her rescuer said, his voice matter-of-fact as he refused all offers of help and ignored

Holliday's wriggles as she encouraged him to put her on the ground. 'Not a wildcat confrontation, just ice – and for that I'm thankful,' he added, his tone dry.

'Wildcats?' Bonnibell's forehead wrinkled, then she chuckled. 'You're joking of course. Why don't you take Holliday upstairs to her bedroom and I'll get my medical kit?'

'Oh no, really,' Holliday complained, her cheeks reddening.

'Ach, lass, we should make sure it's nothing serious – and it's warm in your room so it'll be easier for me to check you over in there. Leo's just dismantled the fireplace in the sitting room because it's been smoking. He's called someone out to look at the chimney but everything's upside down and there's nowhere to sit. Just head to the top of the stairs and it's the first door on your right along the corridor,' she told Damon briskly. 'I'll be with you in a minute.' Bonnibell frowned as she noticed his footwear. 'Lad,' she gasped. 'Your feet must be freezing. Why didn't you borrow a pair of the resort's snow boots? We've got at least three pairs in every size.' She glanced at Holliday. 'I thought you knew that, hen?' she admonished, shaking her head before her expression turned sympathetic. 'You're usually so attentive to our guests, have I given you too much to do?'

'Um, no, of course not. I just forgot,' Holliday puffed, mortified. She tried to unwind herself from Damon again but the man held on.

'You really shouldn't put any weight on your leg until you've been checked over,' he said. 'Just in case you've damaged something. Just think, if you're not fit enough to show me around Christmas Resort, I'll miss out on all sorts of experiences I might not have otherwise.' Damon's tone was sarcastic. 'Wild animals for instance, not to mention frostbite.'

Holliday flushed.

'You need to take those wellingtons off too so we can warm up your feet,' Bonnibell said to her guest. 'You must be freezing.'

'I can do it back in Reindeer Retreat,' Damon said.

'Ach, lad, it's started snowing up a storm, you'll have to wait it out.' Bonnibell shook her head and pointed outside, where it was blizzarding heavily. 'Let's at least get you warm before you attempt it – then I'll get Leo to walk with you. If you don't want to go to Holliday's room you can come to the kitchen instead. It's not ideal because the seats aren't as comfy, but at least it'll be warm.' She looked unhappy. 'I can't have you thinking we don't take proper care of our guests.'

'It's okay, Mr MacAndrew can sit in my room,' Holliday relented. 'At least until the snow settles down. It's the least I can do.' She sighed. She didn't want Damon in her private space, but since his cold feet were all her fault it would be churlish to make him sit in the kitchen. Also, the confused look Bonnibell was giving her was making her feel awful. The woman had been like a mother to her since she'd arrived in Christmas Resort two years ago, swaddling her with warmth, making her part of the family, and Holliday hated feeling she was letting the older woman down.

'Thank you.' Damon gave Holliday an assessing look before silently carrying her up the staircase to her bedroom.

It was a large room with a double bed in the far corner, and a white door that led to a bathroom. There was a white cabinet cluttered with Christmas ornaments, pom-poms and a large silver cage where Mr Jingles was currently sleeping. At the other end of the room, an electric fire blazed inside a pretty silver fireplace with a mantle decorated with fresh ivy that had been woven between picture frames. Damon gently deposited Holliday into one of the two high-backed forest-green chairs set to either side of the fire.

'You can sit over there,' she said, pointing to the other chair, and slid to the edge of hers so she could carefully unlace her boots. She winced as she bent her knee to pull off one of them, but when she rotated her foot it didn't hurt as much. She watched Damon glance around the bedroom before he sat in the other chair where he slowly tugged off one wellington and then the other. As he pulled off his socks Holliday saw his feet were a bright shade of fuchsia and she instantly pressed her hands to her cheeks, fighting pangs of guilt. 'Sorry,' she blurted, immediately wishing she could retract it.

'All's fair in love and war, right?' Damon lifted his chin so he could gaze at her, then he opened his mouth just as Bonnibell bustled into the room with her arms full.

'Here are some thick socks and I've warmed two hot water bottles so you've got one for each foot. Innes is organising hot chocolate and cake. A rush of sugar and you'll feel better, I'm sure. Let's take a look at that leg, hen. Which one is it?'

'The left one,' Damon pointed out as he slowly pulled on the warm socks and planted his feet on the hot water bottles. Then he let out a grateful groan and leaned his head back on the chair and closed his eyes.

Bonnibell dropped to her knees so she could examine Holliday's leg, pressing from her ankle upwards.

'It's fine, it barely hurts anymore,' Holliday mumbled. 'You don't need to make a fuss. You should worry more about our guest.'

'Oh, I'm okay now.' Damon opened one eye so he could gaze at her. 'I'll get out of your way, just as soon as I've defrosted.'

'There's no rush, lad. I've got painkillers here to help with any inflammation and you need to stay put until you're properly warm.' Bonnibell handed Holliday a foil pack of pills as Innes tapped on the bedroom door and entered carrying a tray piled high with refreshments.

'We thought you'd be in need of calories,' she said, dolling out slabs of Christmas cake and mugs while Bonnibell fussed over them and Damon gazed at Holliday with an expression she could only describe as confused.

'I've got more mince pies in the oven, but I'll come back and check on you both in a bit. Will you be okay in here?' Bonnibell asked, looking at Holliday.

She nodded because she could hardly say she didn't want to be left alone with their guest. She wasn't sure what Damon would say. He had a right to be angry with her – it was obvious she'd been trying to ruin his time in the maze, but would he call her out on it? If he did, would she admit to what she'd been doing? Her gran had always been such a believer in honesty, and she couldn't help but feel embarrassed at the way she'd behaved.

The older woman rose and followed Innes out of the room. The silence stretched and Holliday twisted round until she spotted a pom-pom on the side table positioned close to her chair. She picked it up and squeezed it between her fingertips, letting the soft material relax her.

'Are you imagining that's my neck?' Damon asked, studying her.

'Bonnibell frowns on us strangling the guests,' Holliday joked, her cheeks warming. She avoided his eyes and studied the two pictures positioned on the mantlepiece. The first was her gran, then her eyes caught on the largest frame. In it Adrian wore a green jumper dotted with multicoloured pom-poms. Holliday gazed at his face, wondering how he would feel about what she was doing.

'I'm sorry about the wellingtons,' she blurted, twisting the pom-pom between her fingertips. 'I hope I didn't spoil your visit to the maze. It would be understandable if you were having second thoughts about buying Christmas Resort.'

Damon flashed a smile, his grey eyes sparkling. 'If anything you've made it even more appealing. I had no idea a place like this could be so... exciting.'

'So you're still thinking about buying?' Holliday's voice was heavy with disappointment.

Damon nodded. 'I can't imagine anything would put me off,' he said with a hint of challenge in his tone.

Holliday picked up her hot chocolate and frowned into the mug, hiding her disappointment. Despite his kindness over the last hour and the slivers of attraction she'd been feeling, she knew she had to put Damon off buying Christmas Resort. But if she was going to succeed, she was going to have to come up with a better plan.

7

HOLLIDAY

All Holliday could think about on her morning walk was Damon MacAndrew. She hadn't seen him since he'd disappeared to his cabin saying he had emails to answer, while she'd spent the afternoon resting by the fire at Bonnibell's insistence. Her calf was completely fine now but she was taking extra care not to slip. Bonnibell had asked her to drop a pair of size twelve snow boots into Damon's cabin today – and she was working herself up to seeing him again.

Back down the hill, Innes was waving something in the air. 'Holliday!' she shouted.

Holliday paused to wait as the housekeeper caught her up.

'You've got to look at this,' Innes yelled, handing Holliday a thick black folder before leaning on her knees, panting heavily. 'Mr MacAndrew took his car into the village so we haven't got long until I need to put it back,' she said, her voice racing. 'I found it in his wardrobe.'

'You were in his room?' Holliday asked, surprised.

Innes nodded and began to fiddle with her blonde plait, looking guilty. 'Bonnibell asked me to restock supplies, make the bed and run a hoover round while he was out.' She shrugged.

'You know she wants us to impress him. Also the heating's not working properly and he mentioned being cold – Leo's in there now trying to fix it, but he's not having much luck.' She grimaced.

'So what's this?' Holliday asked, wagging the folder she was clutching.

'When I opened his wardrobe to put fresh drinks and snacks in the fridge, I happened to see it.' Innes swallowed, her cheeks flushing pink. 'I wasn't looking or anything,' she added quickly, 'but the folder was just sitting there and when I opened the fridge I knocked it and it... sort of fell out. And some of the papers scattered onto the rug.'

Holliday pulled a face. 'Guests' paperwork is private, Innes,' she admonished sharply, clutching the folder to her chest. 'You need to put it back immediately.' She thrust the bulging folder at the housekeeper. 'What would Bonnibell say?'

'You have to look at it first,' Innes pleaded, her brown eyes serious. 'You'll understand why when you read it. Please...' she begged when Holliday started to shake her head. 'If you don't, I'll just tell you what it says.'

'Fine.' Holliday pinched her lips then opened the folder and flicked through the pages, feeling a myriad of emotions churn through her stomach, from surprise to disbelief to rage all seasoned with a large helping of dread. She'd almost come around to being taken in by Damon, he'd been so kind to her yesterday. 'I knew it!' she snapped. 'I knew we couldn't trust him. They're plans, for a hotel!' she said, blinking away tears.

Even though she'd suspected Damon had been planning to change Christmas Resort she hadn't expected this. She'd started to accept him – hadn't trusted him exactly, but couldn't believe he'd been planning this all along. She'd called him *Demon* and now she knew the name suited him.

But was this as it seemed? Or could there be another explanation? Adrian had always told Holliday that to get to the truth a journalist had to approach a subject from all angles, to see all points of view. Perhaps she was being rash. She swallowed.

'He could be preparing to build the hotel somewhere else in Christmas Village,' she suggested feebly, as her attention caught on the heart-shaped lochan by the forest they'd been looking at yesterday. Someone had sketched a section of a golf course around the outside.

'There are too many natural landmarks I recognise for it to be anywhere else.' Innes echoed Holliday's conclusion. 'Although none of the buildings look the same. I never imagined anyone would want to knock down the resort. What's going to happen if he does?' The housekeeper wrapped her arms around herself and her eyes glittered. 'I know I shouldn't be thinking about me, but if Leo and I lose our jobs we're going to be living with his mother for the rest of our lives!' Her voice wavered. 'And what about all the people who come here year after year? What about Bonnibell, Ross, Connell and everyone else who works at the resort – what will they do? And what about you?' Innes's voice rose to an emotional crescendo.

'We need to talk to Bonnibell,' Holliday said calmly as she forced the bubbling anger inside her to cool. Then she began to march towards Christmas Lodge with the paperwork clutched tightly in her hands.

'Oh, hen, I'm sure there must be a simple explanation,' Bonnibell soothed as she gazed at the papers Holliday had spread across the kitchen counter.

The large drawing they'd unfolded showed the full scale of the planned hotel, which included a swimming pool, a vast quantity of bedrooms, a restaurant, bar, spa and golf course. The older woman popped open the emergency gingerbread-man tin and grabbed a snowman-shaped biscuit, swallowing the whole thing down before offering the container to the other two women.

'Oh, there is,' Holliday said icily, taking a biscuit and dramatically snapping off its head. 'Mr MacAndrew wants to buy Christmas Resort so he can knock it down and build a hotel in its place.' She chewed fitfully, barely tasting anything, fighting the roils of anger and fear. She'd lived here for two years. It had been her escape when her world had come crashing down, a sanctuary from the loneliness and grief of losing Adrian. 'We have to talk to Mr Gray.' If Damon got his way, Holliday knew she wouldn't survive the changes.

The older woman's mouth pinched and she grabbed another biscuit. 'I spoke to him this morning, hen. Apparently Mr MacAndrew has asked his solicitor to proceed with the sale. He said Christmas Resort is everything he's looking for, he's happy to pay the full asking price and he's keen to move quickly.' She shut her eyes. 'Mr Gray is really excited. He's already put an offer in on a house near to his family.' She sighed. 'The sale's going through whether we want it to or not, there's nothing we can do to stop it.'

She swiped a hand across her forehead and then touched a fingertip to the plans, tracing the plot where Christmas Lodge sat, and where it had been replaced with a large triple-storey building marked up as the reception area and guest suites. The place where Holliday's sparkly reindeer ornaments sat was now a restaurant. The maze had gone too, replaced by a twenty-five-foot indoor swimming pool and spa. Nothing from the original resort had survived.

'There's only one thing for it,' Bonnibell said firmly, carefully straightening the fluffy white collar on her red dress as her mouth spread into a determined line.

'Are we going to make Damon disappear?' Innes said in a low, wavery voice.

'No, hen,' Bonnibell chuckled. 'The lad obviously hasn't

realised how magical Christmas Resort is yet.' She shifted her brown eyes towards Holliday. 'We've got to make him realise that he doesn't want to build this' – she wafted a hand over the plans and screwed up her button nose as if smelling something bad – 'hotel after all. We have to persuade him that he wants to keep the lodge, cabins, maze and all the amazing things we offer here exactly as they are now.' Her eyes sparkled.

'How are we going to do that?' Innes asked, folding her arms.

'By giving him the full Christmas Resort experience,' Bonnibell said enthusiastically.

Holliday drew in a deep breath. Which would mean no sabotaging, no hiding Frosty in Damon's bedroom to make him sneeze, no more freezing cold wellingtons or trying to scare him – and she couldn't go through with her latest plot to add chilli flakes to his hot chocolate and mince pies either. Holliday's shoulders sagged as she realised she'd probably have to be nice to *Demon* too.

'Except there might be a small problem.' Innes winced. 'Just before Mr MacAndrew drove into the village today he told Leo he was planning on leaving early tomorrow.' She picked up another biscuit and bit into it, looking bereft.

'That's two days early!' Bonnibell gasped.

'I suppose he doesn't need to stay any longer since he's already made his decision,' Holliday said sourly, wondering if her acts of sabotage had encouraged Damon to get rid of Christmas Resort for good. It wasn't like she'd made his visit a particularly positive experience. She blinked away guilty tears, then reached into the pocket of her coat so she could squeeze a pom-pom.

'How are we going to persuade him to change his mind in less than twenty-four hours?' she asked, feeling hopeless. 'He won't meet any of the guests. At least if we could encourage him to join in with some of the Christmas activities, if he actually experienced what we do, he might decide this place is worth saving.' She knotted her fingers together. 'We've got no chance at all if he leaves tomorrow.'

Where would she go if the resort was closed down? Not back to Cambridge. She couldn't bear the idea. And if she had no job, how would she be able to afford to keep Adrian's house going? Holliday's stomach pitched.

'Ach, hen, Connell knows a thing or two about cars.' Bonnibell chuckled before winking at them both. 'I'm sure Mr MacAndrew will stay for a few more days if he's got no transport. If we're really clever we could probably stretch it out to a full week.' Her grin widened. 'Our next guests are arriving the day after tomorrow – I'm sure we can make sure he's here to meet them.'

'But where will he sleep? Reindeer Retreat has been rented out.' Holliday said. 'All the lodges are booked up to the end of February.'

'We can offer him Mr Gray's bedroom,' Bonnibell decided. 'I don't normally let guests stopover there, but since Mr MacAndrew is going to be our new owner it's the perfect place for him to sleep.'

Holliday gulped. That room was only two doors down from hers. She'd have to keep Frosty away from him. Ensure she steered clear too...

Innes frowned as she spread her fingers wide on the counter and leaned towards the older woman. 'I can only see one problem with this plan.'

'Yes, lass?' Bonnibell said.

'Won't Damon try to contact the Christmas Village Garage if he has car trouble?' The housekeeper arched an eyebrow.

'Perhaps.' Bonnibell wagged a finger at them both, looking pleased with herself. 'But I happen to know the owner of that particular establishment, and I'm guessing any mechanical work is going to be delayed because of the inclement weather...'

'Oh, you are wicked.' For the first time since Holliday had seen Innes this morning the younger woman relaxed.

'Not wicked,' Bonnibell said, tapping the side of her nose. 'I prefer the word *wily*. Because if my plan succeeds, we're going to convince Damon MacAndrew that he *loves* this place as much as we do.'

'Really?' Holliday asked, wondering if that were even possible. He hadn't seemed remotely impressed so far.

'Yes, really.' The older woman nodded, looking serious. 'And not just that, the lad's going to go ahead with his plan to buy Christmas Resort – only instead of building his hotel, he's going to keep it exactly as it is.' Her eyes skimmed across the plans on the table, and this time when they met Holliday's they gleamed. 'We're going to make sure of it.'

Innes let out a loud cheer. Holliday gnawed on her lower lip, hoping Bonnibell was right. She had a sneaking suspicion *Demon* MacAndrew would be hard to convince.

8

DAMON

Damon heaved his small suitcase and laptop bag out of Reindeer Retreat and dumped it next to his car before looking up into the sky. It was still dark, barely seven o'clock in the morning, but he'd decided yesterday that there was no point in staying for longer. He'd already told his solicitor to go ahead with the sale and didn't need bothersome things like a guilty conscience, or ill-advised attraction to a woman who seemed to loathe him, getting in the way of the deal. Once the sale had gone through he'd return, have an honest conversation with the team, offer them all new jobs and pay rises. By then nothing would give him any trouble. Least of all his conscience.

Damon scraped an armful of fresh snow from the driver's side of his Jeep before pulling open the door and slinging his now icy belongings onto the back seat. He took a quick moment to glance back at Christmas Lodge, to where Holliday was doubtless just rising – probably already plotting today's clever sabotage, while Bonnibell baked something to tempt him in the pretty, festive kitchen. He shook his head, pushing down the slivers of confusion twisting in his gut, climbed in the car and slammed the door, staring down the long driveway in the direction of his escape. The next time he drove along this path, the whole place – fir trees, ridiculous shiny baubles, pom-poms and all – would be gone. The final memory in his nightmare of a marriage would be destroyed, giving him the peace he craved. Perhaps then he'd be able to move on.

He pressed the ignition button and frowned when the engine didn't turn over, then tried again and again with the same result. 'What the hell?' Damon shoved the door wide open and strode around to the front of the Jeep so he could glare at the grille. 'You worked fine yesterday afternoon,' he complained, striding back to jerk the lever that opened the bonnet. Not that he knew what he was supposed to be searching for – everything looked perfectly fine to him. 'Bugger it,' he snapped, pulling his mobile from his pocket so he could call a car rescue service.

But there was no signal.

'Typical.' He slammed the door again and turned before slipping and sliding his way up the pathway towards Christmas Lodge, barely managing to stay upright. He'd worn his work shoes because he'd had no intention of getting out of the car until Christmas Resort – with its icy trails and oddly appealing team – was an inconvenient and distant memory.

Damon pressed the bell at the front of the lodge as soon as he climbed onto the decking and then he shoved his hands into the pockets of his coat and tensed as it chimed 'Santa Claus is Coming to Town' at a high volume, and a memory of Willow humming along to the tune and wriggling her hips caught him unawares, twisting his stomach.

Bonnibell answered the door in seconds. She was wearing another Santa-style dress today, only this one was royal blue with furry white edging. The colours suited her. 'Come in, come in.' She waved Damon inside. 'Did you need something, lad? Innes was going to drop some breakfast in presently – you didn't eat much last night, you must be famished.' Her eyes glided to his stomach as if she expected it to murmur its agreement.

'I... um.' Damon cleared his throat, feeling even more awkward, and looked at the ground, avoiding the older woman's dark-brown eyes which were far more canny than he'd initially thought. 'I was leaving – work emergency,' he lied, hoping the handyman, Leo, who'd been attempting to fix the heating in his lodge yesterday morning hadn't mentioned that he was leaving after he'd shared the news in a moment of weakness. Damon had been meaning to tell the Bakers that he was going, but something had stopped him. Guilt probably. Although he had nothing to feel guilty for.

'My car won't start.' Damon pointed back towards the Jeep which was still sitting in the same spot. A dusting of snow had already replaced the avalanche he'd just cleaned off the driver's door and windscreen.

'Ach, lad. That's a shame,' Bonnibell said, looping an arm through his elbow and leading him slowly towards the kitchen.

Damon considered refusing but decided to follow – where would he go otherwise?

'Why don't you sit, have a coffee and I'll see if Connell can take a look at your car? I've just made mince pies,' she added at the exact moment the tempting fragrance reached Damon's nose and his stomach made a loud growling sound. 'Take a seat,' Bonnibell insisted, smiling. 'Holliday will be along in a moment – I believe she has some plans for you both so it's fortuitous you're not leaving us quite yet.' She bustled around the kitchen, grabbing a Father Christmas mug and filling it with coffee before placing it in front of him.

'I'm still planning on leaving.' Damon checked his watch and frowned. 'There's really no need for Holliday to entertain me,' he said as the woman in question strode in from the dining room wearing a short, red belted jumper dress that hugged her slender frame.

She immediately grabbed an apron and pulled it on. 'Showing you around will be my pleasure,' she said, her eyes glittering with something Damon couldn't read. It didn't seem friendly, but that didn't stop his body from tightening when she gave him a long look. 'Some of our guests are arriving tomorrow so I thought you might like to come shopping with me in Christmas Village. I've had lots of craft supplies posted to me and when the weather's this unpredictable the postman doesn't always like to come out this far. The post office is often shut so The Corner Shop takes care of it for me. It'll give you a chance to see the village and to meet some of the people who live there. If you're planning on buying the resort' – her tone of voice was challenging – 'then I'm sure you'll want to meet your new neighbours in advance.'

'And while you're there I'll ask Connell to take a look at your car. If he can't fix it I know of a garage just outside the village,' Bonnibell said. 'I can give them a call later if it's necessary.'

'Um. I was planning on calling a breakdown service,' Damon said.

'Ach, it'll be far quicker if we help you sort it out,' Bonnibell said firmly. 'Lots of those companies struggle to get their trucks out this way and you could be waiting for days. Just leave it to me.'

Damon reluctantly nodded. 'Okay, thank you. But please can you tell Connell and the garage that it's *very* urgent?' He didn't want to stay any longer than necessary, couldn't risk being drawn further into the sugary web these two women were weaving. He knew his defences were cracking, knew it was only a matter of time before he began to question his plans.

'Of course.' Bonnibell gave him a bright smile.

'I usually walk in, I assume you're okay with that?' Holliday gave Damon a thoughtful look he didn't understand, although the sideways kick of her mouth suggested she was happy about spending time with him, which was confusing. 'I've got some new snow boots for you,' she added, glancing at Bonnibell. 'A gift from the resort.'

'No wellingtons today?' Damon risked a joke, then he picked up his coffee and sipped, watching the two women exchange a look before Holliday's smile brightened by about a thousand watts.

Something odd was happening, either that or his senses were off. Why did the woman keep beaming at him? Why was his body responding? Damon blew out a breath and reached for one of the mince pies Bonnibell had left out. If he watched Holliday carefully when they went into town, he'd probably puzzle it out.

'What are those?' Damon asked, pointing to the stocky hedge that followed the pavement as he walked beside Holliday in the direction of Christmas Village. It was still snowing heavily which gave their surroundings an oddly unreal hue, but the knitted garlands he'd seen hanging from almost every shrub, tree and fence during their walk were both attractive and baffling.

'The villagers make them in a knitting club I run and we've been hanging them in the square and along the roads that lead into the high street,' she explained.

'That's a lot of knitting,' Damon said, checking to see where the decoration finished but there was no visible end in sight. From where he was standing it looked like it might go on for miles.

'We had a surge in members as word spread so we've been able to decorate even further out than expected. I'm sure you will have noticed lots of knitting around the resort too,' Holliday said, stopping so she could point out a knitted donkey, castle, cottage, turkey, tiara and tool belt that had been painstakingly crafted from multicoloured wool. 'The decorations represent the people and places of Christmas Village.' She turned and studied him through glorious blue eyes. 'If you keep an eye out during our walk you may spot Frosty, Claus and Bonnibell too.'

'What about you?' Damon asked, wondering what Holliday would look like recreated in wool.

She flushed. 'There's someone with long brown hair wearing a white apron filled with pom-poms that Innes made. I don't know how many people would realise it was me...'

'I would,' Damon said, instantly regretting the confession when she looked surprised. He cleared his throat. 'So, you run a knitting club?' he deflected. The decorations were charming and for some reason he wanted to know more. He couldn't help being enchanted by a person who spent her days creating and teaching others to do the same. Willow had been in mergers and acquisitions like him; she'd been ruthless and ambitious – both qualities he'd admired. But she'd never been warm. She'd never cared about anyone or anything aside from herself. Damon probably should have seen that as a warning but he hadn't looked beyond her beautiful face. He shook himself and frowned. He was thinking about her again.

'We host the knitting club at the resort every Wednesday evening and a number of our guests and a few of the locals join in,' Holliday explained.

'The villagers come?' Damon asked, surprised. He hadn't paid much attention to the village when he'd visited with Willow – had paid even less since coming back.

She nodded. 'Having local connections is important to us. We get a lot of business from word of mouth, but also our guests love exploring Christmas Village. It's all part of the experience.' She shrugged. 'Perhaps you'd like to come along to the club while you're staying? You don't need to be able to knit, I can teach you the basics in half an hour.'

Damon cleared his throat again. 'I hope to be in London by this evening.' He didn't add that a small part of him was keen to see Holliday at work. To watch her interact with people she actually liked. He wondered what he'd learn about her if he did. 'Tell me about the pom-poms,' he asked instead, pointing to a couple of trees on the other side of the road which were speckled with dozens of them in various colours and sizes.

'Ah, I made them.' Holliday gave him a smile tinged with sadness. 'I think they look pretty, don't you?'

Damon nodded, because he agreed, although a part of him – the sensible part – wished he wasn't telling the truth. It was easier that way – he wasn't looking to invest emotionally and the longer he stayed, the harder it was going to be to keep his distance. Which was why he hoped Connell had fixed his car. If he left soon he'd be back in London by late evening and this whole experience would be a dim and distant memory. A pinprick in his quest to rid himself of Willow's memory once and for all.

'We'll go to The Corner Shop first to pick up my post,' Holliday said. 'Then I'll take you around some of the main shops on the high street. It's a close-knit community and I'm sure people will get a kick out of meeting the new owner of Christmas Resort.'

'Ah... okay,' Damon said, looking down at the pavement, hoping he'd think of a way of getting out of that before they arrived. He could see Christmas lights in the distance and guessed they were getting closer to the shops so he'd have to think fast. 'What's in the road?' he asked, squinting through the snowflakes which were now coming down in thick droves. 'Looks like a... donkey.' Or was it a hallucination brought on by Bonnibell's sugary mince pies?

'Yes, that's Bob,' Holliday said. 'He belongs to Edina Lachlan who owns Evergreen Castle on the other side of the village. You'll often see him wandering the streets, he's a big favourite with the kids in our local primary school. When Edina visits the knitting club, he often comes to the resort too.'

'I'm amazed she lets a donkey roam free with all the cows, wildcats and boar running loose,' Damon said dryly. The creature studied them as they drew closer before turning and trotting away.

Holliday flushed and fell silent until they reached the end of the high street where Damon spotted The Corner Shop, situated a few metres along from the post office. Adjacent to that sat a café, belonging to someone called Rowan, which had steamed-up windows and a small queue of people waiting outside. The Workshop was further down the high street and Damon recalled Willow had frequented the beauty salon a few times while they'd been holidaying at the resort. Just the memory of her had his stomach twisting in annoyance.

He watched Holliday open the door and stride into The Corner Shop, then stopped just outside, taking in the pretty, festive window before following. A man with silver hair, wearing a garish red-and-green Christmas jumper, was standing behind the long counter at the far end of the space.

'Tavish Doherty,' Holliday said, striding up to the counter. 'Let me introduce you to Damon MacAndrew. He's hoping to become the new owner of Christmas Resort.' Her voice was friendly but Damon couldn't help feeling she was issuing a warning under the words. Perhaps hinting that the older man should be on his guard?

'Pleased to meet you.' Damon stepped forward and took the offered hand.

'Aye. I hope I can say the same.' Tavish frowned, the creases across his face deepening. 'My son Matt runs this shop now, I just work part-time.' His eyes narrowed and his expression grew more serious. 'The resort's a good place, important for the village,' he said gruffly. 'It employs a lot of people and brings plenty of custom to the area, especially to the shop – I'm assuming you're planning to do right by it?'

Damon cleared his throat. 'Absolutely,' he lied, wavering a

little. 'Nice place.' He waved a palm around, trying to appear harmless. Once the hotel was up and running, he was sure the locals would welcome the new clientele it would bring – but he couldn't afford to stir up any ill-feeling in advance. Planning objections would delay the work and he just wanted this whole thing done.

'Aye,' the older man said, his back ramrod straight and his demeanour far from friendly. Then his eyes shifted to Holliday and immediately softened. 'You here for your post, lass?' he asked, reaching under the counter and pulling out two brown parcels. 'Matt mentioned he'd put them aside for you. One's from that craft shop you use and the other one's been posted from Cambridge. Looks like the same handwriting as the usual monthly parcels you receive.' He raised an eyebrow as if inviting Holliday to confide.

'Thank you.' She took the parcels and wrapped her arms around both bundles. 'Bonnibell asked if I could pick up a dozen bottles of that new Secret Cider you've been selling? Connell's really taken with it and she wants to put some in the lodges too. We've got new guests arriving tomorrow.' She glanced around. 'I couldn't see any as I came in – have you sold out?'

Tavish jerked his chin. 'We're hoping for a delivery soon. The cider's proving very popular. It's made by a contact of Matt's. I sold three dozen bottles to someone who was driving through the village yesterday afternoon – he'd heard about it from a friend who was visiting last week. But...' Tavish narrowed his eyes at Damon before shaking his head once, then he bent to tug some bottles out from under the counter. He kept glancing at the door of the shop as he expertly wrapped each of the six bottles in brown paper before placing the whole lot inside another paper bag. 'I kept a few aside for special customers, but I'm afraid there are only these left.' He winked at Holliday. 'I'll put it on the resort's account – tell Bonnibell

I've listed it as red wine.' Tavish tapped the bridge of his nose before glancing at Damon as if suddenly recalling he was there. 'It's a new brand and we haven't added it onto the system yet,' he muttered.

Holliday looked surprised. 'Okay, I'll tell Bonnibell when I get back. Are you expecting more in soon?'

Tavish shrugged. 'Who knows, lass. The deliveries are intermittent and we're getting more and more demand. Bram McGregor who runs Christmas Pud Inn is trying to stock it too, but he's not been able to get hold of any yet. I'll give the resort a call when more turns up and keep a couple of dozen aside for you.'

'Thank you,' Holliday said as Damon took the bag Tavish offered. 'We're going to visit some of the other shops in the high street. I want Mr MacAndrew to get the full Christmas Village experience while he's here.' She turned to look at him and blinked innocently.

'Can't wait,' Damon said as he turned, wondering if Holliday was up to something. He was going to have to think of an excuse fast, because the last thing he wanted to do was meet any more of the villagers. Even if a small part of him wasn't completely unhappy about the idea.

9

HOLLIDAY

'The snow's getting heavier,' Holliday remarked as they made their way back from Christmas Village to the top of the resort's driveway. She saw the lights twinkling in Christmas Lodge and immediately spotted an unfamiliar dark green Volkswagen Passat Estate parked outside.

'Expecting someone?' Damon asked, swinging the large bag he was holding into his other hand. He'd insisted on carrying the cider and parcels Holliday had picked up in The Corner Shop, but had snubbed all the other stores along the high street. First he'd balked at the queue outside Rowan's Café, then he'd taken one look inside The Workshop where the owner Kenzy Campbell had been painting someone's nails fire-engine red – and had vehemently shaken his head as if he were afraid she'd somehow try to paint him.

In the end, he had asked if they could explore the village square and Christmas tree that Mr Gray had allegedly told him so much about. Then he'd spent half an hour admiring the pompoms, bunting and baubles the knitting club had made, showering the creative work with a raft of insincere compliments until Holliday had grown irritated. It was obvious the man was avoiding meeting any more of the villagers – and since she knew about his plans for the resort she understood why. She also knew he wouldn't be able to get away with it for much longer, not now he was going to be stuck here.

'I've no idea.' Holliday perused the Passat. 'I don't know of anyone who owns that make of car,' she answered, stopping just outside Reindeer Retreat where Innes was inside changing the sheets. 'Looks like you'll have fresh bedding if you need to stay tonight.'

The housekeeper waved from the window when she spotted them, then indicated that they should make their way up to the lodge.

'Your car's gone,' Holliday remarked as they passed the place where it had been parked earlier. There were no tyre tracks – the ground already layered with crisp, pillowy snow.

'Hopefully Connell's fixed the problem. Perhaps he's taken it for a quick drive?' Damon suggested.

Holliday nodded, wondering where the shrewd old man had decided to hide it. There was plenty of room in the grounds, and at least three barns where he could stash the Jeep. Even if Damon went for a walk he'd be unlikely to stumble across it. She tracked to the front door and held it open until they were both inside.

'Holliday!' Bonnibell appeared the instant she shut the door and Claus bounded from the entrance to the kitchen before seeking out Damon, wagging his hellos. 'Barney Price and his family, the Bennetts, have arrived a day early,' Bonnibell whispered, pointing towards the kitchen and waggling her generous eyebrows. 'Mabel Price passed six months ago apparently and they're all over the place with dates. She used to manage everyone's diaries.'

'Mabel died?' Holliday gulped, remembering the sweet grandmother who'd always had such a kind smile for everyone – even the sour-faced husband she'd been married to for almost sixty years. She'd been an incredible knitter and had often helped out when Holliday ran the club. 'But she comes twice a year...' Holliday's voice faltered and she momentarily bit her lip to stop herself from acknowledging the bubble of distress that had lodged in her airway.

'Aye, lass,' Bonnibell said, reaching out to gently squeeze her shoulder. 'The family are booked into Gingerbread House and Barney is moving into Reindeer Retreat just like always. It's been incredibly popular lately. I had an enquiry from some honeymooners last month who were very insistent they wanted to stay in that cabin too. I asked Barney if he'd take another one but he refused.' She shrugged. 'He's insisting on staying there alone – but from what I understand he wasn't keen on coming at all.'

'How is he?' Holliday's voice sounded scratchy and she turned her attention to the fluffy red rug on the floor to get her emotions under control.

'About the same – perhaps a little *less* accommodating.' Bonnibell gave Holliday a rueful smile. 'But I think we can forgive him for that.' Bonnibell turned to Damon. 'I hope you don't mind, but I thought since you'd already moved your things out of Reindeer Retreat this morning, that we could just pop your suitcase straight into Mr Gray's room upstairs? Connell brought your luggage in from your car. There's plenty of space. You'll have your own bathroom, sofa area and Frosty rarely strays into the other bedrooms so you won't have to worry about unexpected guests. Especially if you keep your door closed.'

'What about my car? I'm supposed to be leaving later,' Damon said, frantically looking around.

'Ach, Connell couldn't do a thing with it.' Bonnibell waved her palms. 'I called the garage and they towed it forty minutes ago. They'll take a look. I gave them your mobile number and they promised to give you a call as soon as they could. Did you know two of your tyres were almost flat?'

'No.' Damon's eyes widened. 'Are you sure? They looked fine this morning.'

The older woman shrugged. 'Tyre pressure can sometimes drop in the cold, don't fret. It's good it was spotted before you left. Nothing worse than losing a tyre when the weather's taken a turn for the worse. It's a long way back to London, you wouldn't want to break down.' Bonnibell shuddered. 'Don't worry, hen, you can stay with us for as long as you need. There's lots here to keep you entertained. We run the knitting club tomorrow evening, so it's fortuitous you might still be around and be able to go. All our guests love it.'

'Oh. I really don't think I'll still be here.' Damon's cheeks paled. 'Don't you have trains?' Clearly panicking, he whipped his mobile from his pocket and began to search an app.

'Ach, lad, you won't get anything this time of the day, Connell already checked. Besides, even if there were trains the service is likely to be affected by the weather,' Bonnibell said. 'Stay the night, we can see how things look in the morning. I'm sure you don't want to leave your car in Scotland if you can help it?'

'I'm sure it'll be fixed by then,' Holliday jumped in, shoving down the slivers of guilt. She wanted to come clean, but instead she visualised the hallway they were now standing in reduced to a pile of rubble and the opulent hotel reception Damon planned to build in its place. If Christmas Resort was razed, she'd never be able to keep the house in Cambridge and she couldn't imagine what she'd do if she had to leave here. Perhaps in a few years she'd be ready for something to change, but right now she couldn't contemplate the idea. She patted Damon on the shoulder before picking up the bag he'd placed on the floor. 'I ordered some new wool and knitting needles so we've got plenty of spare equipment if you are still around—'

'I really don't think—' He held up a palm.

'It'll be a good way for you to get a feel for what we do day to day,' Holliday interrupted. 'I know you'll enjoy meeting more of the locals, especially since we saw so few of them this afternoon.' She stared at him, and when his eyes met hers and lingered she felt the sizzle reach her toes and immediately broke eye contact. She gulped. 'Would you mind taking the cider into the kitchen, please? I'll go and put the supplies in the craft room and I've got some letters in here I'd really like to read.'

'From Cambridge?' Bonnibell asked, her smile wavering before she plastered it back on, but not before Damon noticed and glanced at Holliday again, this time with a questioning look. 'Why don't you come and meet our new guests?' the older woman suggested, coiling an arm through his and practically dragging him towards the kitchen before he could satisfy his curiosity.

'I'll see you in a few minutes,' Holliday said, watching until they disappeared – then she tugged off her snow boots and bounded upstairs.

Holliday fed Mr Jingles a handful of muesli before spreading the contents of the parcel from Mr Hornbuckle across her bed and sitting beside it on the duvet. There were nine Christmas cards in all, eight of which were addressed to Adrian. Holliday swallowed and put them – still sealed – to one side. After two years there were still a few people she hadn't told her fiancé had passed. But the fact that her neighbour had chosen to send her the unopened cards rather than place them on the mantlepiece in the house like he did last year, suggested he'd decided it was high time Holliday did.

She sighed and opened the Christmas card from the older man, recognising the narrow, spidery handwriting on the envelope immediately before reading the innocuous festive message and popping it onto her dresser. Then she undid the folder containing the month's household bills and cringed at the numbers before putting it to one side ready to deal with when she felt braver – besides, she had a few mystery letters to distract herself with first.

She ripped the top off one and found a flyer for a sofa company Adrian once used, then drew out an invitation to subscribe to a local lottery from another, before carefully opening the final envelope marked *Private and Confidential*. Holliday had to read the handwritten letter twice before she fully understood the senders' request.

Dear Ms Harrison,

I hope you don't mind us writing to you out of the blue but we wanted to contact you about The Ambles. We understand you aren't living locally but hope this letter reaches you somehow. We are a local couple who recently missed out on buying our dream family home nearby and would love to settle in a house just like yours so we can put down roots. There is something very special about your street, and The Ambles in particular. It looks like such a warm and happy place. The kind of home that was created to make wonderful memories in. I'm sure you have many of your own.

Holliday swallowed. Her house was filled with a hundred happy memories – all of which she was doing everything in her power to keep alive.

I don't know what your circumstances are, but I believe your house is currently sitting empty and we wondered if you were thinking of moving.

'Never,' Holliday croaked as emotion clogged her throat.

If you are considering selling at any point, please would you consider contacting us directly? We are chain-free, cash buyers and would be able to proceed at your convenience without incurring any estate agent fees. We are prepared to go above and beyond any current valuation and have included a ball-park figure at the end of this letter along with our contact details in case you are interested.

Yours hopefully,

Adrian and Sandra Leveston

The figure at end of the letter made Holliday's hand shake so much she had to put it on the bed. When she'd inherited Adrian's estate after he'd died, she'd had no idea of how much the house was worth and it had never occurred to her to check. Since his parents had passed years before and he'd had no siblings, she'd been the only beneficiary. And since she was alone in the world, too, she hadn't had anyone to share or discuss her inheritance with – besides, there was nothing to review, beyond the fact that she didn't want to sell or change anything.

Holliday traced a fingertip over the couple's names at the end of the letter and sighed. One of them was called Adrian – was that a sign that she should consider their generous offer? The fact that the sum they'd mentioned, alongside a small mort-gage, might be enough to buy Christmas Resort occurred to her, but her stomach churned, immediately rejecting the idea. She couldn't give up Adrian's home – but she couldn't lose Christmas Resort either.

Then Frosty jumped onto the bed beside Holliday and climbed onto her lap, balancing himself across her knees before curling into a ball and starting to purr. Holliday stroked his head as her mind conjured pictures of her and Adrian still living in The Ambles, of the children they might have had running along the hallways and around the garden. Her eyes filled and she pushed the images away, picturing her fiancé sitting in his favourite chair beside the fire next to the Christmas tree instead. He'd be reading and sipping red wine.

'I'm sorry. I can't,' she whispered, and placed the letter in the pocket of her apron. She wasn't ready to move on and she'd never be able to bring herself to sell The Ambles, even though a tiny piece of her kept whispering it was time.

'I'm so sorry the heating in the lodge has been all over the place this morning,' Bonnibell soothed as she handed fluffy red blankets to their unexpected guests who were now huddled around a roaring fire in the sitting room. 'It's working fine in your cabins, which are almost ready for you to move into. I've got a meal on the go so we can eat together this evening.'

'I should think so too. A place like this should have a constant supply of food in the fridge.' An older man with grey hair, who Holliday recognised as Barney Price, grumbled from the corner of the room where he was picking stray pieces of fluff from the arm of one of the chairs. 'It's freezing in here and the mince pies aren't as tasty as usual,' he complained, placing his empty plate on the floor beside his feet, which Claus made a beeline for. 'Are you sure they're fresh?' he added.

He earned a patient nod from Bonnibell. 'I cooked them myself, this morning,' she said gently.

He huffed and Holliday frowned. The man had always been sour, but his sweet wife Mabel had somehow softened the affect. What would balance him now the nicer half was gone?

'Ah, there you are.' Bonnibell beamed as she spotted Holliday standing by the entrance.

'It's so wonderful to see you again!' Kate Bennett immediately put down her mug of hot chocolate and hopped up from where she was sitting so she could give Holliday a hug. 'I can't believe it's been over seven months,' she said sadly, staring into her eyes. 'You heard about Mum?' Kate pushed one of her blonde curls away from her face. She was a pretty woman in her mid-forties with a wicked sense of humour and a penchant for early morning runs which Holliday had never understood. The exercise kept her petite frame slim and her complexion glowing, although it was dull today and there were bags under her eyes.

Holliday could understand more than anyone – she hadn't slept properly after Adrian had passed until she'd arrived here. Hopefully Kate would start to feel better after a few days at the resort.

'I'm really very sorry,' Holliday said, her voice heavy with emotion.

'Don't be, it's the cycle of life, nothing more, nothing less,' Barney piped up from the corner. 'I keep telling you all that.' He pushed out his bottom lip, making his face look skeletal. He'd lost weight, suggesting he was missing his wife more than he was making out. 'Mabel wouldn't want to spoil Christmas and if I have my way we're going to celebrate it exactly as we always have. With craft, crackers, presents and as much food as we can eat.' He folded his arms across his chest and stared at them, his expression belligerent.

Kate gave him a tense smile. 'You're right, Dad, it is what she would have wanted.' She sighed softly. 'Which is the reason we all agreed we'd still come. I'm only sorry we arrived a day early. I'm sure I put it in the calendar correctly. I've no idea where my head's been these last few months.' She rubbed the back of her neck.

'Looking after everyone else, as per usual,' Kate's husband Robert said, coming up to pat her shoulder. 'Good to see you again, Holliday.' He gave her a crooked smile, but despite the attempt he looked tired and his dark hair was a little unkempt and longer than he normally kept it.

'And you. Are the children here?' Holliday asked, glancing around the room, expecting to see Arthur, their teenage son, and Lucie, their eight-year-old, lurking somewhere, attached to their devices.

'You just missed them. They popped out a few minutes ago for a walk around the maze with Claus and Connell,' Robert explained. 'It was a long drive up from Brighton and they were climbing the walls, so he offered to help them work off some energy.'

'They'll be getting up to mischief by now no doubt,' Barney moaned. 'They complained so much on the journey here.' He rolled his eyes, clearly missing the irony.

'Well.' Bonnibell clapped her hands. 'The good news is Innes has just got back and your accommodation is ready for you to move into. Leo's transporting your luggage there as we speak. Why don't you make yourselves comfortable and we can meet back here at' – she glanced at her watch – 'six o'clock? I've got a treat for you all this evening.'

'What?' Kate asked.

'The potential new owner of our resort is staying here. He's just settling in upstairs, and you'll get to meet him over dinner.' She winked at Holliday. 'He's really handsome and quite charming and he's staying so he can learn about everything we do at the resort. I'm hoping you'll be able to tell him about the things you most love about coming – and what in particular makes you keep coming back.'

'Well.' Barney sniffed, looking around. 'It'd be a lot easier to do that if the heating worked and the mince pies tasted like they usually do.'

'Dad,' Kate admonished, giving Bonnibell an apologetic grimace. 'Please ignore him.'

Bonnibell shrugged. 'It's fine, hen. I'm baking up a batch of gingerbread biscuits which I remember are a particular favourite of your dad's, and I'm sure the heating will be fixed very soon. Meanwhile, we'll keep the fires burning and there'll be plenty of free whisky in your rooms to help you to thaw out,' she promised.

She nudged Holliday's arm as the family began to make their way towards the front door where their shoes and coats were waiting. 'Hen, why don't you go and see how Damon's settling in? Make sure he's got everything he needs and I'll meet you back here in an hour so you can help me get dinner ready? This is our chance to dazzle and we all need to be involved.' With that the older woman marched into the hall.

'Of course,' Holliday said, her eyes skirting the room, wondering if it was even possible to impress Damon – and what in the world they would have to do to ensure he fell in love with Christmas Resort.

10

DAMON

The bedroom that Bonnibell had allocated to Damon was absolutely freezing. He checked the radiator, which was cold, then rubbed his hands together and loaded another large log onto the fire that had been lit in the pretty fireplace opposite his bed. Then he paced around the space in front of it, stopping momentarily to kick the edge of his suitcase before striding around some more. He should be halfway to London by now, instead he was stuck in Christmas Lodge, a few doors down from the tempting art teacher who kept looking at him as if she were imagining wrapping his body in some of her knitting and dumping him in a snowdrift far, far away. If the garage couldn't fix his car by the morning he'd call a taxi and persuade them to drop him at the closest train station – which according to Google was twenty-two miles from here.

Damon almost jumped out of his skin when his mobile rang in his hand. He didn't recognise the number so immediately picked up, praying it was the garage calling with good news. If he got the car back and left soon, he'd be in London before morning and this whole nightmare would be done. 'Hello,' he said hopefully.

'I suspected you were still ignoring my calls because the other number I had doesn't seem to work anymore,' Scarlett complained. 'I was giving you the benefit of the doubt, then I thought I'd use another mobile to see if you'd pick up. Where are you exactly?'

'Somewhere between Hades and hell,' Damon grumbled, slumping onto the king-sized bed and resting his head onto one palm. He could hang up now, but knew that wouldn't stop his sister from finding another way of tracking him down.

'I would say I felt sorry for you, but we both know this is all your own fault,' his sister said without sympathy.

'How's that?' he asked, frowning at the phone.

'I'm assuming you've heard of karma?' she asked sarcastically.

'Of course,' Damon snapped. 'Which is why I know I'm due some good luck soon.'

'I'm not sure I agree. Where are you now? Have the team at Christmas Resort figured out what you're up to yet?' Scarlett enquired.

'Still here and I'm not entirely sure...' Damon said slowly, thinking about some of the looks Holliday had given him earlier, ignoring the way his body immediately reacted to the thought of her. Before Willow he hadn't been masochistic – had the relationship twisted something in his brain? 'They don't know about the hotel, but I think at least one of them might suspect something's off.'

He got up and strode around, then stopped to open the minibar he'd just spotted to the right of the room, immediately picking out a bottle of the Secret Cider he'd tried the night before.

He popped the lid, poured some into the glass perched on the top of the fridge and sipped. It really was very good. It might be worth getting in touch with the people who made it before he left for London – if the shopkeeper Tavish had been telling the truth it had a lot of potential. Perhaps he could add it to his growing portfolio? It would be nice to be involved in a project from the ground up.

'My car's out of action for now, so I'm staying here for one more night.' He winced. 'I'll be back in London tomorrow and then it's all systems go on the sale.' He strode to the window so he could gaze at the view, trying not to admire the beautiful rolling hills, or three reindeer decorations he could see glowing on top of one of them. He guessed you'd be able to see them from all sides of the valley, like some kind of beacon welcoming visitors home.

'Seriously?' he grumbled under his breath, almost choking on the cider. What was happening to him? It was like this place was turning him into an emotional marshmallow – making him buy into the cheesy Christmas promises it could never deliver on. The sooner he got back to his real life, the sooner he'd get himself under control.

'You've not come to your senses then?' Scarlett asked, sounding disappointed. 'I'm not surprised. Perhaps a few more days up there will help you change your mind. I've been reading articles about Christmas Resort. It's really very special. I've been thinking I might book the family in for a break.'

'There are no vacancies. Besides, you'll like my new hotel better,' Damon said mildly because he knew his sister was trying to wind him up. 'There'll be a golf course, spa, but no Christmas trees or glitter and...' He pressed a hand on the radiator again. 'Crucially, the heating will work.' He scanned the room. It was clean, comfortable and oddly appealing, but could do with redecorating, something sleeker and more sophisticated. Even the minibar was an older model and he guessed the humming noise coming from it would keep him up for most of the night. 'I'm doing them a favour, the lodge and all the cabins need a total revamp, I'm thinking classy rather than cosy.' He frowned. Was he trying to convince his sister or himself?

'Then why not consider giving it to them?' Scarlett asked quietly. 'Instead of destroying, build on what you have. I've said it before, brother, and I'll say it again: you don't get over a bad memory by pretending the old one didn't exist. It's better to acknowledge and build on what you've learned. Otherwise you'll just make the same mistakes over and over.'

Damon bristled and clenched his jaw. 'I know you want the best for me, sis, which is why I'm going to agree to disagree. When I'm home tomorrow I'll visit and show you what I'm going to do.' He sighed, deliberately releasing the tension in his body. 'Besides, how is this any different from what you did with *he-who-must-not-be-named*? You've got a new husband, you've redecorated and extended your old house. Isn't that the same?' He wasn't sure why he wanted to know. It was that feeling in his chest again, like someone had opened it up and sprinkled glitter between his ribs. Now it was prickling his insides, making him feel uncomfortable and out of sorts.

Scarlett snorted. 'You can't compare it, Damon. The man left, but I didn't torch his car or cut up his clothes, and I'm still living in the same house. I've claimed it as my own, made new memories, made it even better. That helped me to heal because I haven't ignored what happened, I haven't destroyed what was here. I've chosen to build my new life on the same foundations. You should try doing the same. Stay for a couple more days, forget about Willow and give the place a fresh chance. See it through new eyes, not Willow-tinted spectacles. You've got nothing to lose.'

Damon thought about Holliday and shook his head. He couldn't afford to get distracted from his mission here. 'I know what you're trying to do, but my mind's made up. Look, I need a shower and change of clothes. I'm supposed to be heading down to dinner in an hour to meet some guests. I'll call as soon as I'm back in London.'

Damon heard his sister sigh and didn't wait for her to argue more. Instead, he hung up and finished his cider, instantly dismissing everything she'd said.

It wasn't to Damon's taste, but the en-suite bathroom was large and immaculately clean, and there was a walk-in shower in the far corner with enough toiletries to satisfy a football team. Damon picked up the shower gel and sniffed, then thumped it back in the same place when he detected the scent of gingerbread and immediately recoiled as he remembered Willow stepping out of the bath in Reindeer Retreat smelling just like it. If he needed a reminder of why he was doing the right thing, fate had just delivered one in spades.

He gritted his teeth as he strode out of the bathroom and grabbed a fresh towel from the end of the bed. Then he slipped out of his clothes and, shivering, made his way back and switched on the water, groaning when a dribble of hot water emerged from the showerhead.

'Does anything in this place work properly?' he complained, wriggling the head a little and praying the movement would release a cascade of water worthy of Niagara Falls. When the dribble became a slow trickle he gave in and stepped into the cubicle before pouring a dollop of minty shower gel he'd found beside the gingerbread one onto his palm. Damon shut his eyes and massaged the cream into his scalp, moving back and forth under the spray, hoping the water flow would miraculously fix itself.

When the pipes started to rattle and clunk he looked up, then swiped at his left eye as a droplet of foamy soap slid into the corner – at the exact moment the water shut off. 'Dammit,' he cursed as his eyeball screamed. He blinked furiously, leapt out of the cubicle and grabbed the towel, rubbing his face before he stood, still squinting, watching the showerhead for signs of life. But it wasn't even dripping now.

'Seriously?' He fiddled with the on/off switch, shivering as the frigid air set off a wave of goosebumps across his wet skin. Sighing, Damon turned to the sink and switched on one of the taps – he could at least sluice water on his head and get rid of the worst of the soap. When nothing happened, he cursed again and stepped into the bedroom before wrapping the towel around his waist. *What was he going to do?*

Damon slung the towel a little higher and made sure he was decent before peering out of the doorway into the long landing. He could hear voices downstairs and someone was humming a Christmas carol, which meant Bonnibell was probably baking in the kitchen. Maybe Holliday was there too?

Damon knew he could make his way down to see them, but hated the idea of being caught half naked. What if the new guests were there? He could tug on some clothes but was covered in foam and didn't want to risk transferring it to what remained of his clean wardrobe. If he could just rinse the shower gel from his hair, he could dress and talk to someone about the problem. Damon drew in a shuddery breath and crept down the hallway towards Holliday's bedroom. She'd left the door open and he could see the fire wasn't switched on, which meant she probably wasn't upstairs. There was no sign of the cat either.

He turned and knocked on the door opposite. When no one answered, he pushed it open. It was a small room and a lot less fancy than his, but Damon could see no one was using it because the wardrobe door hung half-open and there were no clothes or suitcases visible. He checked the hallway again and crept inside the bedroom, shutting the door before hurrying across the room in the direction of the bathroom. The bed was made up, and there was a small fireplace in the corner, but it hadn't been lit. Shivering, Damon pushed the door to the bathroom open.

It was similar to his, although a little smaller. He glanced back into the bedroom again and quickly made his way to the shower. Then he switched it on and almost cheered when a torrent of hot water immediately gushed out. He quickly checked the bedroom again before pulling off the towel and stepping into the jet of warm water. If he was fast, no one would know he'd been. Damon took a moment to enjoy the spray of heat and twisted around inside the cubicle, rubbing his hair and taking his time to ensure the suds were fully purged. He looked up with his eyes still closed and pressed his fingertips onto his eyelids, massaging them to get any remnants of soap out. For the first time since arriving at the resort he began to relax.

Then Damon heard a loud squeal and when he twisted around he saw Holliday standing at the entrance to the bathroom with her jaw open wide. Her eyes, which were scanning his body, were filled with something he couldn't read. Damon felt his body react and immediately shoved his hands downwards, trying to hide himself – because the goosebumps now hopping across his skin had nothing to do with the cold.

11

DAMON

'Oh, I'm so sorry!' Holliday moaned. She grabbed the white apron she was wearing and pulled it over her face. Multi-coloured pom-poms, a knitting kit, folded pieces of paper and four small tubes of craft glue spilled from the wide front pocket onto the tiled floor. She started to blindly back out, bumping her hip on the architrave and yelping. 'I mean, I heard a noise and I wondered who was in the bathroom because no one's supposed to be in this bedroom. Only you and I are sleeping upstairs.' The words tumbled from her lips and she sounded stressed. 'I thought maybe Claus or Frosty had got themselves stuck – which was stupid because I heard the sound of running water. I shouldn't have come in the bathroom. It never occurred to me that you'd be in here and you'd be naked, *gahhhh*,' she babbled from the other side of the door, clearly appalled as Damon shut off the water and stumbled from the cubicle and grabbed the towel.

'Wait there,' he demanded, quickly drying himself and searching the room for a dressing gown or something he could use to cover more of himself, but there was nothing. When he eased the door of the bathroom open Holliday was standing across the bedroom with her back to him. 'Are you alright?' he asked, taking a step closer until he remembered he was still mostly naked. He should have been horrified, even desperate for her to leave, but inexplicably his only instinct was to soothe.

'I'm fine.' Holliday's voice shuddered. 'I'm sorry, I have to apologise. This is so embarrassing. I had no idea—' She shook her head, her shiny brown hair bouncing across her shoulders.

'It's okay,' Damon said. 'Honestly, I understand – I probably would have done the same.'

'Why are you using this bathroom?' she asked, clearly confused.

'The shower in my room stopped working when I was halfway through a wash,' Damon explained, wrapping his arms around his chest when he started to feel cold. 'I was covered in foam and thought if I used another bathroom to rinse off, I could dress and find Leo. See if he could fix it. I knew no one else was staying up here. I knocked on your door first, but—'

'I was downstairs with Bonnibell.'

Damon hesitated. 'I'm sorry too.' He suddenly wished he could see Holliday's face, see what she was thinking. 'I didn't mean to...' He glanced at the towel which he'd slung around his hips, making sure he'd fully covered himself. 'Please turn around, there's nothing to see.'

'*Oh God,* I'm just... I wasn't looking before.' Holliday slowly rotated, her cheeks flaming, but her eyes immediately shot to Damon's chest, before skimming lower, almost as if she couldn't control where they went.

Was she attracted to him?

Damon adjusted the towel and saw Holliday's breath catch, noticed the flush on her cheeks, the way she was biting her lower lip.

'*No, no, no!*' she moaned. Then her eyes darted to Damon's face and she scoured his features before shifting her gaze until she was staring at something beyond his left ear.

She *was* attracted to him. His heart started to hammer.

'Um,' Damon said, feeling the fast pump of blood. He'd barely looked at a woman since splitting with Willow. He'd been far too fixated on snuffing out every memory they'd ever made. So why was he responding to Holliday now? Could he stop it? And more importantly, did he really want to? 'Um, look, let's keep this between us. We don't need to mention it again,' he said roughly. 'I'll be leaving soon and there's no need to be embarrassed...'

'I might end up working for you and I've seen you naked,' Holliday moaned, looking flustered. Her gaze fixed on his shoulder. 'I have to go, you should go back to your room.' She rubbed a hand across her forehead, wincing. 'And for goodness' sake, please put on some clothes.' Her eyes dipped to his chest again, widened, and his skin prickled. 'You look...' She hesitated. 'Um, cold.' Then she turned her back again as if she couldn't bear to look at him.

'What about your things?' Damon asked, half-smiling. The contents of her apron were scattered on the floor.

'I'll pick them up later,' Holliday promised, before opening and practically sprinting through the door.

Damon took a few moments to collect himself once Holliday had gone. He had no idea what had just happened. He should have been embarrassed about being caught naked in the shower, but he wasn't. He wasn't cold anymore either. But he was confused. He wandered back into the bathroom so he could collect the pieces Holliday had dropped on the floor, carefully gathering the multiple pom-poms, glue and paper in his hands.

He peered through the doorway, making sure no one was around, then crept onto the landing. He paused outside Holliday's door, contemplating knocking so he could hand her the items she'd dropped – then he heard a flurry of voices downstairs and the scatter of doggy feet and decided he didn't want to risk getting caught with his towel around him.

When he got back into his bedroom he shut the door and put everything on the bed, immediately adding another log to the fire. He dried off and tugged on underwear, jeans and a long-sleeved T-shirt before running a hand through his still-wet hair, trying not to think about Holliday. His nose began to itch and he wriggled it, quickly searching the bathroom and bedroom to make sure Frosty hadn't sneaked in. He got down on his knees and checked under the bed, immediately spotting a set of almond-shaped eyes and the tell-tale shape of a cat.

'Dammit.' His nose itched and he fought a sneeze, so he stood and swiped his hands across his eyes which were already streaming. Then he opened the door and waved. 'Shoo!' Damon snapped, nudging the bedframe, hoping the movement would spook Frosty. He didn't bargain on his own strength or the lightness of the frame because the furniture skidded across the wooden floorboards, dispersing all the items he'd collected across the duvet.

Damon watched as the cat suddenly showed himself and jumped onto the bed, bending to sniff one of the pom-poms and prodding the piece of paper with a paw, seemingly unperturbed.

'Seriously?' he grumbled, pinching his nose, as Frosty turned to look at him with a grave expression.

Then the cat let out a small miaow and launched itself from the bed before slowly sauntering out of the bedroom into the hallway. Damon quickly shut the door and went to put the bed back in its rightful place before carefully rearranging Holliday's art supplies into a neat pile. There was an endless stream of pom-poms, a knitting kit, four tubes of glue and the single piece of paper that Frosty had seemed so interested in. Had the cat been trying to tell him something?

Damon snorted, feeling absurd, but he still picked it up and unfolded it. It was a letter. He knew he shouldn't read it, but there was so much about Holliday he didn't know. She was suspicious of him, and he didn't understand why. Would the letter reveal all? Or was there something in it he could use to persuade the sexy art teacher that the hotel was a good idea?

He quickly scanned the contents, then read it again to ensure he understood. If this were true then Holliday owned a property in Cambridge, so why wasn't she living there? The sum the buyers had mentioned was significant – so the property was either large, or set in an area of the city that was sought after. He'd check the address later and see. Was it Holliday's family home? She hadn't mentioned anyone in her life. What did it mean that no one was living in the house now?

Frowning, Damon played with the letter, folding and unfolding it. His marriage to Willow had taught him you couldn't trust anyone. Despite the chemistry between them, he knew he couldn't let himself trust Holliday now.

He refolded the paper and placed it on the bed with the art materials. He'd drop it all back as soon as he'd made a few discreet enquires about Holliday Harrison to ensure he understood exactly who he was dealing with.

12

HOLLIDAY

The following day, Holliday collected the large basket of knitting needles and wool from the cupboard at the back of Christmas Lodge and nudged the door open with her hip just as Bonnibell came blustering in from the hallway.

'The garage just called Damon to let him know it's going to take them a few days to fix the car,' she whispered, glancing over her shoulder before continuing. 'I asked them to tell him there's something wrong with the starter motor and it's going to take a while to get hold of the part.' She gently pushed Holliday back into the storeroom and zipped a finger over her lips, checking the corridor again before shutting the door. 'I know it's sneaky and I feel quite guilty.' She blanched. 'But if Damon stays longer I'm sure we'll be able to convince him to keep the resort as it is. I know he'll love it if he just gives it a chance.'

'How's he taken the news?' Holliday asked, pushing away the memory of his naked body as it zapped into her mind, setting off a tsunami of tingles.

Bonnibell winced. 'He's in the kitchen with Connell now. He was determined to get a train to London tonight but apparently they've all been cancelled because of a signal failure on the line.' As she said the words, the tension across her shoulders visibly eased. 'I think that means luck's on our side. But we're going to have to work extra hard to impress him today because the trains will probably be running again tomorrow and time's running out.'

'He didn't seem very captivated by anything last night,' Holliday sighed. 'After the heating broke and the fiasco with the shower in his room.' She gulped. 'You know, when it wouldn't work...' she added quickly as her cheeks went up in flames.

She hadn't told anyone about their encounter in the bathroom and had no plans to share it now. She closed her eyes, attempting to block out the memory of Damon naked again. If she'd thought he was attractive before, it was nothing compared to her opinion of him now. He was lean but muscular, and his chest broad with abs she was more used to seeing on comic-strip heroes in body-hugging suits. He was either naturally lucky or the man had spent the last few years pushing the equivalent of a woolly mammoth in the gym. It made her wonder why someone hadn't snapped him up before now. Holliday gulped, instantly feeling guilty. She'd barely thought about a man since Adrian; why was she suddenly obsessing about Damon?

'So you don't think he's impressed?' Bonnibell asked worriedly.

Holliday's mouth pinched. 'I don't think Barney helped,' she said, recalling dinner when the older man had complained bitterly about everything from the temperature of the room to the food to the decorations in his cabin. Mabel had always been such a welcome antithesis to her husband, Holliday had never realised or acknowledged how exhausting Barney could be. Perhaps losing his other half had made the world an even darker place, squashing any positivity he'd previously had. If she hadn't come to Christmas Resort, she might have been the same.

'Ach, don't worry about him, hen.' Bonnibell waved her hand. 'I think being here without Mabel must be difficult, whatever he says. We need to be patient. I'm sure after a few days he'll settle. Even if he doesn't, it's up to us to ensure he enjoys his time here. He needs to make some new memories or perhaps just grow more comfortable with the ones he has. The family came to celebrate her; I'm just not sure Barney's ready for that.'

'Of course we'll do everything we can,' Holliday murmured as Bonnibell checked her watch.

'Isn't the knitting club due to start in half an hour?' the older woman asked, frowning.

Holliday nodded at the basket she was carrying. 'I'm just getting everything ready now.'

'Is Damon planning to take part?' Bonnibell asked.

'I've no idea.' Holliday sighed, nudging the door open again and making her way towards the sitting room where she hosted the club.

Bonnibell's mouth fixed into a determined line. 'Then I'll head for the kitchen now and make sure he does...'

Holliday finished moving the sitting-room furniture into the usual arrangement for the knitting club. She never knew how many people would turn up, so allowed for at least twenty guests, ensuring the long sofa, green velvet armchairs, dining-room seats and stools all faced the roaring fire. She shuffled the coffee table to the right of the Christmas tree and piano and set out the biscuits and mince pies Bonnibell had just baked, sliding them away from Claus, who'd already planted himself on the rug in front of the fire. Then she put on Christmas music before placing a high-back chair to the right of the flames, adding a bucket of wool alongside it, and another filled with knitting needles. Some of the members brought their own gear, but Holliday always made sure there was plenty available for everyone who decided to drop in.

'Where should I sit?' Damon enquired quietly from the doorway.

Holliday's heartbeat danced and she immediately fought to tamp it down as guilt flooded her. She shouldn't be having a reaction to this man. Especially while she could still picture her fiancé living in their house in Cambridge; could still imagine he was a part of her life.

'How about you take that seat to the right of the fire?' she said, her voice breathless. 'That way if you get stuck I can help. I didn't expect you to join us this evening.'

'I wasn't going to but Bonnibell insisted.' From his tone Holliday could tell he wasn't happy about being here. 'She said it'd be a good opportunity for me to meet the guests again and to familiarise myself with some of the locals. She's very keen that I learn all about what you do here.' His shoulders hunched. 'Apparently Mr Gray has been asking how I've been getting on.' His forehead stretched. 'I hear you started the club in January and it's already the most popular activity at the resort.' He sank into the chair she'd pointed to perusing the room. 'At least it's warm,' he growled.

'I believe Leo finally got the heating to work,' Holliday said briskly, handing Damon a ball of red wool and a set of knitting needles, ensuring their hands didn't brush. 'He said he'd sort out your shower later because the part he needed just arrived, so there'll be no need for you to use a different bathroom.'

Damon humphed, obviously embarrassed, and their eyes met. Holliday cleared her throat and shoved her hands back into her apron, searching for a pom-pom but found none. That's when she remembered she'd dropped them when she'd seen Damon naked and her cheeks flooded again.

The bell at the front of the lodge jingled, breaking the charged atmosphere.

Holliday's body sagged with relief. 'I'm guessing that'll be some of our members,' she said roughly, stroking her hands down her apron as an older woman with white hair wearing a ruby tiara wandered in. 'This is Edina Lachlan,' Holliday explained to Damon, welcoming her into the room. 'I mentioned her when we walked into Christmas Village. She lives in Evergreen Castle, and owns a donkey called Bob. Edina, this is—'

'Damon MacAndrew. Bonnibell's told me about you already,' the older woman said, scanning Damon with wily green eyes that sparkled mischievously. 'I hear you're going to buy Christmas Resort?' She pulled off her coat and took a seat on the sofa before lifting a set of knitting needles and a ball of wool from her green tartan tote. 'What do you plan to do with it?'

'Um.' His forehead bunched as he hesitated. 'What you'd expect,' he said carefully. 'Encourage people to come and stay.' He stiffened and Holliday suspected he was trying not to give anything away.

Edina's eyes narrowed, as if she sensed something was off, and a part of Holliday hoped she might interrogate him more. It was unlikely he'd expose what he was up to easily, but he might accidently reveal something she didn't know.

Edina stared at him for a beat, scrutinizing his face, before nodding. 'And what do you do when you're not here?'

'I work in mergers and acquisitions,' Damon said, avoiding her eyes.

'What does that involve?' Edina asked, leaning forwards, almost poking herself with the knitting needles on her lap.

'Buying, selling, repurposing...' Damon said vaguely, looking even more uncomfortable.

'Well I hope you're planning on doing right by the resort,' Edina said firmly. 'Have you knitted before?' She continued to study Damon carefully. 'I think you can tell a lot about a person from the way they hold a stitch.'

'This is my first time,' he said, staring back, his expression blank. 'So I doubt I'll give much away.' His smile was strained.

'Shame.' The older woman cocked her head and gave Damon another penetrating look before turning to Holliday. 'Is it just us tonight?'

'I'm expecting more,' she said as a beautiful blonde wearing a figure-hugging red dress wandered in and immediately bent to give Edina a hug. 'Damon, this is Kenzy Campbell who runs The Workshop in the village.' She gave him a long look because he'd avoided visiting the salon when they'd been in the high street. 'Kenzy, Damon's thinking about buying the resort.'

The younger woman tilted an eyebrow and gave him a stunning smile. 'There's been a lot of chatter about you in the village,' she purred in a sexy American drawl. 'And now we're face to face, I've got the oddest feeling I may have met you before.' She eased herself down on the sofa next to Edina and her full lips pursed.

Damon paled. 'I don't think so,' he murmured and his eyes darted to Holliday. 'We were in the high street yesterday, perhaps you saw me then?'

Kenzy shook her head. 'That's not it.'

Holliday frowned. Hadn't Bonnibell also said Damon looked familiar? Was it a coincidence or had both women seen him before? If so, it must have been in Christmas Village as neither woman strayed far from the area. But if Damon had been here before, why keep it a secret?

'I said exactly the same when Damon first arrived, but he hasn't been up this way,' Bonnibell sang as she strutted into the room, her red velvet skirt swishing, and placed a dish of freshly baked sausage rolls on the table with a flourish. 'For those of you who haven't got a sweet tooth!' she declared. 'Please help yourselves. I believe we have a few more members coming along later, but in the meantime, you should probably get started.'

'Wait for me,' Innes said, rushing in to join them and taking a seat to Holliday's left before digging into her bag for her knitting, looking flustered.

'Is Mairi coming tonight?' Bonnibell asked, flopping onto one of the chairs situated further away from the group. She wasn't very good at kitting, but enjoyed coming along for the chatter and company.

Innes's face fell. 'I think she might be popping in later,' she muttered, burying her face in her ball of black wool. 'She wanted to cook something special for Leo's tea first.' Her chest heaved. 'I already made a bean chilli but apparently that's not good enough for a working man – or a woman of indeterminate age for that matter.' Her eyes glittered. 'Seems I can't do anything properly.'

'I'm sure Mairi didn't mean it like that, hen,' Bonnibell said sympathetically.

Innes frowned and flicked her plait over her shoulder, looking unhappy. 'After my mam died I hoped we might become close...' She sighed heavily. 'But Mairi's never liked me. And Leo – well, he always sides with his mam.' She blinked, her eyes shining, and Bonnibell opened her mouth just as Barney hobbled into the room.

'It's a little empty tonight, isn't it?' he observed as he set his sights on the velvet chair to the right of the fire. He grimaced and stopped, leaning on his cane so he could examine the cakes, sausage rolls and biscuits on display. 'Looks like you forgot my favourites again,' he said to Bonnibell before taking the seat he'd been eyeing. Then he picked up a set of needles and a ball of wool from the buckets without being asked.

'I thought gingerbread was your favourite?' Holliday asked innocently. 'I happen to know Bonnibell made a fresh batch this afternoon just for you.'

Her boss nodded.

Barney arched an eyebrow. 'I prefer chocolate,' he said

airily, glaring at the needles and wool he was clutching in his hands.

'It's good to see you again, Barney.' Edina leaned across to hold out her hand and then adjusted her tiara as it slipped over her forehead. 'I was sorry to hear about—'

'Thank you, but it's fine, I'm all okay.' Barney held up a palm. 'I'm here to make some socks to keep my feet warm in bed, not to blather about things best forgotten.'

Edina raised an eyebrow, looking surprised.

'Where's Kate?' Bonnibell asked, easing the conversation away from the touchy subject.

'She's drying her hair – but that might take all night,' Barney said, unwinding his ball of grey wool before looping some over a knitting needle. His fingers were nimble and he was far quicker than Holliday remembered. Perhaps he'd been practising at home?

Holliday glanced at Damon who was still staring at the equipment he was holding. 'Do you need some help getting started?'

'My sister used to knit at home, she always made it look so easy.' Damon continued to frown at the needles and yarn as if hoping they'd start doing something without his help. 'I've never tried.'

'What do you want to make?'

Damon's eyes rounded and Holliday almost wanted to laugh.

'How about we start with something simple?' she suggested.

'Like what?' he asked, looking out of his depth.

'How about a dishcloth?' Innes suggested. 'It's easy and it won't take long.'

Damon shrugged.

'Okay, so you begin like this.' Holliday shifted closer, ignoring the tingles that shot through her body when their shoulders brushed. Then she carefully showed him how to cast on, watching Damon's forehead crease in concentration as he mirrored her movements, his grey eyes darkening as he worked.

'That's a good start,' Holliday said, smiling.

He looked surprised and mildly pleased.

The next few minutes passed in silence aside from the clatter of needles, which oddly complimented the Christmas music. Holliday kept an eye on Damon, who was proving competent – although slow.

'Hang on,' Holliday said suddenly, placing a palm over Damon's hand when she saw him drop a stitch. The contact made her tremble and she pulled away just as their eyes met and held. 'Um.' Holliday swallowed and dropped her gaze, reaching for the needles so she could get him back on track. All the while her heart was pounding, the noise flooding her ears.

'Is everything okay?' Damon asked softly, huddling closer as she handed the knitting back without looking at him.

'Have you seen this?' Arthur Bennett suddenly sprinted into the room, searching for his grandfather, holding up his mobile phone. Holliday let out a sigh of relief when Damon shifted away. 'Where's Mum?' the teen asked, checking the sea of faces.

'Still doing her hair, I expect,' Barney grumbled. 'What is it, boy?'

'There's someone on TikTok posting about Secret Cider,' he said excitedly, rushing further into the room. 'Dad had a bottle in the cabin last night and said it was really good.'

'TikTok?' Bonnibell queried, sounding confused.

'It's a social media site,' Damon explained, eyeing the phone. 'People post videos about all sorts of things.'

'Not many get this many views in a day though,' Arthur said proudly, striding over so he could show Barney his screen. 'The people in this video are saying no one knows who makes the cider. That it's a big secret.' He lowered his voice. 'They're saying they're going to visit Christmas Village so they can track down whoever makes it and lots of people have commented to say they're going to do the same. It's turned into a treasure hunt. Do you know who makes it?' He turned towards Bonnibell.

'No, hen.' She frowned. 'All I know is they sell it at The Corner Shop.'

'Does anyone know who makes it?' Arthur asked, skirting the room, but everyone shook their heads. 'This post has got half a million views, who knows what the numbers will be by tonight. Grandad Barney, will you come with me to look for whoever makes Secret Cider tomorrow?'

Barney's mouth unexpectedly stretched into a slow smile. 'Aye, lad, I'll come with you. That sounds like the sort of Christmas adventure I might enjoy.'

As the boy and his grandfather continued to chatter, Holliday sat back and watched Damon work, taking care not to catch his eye. Something was happening between them but she wasn't going to explore it. She had to remember Adrian and focus on what was best for Christmas Resort. The fact that Damon was still here and had taken to crafting so quickly was surely a good sign. It wasn't in keeping with the man Holliday had thought he was. If he could enjoy something as simple as knitting, surely he could learn to love the resort. For the first time since he'd arrived Holliday started to feel hope.

13

DAMON

Damon stomped out of the front of Christmas Lodge the following morning and made his way onto the snow-covered driveway. It had been snowing all night and the ground was covered in a thick layer of ice. He contemplated taking a long walk to work off his bad mood, but one look at the moody sky told him it wasn't a good idea.

'Everything okay?' Leo shouted above the howl of the wind as he climbed out of his truck and shut the door before grabbing a container of tools from the back seat.

'My car's still not ready,' Damon complained, keeping pace with the younger man. He might as well walk in the same direction – he had nowhere else to go. Besides, Frosty had been hanging around downstairs in the lodge and he didn't trust the cat to leave him alone. He wondered idly if Holliday would put her pet up to it – then again, perhaps not now they were on slightly better terms? He'd enjoyed the knitting last night, had even found himself relaxing and listening to Holliday chat with the guests. There'd been an oddly tense moment between them, but despite that, he hadn't felt so at ease in a long time. The calm had disappeared instantly when the garage had called first thing that morning.

'When do you think the car will be fixed?' Leo asked.

'The garage said it might be another two days.' Damon sighed. 'The trains aren't looking good either. I tried to book today, but the wi-fi cut out halfway through and now there aren't any seats available.' He ground his jaw.

'Maybe you should just stay until it's ready?' Leo suggested. 'Or is there something in particular you've got to get back for?'

Damon thought about his flat back home and grimaced. For some reason the space he remembered now felt empty. Besides, the food here was good and he'd enjoyed himself more than he'd expected since he'd been stuck. 'Perhaps not...' he murmured.

Besides, once he was home he knew Scarlett would visit with the twins as soon as she got the chance. Then she'd nag him about his plans for the resort – giving him a million reasons why he should leave it exactly as it was. If he were honest with himself, the thought had even occurred to him once or twice since he'd arrived, but he couldn't – not while every step he took here reminded him of Willow and the way she'd made him feel. Unfortunately, no matter how many times he explained that, his sister would never understand.

But if he stayed at the resort for longer he could avoid Scarlett and spend more time brainstorming ideas for the new hotel. He might even be able to subtly convince some of the team that a change would be a good idea. He rubbed his chin.

'What are you up to?' Damon asked, pointing to the toolbox.

Leo pulled a face. 'We've got new guests arriving later. They're celebrating their first anniversary and are supposed to be staying in Plum Pud Inn. But when Innes went in to stock the fridge this morning she realised the roof's been leaking. Hopefully it'll be an easy fix.'

'A lot's gone wrong here since I arrived,' Damon said thoughtfully.

The younger man shrugged, dodging a robin as it hopped into his path. 'Mr Gray hasn't invested any money in this place for a while. I think he's been hoping to sell and didn't want to sink in funds when he knew he wouldn't be involved anymore. I know some of the others are concerned about a change in ownership, but I'm really glad you're here.' He patted Damon on the shoulder. 'We need fresh blood, someone with energy and enthusiasm. The resort needs a big influx of cash too – and you're just the kind of person who could really help take it to the next level.' He looked over at Damon, his eyes shining with excitement. 'I've got a few ideas if you ever want to talk. I know Holliday's probably told you everything you need to know, but it's always good to have another perspective.'

'Sure,' Damon murmured, looking at the ground, fighting off a fresh rush of guilt.

Leo grinned. 'If you're at a loose end, would you mind coming along to the cabin with me? Connell's gone to buy more supplies and I need someone to hold the ladder while I look at the roof. Also...' Bright wings of colour stained the tips of Leo's cheeks. 'I wondered if I could talk to you about something personal?'

'Um, okay.' Damon gulped nervously and shoved his hands into the pockets of the thick coat he'd borrowed, wishing he'd thought to borrow gloves too. At least his feet were warm – thanks to the snow boots the resort had gifted him. 'What about?' he asked, hoping it had something to do with a pay increase or a new position in the company. Perhaps he could start to feel Leo out about a new job?

The younger man sighed, looking at the ground. 'It's Innes. We're living with my mam at the moment and they don't get on.' He hissed air between his teeth. 'I started a small business – trying to earn some extra cash. It was all going well and if things had continued as they were we'd be in a position to put a deposit down on a house in the next six months, but...' He scrubbed his hands on his jeans. 'The situation's changed and things have got a bit... sticky.'

'What does sticky mean?' Damon asked bluntly.

'It's complicated.' Leo pressed a finger to his lips as they got to the end of the path and spotted Bonnibell heading towards them wearing a billowing red coat. 'Can we talk about it later, please?'

'Sure,' Damon promised, wondering what had got the younger man so wound up.

'I brought supplies. Innes told me she'd spotted you both walking this way.' Bonnibell shoved a tin into Damon's palm and handed them each a small flask. 'Something sweet and a hot coffee. I know how you both take it.' She looked up and swiped snow from her rosy cheeks. 'Looks like the weather's turning stormy.' She examined Damon's coat. 'Are you warm enough, hen? I could send someone out with more clothes if you want?'

'I'm okay.' He opened the tin and inhaled the wonderful scent of freshly baked mince pies. 'Ah,' he hummed, wondering if he was going to start drooling every time he saw the older woman from now on. Bonnibell would be an asset to the new hotel, but would she take a job if he offered her one? Damon tried to picture her amongst the chrome and steel cabinets he'd envisaged in the main kitchen but the image simply wouldn't come to mind.

Leo reached into the open tin and grabbed a mince pie. 'They're good,' he said between bites. 'You ready to go, partner?' He thumped Damon enthusiastically on the back.

'You don't need to help.' Bonnibell turned to Damon, looking concerned. 'I'm sure Connell will be back from running errands soon.'

'It's okay,' Damon said. 'I'm only going to hold the ladder...'

'Well, be careful,' she demanded before turning and heading back towards the lodge.

The cabin was the smallest Damon had seen since arriving at the resort, but it was set back from the driveway, in between dozens of fir trees loaded with fresh powdery snow. There were fairy lights scattered across the cabin roof and around the door and someone had decorated the surrounding shrubs and bushes too. He wondered idly what the wild boar and wildcats would make of the twinkling colours.

He chuckled to himself as his mind wandered to Holliday and the charged moment between them when he'd been sitting beside her at the knitting club. The woman baffled him. On the one hand he knew she'd been doing everything she could to put him off buying the resort, but on the other she'd happily spent a couple of hours teaching him how to knit. Her generosity humbled him, but he knew he couldn't trust it. He knew absolutely nothing about her apart from that she owned a property in Cambridge – and he wasn't supposed to know that.

'Everything okay?' Leo asked, looking at Damon strangely when he let out a growling sound.

Damon was annoyed at himself because he knew he had been starting to let his guard down around Holliday, which meant he'd learned nothing from the past. 'Fine,' he said, rubbing a hand on his throat. He pointed to a white ladder which had been propped against the side of the small building. 'You really going up there?' he asked, stepping forwards to grab hold of the bottom as the younger man scraped an inch of snow from the lower rungs and hopped on.

'Can't have the lodges leaking. We'll get complaints and it'll ruin the magic for our guests,' Leo said, stopping on the second rung and pulling work gloves from the pocket of his coat, stretching them over his large hands. Then he turned his attention back to Damon, and his youthful face grew serious. 'This place means a lot to us all,' he said quietly. 'It's special.' His blue eyes shone. 'Innes and I got married here earlier this year. But it's more than that. It changes people...'

'How?' Damon asked.

'I dunno, maybe it's the Christmas magic.' Leo shrugged. 'All I know is it does. Stay here for long enough and you'll experience it for yourself. Can you hold the toolbox while I take a look, please?' He shoved the box into Damon's hands and scrambled to the top, then slithered onto the roof and disappeared out of sight.

Damon stayed where he was, afraid if he moved he might accidently jog something and Leo would come tumbling down. Wind whistled around his ears, blowing snow into his eyes, and he had to blink a few times.

'It doesn't look too bad, just a misplaced tile,' Leo yelled from above. 'I can definitely fix it. Do me a favour, please, can you grab a hammer and bring it up?'

'Sure...' Damon said, putting the box onto the ground and lifting the tool out before climbing up. The ladder wobbled but he forced himself up to the top rung where Leo was calmly sitting cross-legged on the tiles, waiting for him.

'Thanks,' the younger man said, reaching out to grab the hammer. 'It won't take long, then we can look inside the cabin and see if there's any damage. This is a good way for you to see the types of things I do on a day-to-day basis. It'll also give you an idea of what needs investing in first.' He smiled before shifting around so he could hammer at some of the tiles, adjusting a couple, presumably to cover up whatever hole had emerged.

Damon stayed where he was and twisted his neck. The view was magnificent, and despite the forest of trees surrounding them he could see for miles – down into the valley where he planned to put the golf course, past the lodge where

Bonnibell was probably already baking something mouth-watering in the kitchen, then up onto the hill where the three twinkling reindeer ornaments glowed on the site his architect had allocated for the restaurant. He felt a pinch in his chest and forced himself to look beyond them. Getting sentimental wasn't going to get the job done.

'Finished,' Leo shouted. 'We can climb down now.' He started to shift across the roof and as he did a large patch of ice loosened from the top of some of the tiles and he lost his balance. He let go of the hammer and the tool tumbled down the incline before sliding off the edge and plummeting to the ground. 'Dammit!' Leo yelled, sounding scared as he carried on gliding, scrambling around frantically. He continued to topple until his foot caught on the edge of the ladder, at which point he finally managed to grasp onto the small chimney at the same moment the ladder started to swing back.

Everything happened so quickly, Damon didn't realise Leo was moving until the ladder was suddenly floating upright in mid-air. 'Um...' His stomach somersaulted as he shunted his hips forwards, hoping the momentum would force it back towards the roof. 'Nooo!' he yelled as it swayed and he felt the whole thing pitch backwards. He saw Leo stretch out in an effort to catch the tip of the ladder, but it was way beyond his reach. Then gravity took over.

Damon heard a shout in the distance and then a scream as his body hit the floor with a loud thump – then he passed out.

'Dammit, you're not supposed to kill him!' a worried voice wailed. 'We want him to fall in love with the resort, remember?'

Pain reverberated around Damon's head and he opened one eye. Someone was speaking through the fog in his brain but he couldn't work out who it was. Willow? No, he remembered now and felt a wave of relief. She wasn't in his life anymore – and in a few months nothing would remain of their courtship or marriage to remind him of her. In the new world he was creating, she'd no longer exist.

He gazed at the sky as snowflakes tumbled from the clouds and melted on his cheeks. Was he skiing? He couldn't exactly recall – perhaps he'd drunk too much last night and passed out on his way home?

He pressed a hand to his forehead and realised he was wearing a glove. When he studied it he saw it was bright red with green pom-poms sewn across the top. Definitely not skiing, perhaps he'd signed up for clown school and slipped on a banana? The witticism didn't make Damon laugh and he swallowed a wave of pain as he tried to move. Perhaps he was hallucinating – or could he have some kind of brain injury?

'What's happening?' he croaked as he tried to shift himself upwards to look around. But then someone reached out and pushed him gently back onto the ground.

'I think you're okay but you might not want to move yet – at least not until you're sure nothing's broken,' Holliday murmured, carefully brushing snow from his face and trying to look into his eyes. Suddenly Damon remembered – he was in Christmas Resort and the woman he was finding it increasingly difficult to ignore was murmuring something soothing and holding his hand. 'The ladder you were standing on fell backwards into the snow and I'm worried you hit your head,' she explained softly.

'What am I wearing?' he asked, gazing at the woollen creation and wriggling his fingers. He was finding it difficult to breathe now and tugged at his neck, realising when he unwound the material strangling him that he wore a matching scarf.

'I knitted them for you,' Holliday said, shyly. 'I make things for all the guests at the resort. *All of them,*' she repeated, looking embarrassed.

'Why?' He croaked, confused. Maybe it was just shock from falling but he didn't understand. Up until now Holliday been trying to put him off buying the resort, now she was taking care of him. As much as he appreciated it, he couldn't help being suspicious. What was in it for her?

'Bonnibell told me you were helping Leo with a leaking roof and she was worried you'd be cold. I decided to find you so I could give you the extra layers.' She leaned over again so Damon could see her face. She looked deathly pale and her eyes were wide like a rabbit's caught in the glare of a headlight. 'I was on my way when I saw the ladder fall.' Her voice wobbled. 'I thought...' She gulped. 'I didn't think I should move you so I put the gloves and scarf on you to keep you warm. Your fingers were so cold.'

'Is he hurt?' Leo interrupted as he trotted over. 'Sorry. It took me a while to get down from the roof without the ladder.' He leaned down so he could study Damon too, his voice choppy with nerves.

'His eyes look fine, so I don't think he's concussed,' Holliday said, staring into his face again.

Leo nodded, looking relieved. 'You were lucky you landed on a pile of fresh snow and there weren't any shrubs or bushes in the way. You don't look too bad and there's no blood that I can see.' He paused as his eyes scoured the ground. 'Do you think anything's broken?'

Damon shifted and eased himself slowly up onto one arm. 'I don't think so, just a few bruises.' He rubbed a hand over the back of his head, checking for bumps, but there were none. 'No matching hat?' he asked Holliday when he realised his head was bare.

She blushed. 'I haven't finished knitting it yet. We should get you indoors, if you think you can walk?' she asked, glancing uncertainly towards the lodge.

'I'm alright, really. Just a little winded,' Damon said, moving into a sitting position and wriggling his shoulders. He felt a bit sore, but other than that he was fine.

Holliday nodded, her tense expression softening. 'Bonnibell's just made hot chocolate – she guessed you'd have finished your coffee by now.'

'We didn't drink them – but I'm sure Damon will feel a lot better after a mug full of that. Sugar's supposed to be good for a shock,' Leo said, looking far more cheerful than he had a few moments before. He glanced over his shoulder. 'Look, I need to check inside the cabin so I'll catch up with you inside if you're sure you're okay to walk?'

Damon nodded.

'Okay, well thanks for the help,' Leo said. 'Sorry about...' He waved at the ladder and pulled a face.

'No problem,' Damon said, easing himself onto his knees. The snow had seeped through his trousers but he didn't care.

Holliday hooked a hand under his elbow and carefully helped him to his feet. 'You really feel okay?' she asked.

'I think so,' he said, twisting his body into a few more shapes. 'I guess I was lucky.' He turned so he could study the dent in the snow where he'd just been lying. A few inches to the right, a shrub waved its spiky talons into the sky – if he'd fallen on that things might have been quite different. The sudden realisation gave Damon a jolt and in his imagination he heard Scarlett mutter something about a wasted life.

'Come inside,' Holliday said when he started to shiver. 'The fire's on in the sitting room. We need to get you warmed up.'

'What about the cat?' Damon asked suspiciously. Was she setting him up?

Holliday's eyes clouded. 'I'll make sure Frosty's out of the way.' She nibbled her bottom lip. 'I wouldn't set the cat on you when you were hurt — I'm not really made like that.' Then with a sad twist to her mouth she turned and steered him back towards the lodge.

. . .

The fire was already glowing as Holliday helped Damon into the sitting room, assisting him with taking off with his coat, snow boots, scarf and the psychedelic gloves. She guided him into the chair and studied him for a moment before nodding. 'You look better now you're inside. I should probably check your eyes again to make sure you're not concussed.'

'Ach, the lad's fine – nothing a dash of sugar won't cure. I've just been on the phone with a doctor I know and he told me we need to keep an eye on you, that's all,' Bonnibell said, busting into the sitting room and motioning to the chair facing his. 'Take a seat, lass. You look worse than the lad does.'

Damon took a moment to examine Holliday's face. Her cheeks looked pale and she kept fiddling with something in her apron. More pom-poms? Had she already replaced the stash he still had in his bedroom? She'd even sewn them on his gloves and scarf. Did they have some bigger significance?

'Fine,' Holliday sighed, slumping into the chair and gazing into the fire as the older woman laid out festive mugs of hot chocolate and reindeer-shaped biscuits onto a plate. 'I'm supposed to be running a craft class in half an hour,' she admitted.

'I'll gather everyone in the kitchen. It's only Barney and the Bennetts until this evening so there's room for me to host a cake-decorating class. You relax for a while, hen, you look done in,' Bonnibell said, squeezing Holliday's shoulder. 'I'm guessing that was a bit of nasty surprise for you. I hope it didn't bring back any bad memories.' She glanced back at Damon and disappeared into the hall.

The room fell silent and Damon took a moment to gather himself and stare into the fire, wondering what Bonnibell had been referring too. It was on the tip of his tongue to ask – he wanted to know more about Holliday – but he found himself hesitating. He was already feeling mixed up, did he want to make it worse? He could hear the snap of logs as they heated in the grate, could smell pine needles and realised the fragrance was wafting from the nearby Christmas tree. A few days ago the scents would have made him think of Willow, now they only conjured images of Holliday. What did that mean?

Holliday let out a long sigh which sounded more miserable than content. Then she leaned forwards and picked up her hot chocolate, rubbing her hands thoughtfully up and down the mug.

'Something wrong?' Damon asked, studying her. She was wearing a short woollen green dress today, which suited her skin tone, and the white apron she never seemed to take off. He wondered again if the pockets had been refilled with pom-poms and glue. For some reason he liked the idea. Liked that he knew that about Holliday. If he knew her better he'd have said for the first time in a long time he'd met someone he wanted to trust. Which was crazy. She didn't even like him. Perhaps Leo was right and this place did change you? That, or a bump on the head had affected his brain.

Holliday's mouth moved as if she were considering how to respond – and for a moment Damon thought she wouldn't. But then she dipped her chin and he watched light from the fire play across it, emphasising the rosy bloom of her lovely clear skin. He swallowed.

'We're not doing a very good job of getting you to fall in love with the resort,' she said, her voice hoarse. 'It doesn't seem to matter what we do or how hard I try.' She cleared her throat. 'Everything keeps going wrong.' She looked upset.

Damon leaned closer and placed his palms on his knees. There was something raw in her voice and he could almost feel how much her admission had hurt. As if it was somehow circling around him, trying to find a crack or way in – a way to make him feel it too.

He looked around. This was a pretty place, he understood that, but the areas he'd already planned for the hotel would be far glossier, shinier – and newer too. He'd use an interior designer, get the most fashionable furniture, curtains – even the heating system would be cutting edge. Perhaps he'd hire someone to decorate it for Christmas each year – ask Holliday to select her favourite ornaments, maybe see if she'd like to be involved? Although it was difficult to imagine her in the new space – because she'd hate it, he realised with a jolt.

'Why does it matter so much that I like it here?' he asked.

He waited while she considered the question. Felt the tension in his shoulders bite when she put down the mug and rose. Then, speechless, he watched her stride from the room.

'What just happened?' Damon murmured, staring at Holliday's empty chair, wondering if he'd somehow offended her. There was a ball in his throat now and it felt... awful. He hadn't let himself feel anything for so long, he wasn't sure what to do now he did. He had to force himself not to follow her so he could find a way to put things right. He was glad he hadn't when Holliday returned a few moments later. Relief flooded his limbs.

'My answer's in here,' she said, holding out one of the photo albums from the dining room – making all the breath whoosh from Damon's throat.

14

HOLLIDAY

Holliday hugged the heavy black album to her chest as she watched Damon pale and for an uncomfortable moment wondered if he was going to faint.

'Are you okay, does your head hurt?' she asked, stumbling forwards and dropping to her knees. Lifting a palm to cup his face, she stared into his grey eyes, steeling herself so she wasn't affected. She wondered why the idea of him being hurt was so distressing. 'Are you feeling dizzy or sick because of the fall?' Her heart raced.

'The album...' Damon mumbled, leaning away from her, his voice raspy. 'What did you find?'

Holliday studied him for a beat, hesitating as she reconsidered whether she was about to do the right thing. Sighing because in the end she knew she had no choice. 'There's a photo,' she said eventually. 'A picture I need you to see.'

His eyes widened as she flicked through the pages and found the right spot. 'I can explain...' Damon began as Holliday opened the book and handed it to him before rising and wandering to the opposite chair.

She watched as he gazed down at the picture, saw the

instant he realised what he was seeing – then his eyes abruptly shot to hers. 'It's you...' he said, his voice gruff. 'And...?' His eyebrow rose.

'That's my fiancé... *was* my fiancé,' she told him. Holliday hated talking about Adrian, but if she was going to convince Damon to keep the resort – explain why it was so important – she knew she was going to have to come clean. 'He died in a train crash, over two years ago now.'

Their eyes met again and she saw sympathy in his and for a moment wasn't sure if she could deal with it. But the wave of pain passed quickly, surprising her.

'I'm very sorry.' His voice had deepened and she knew he was speaking the truth. He swallowed, looking uncomfortable. 'You stayed here, together?'

She nodded. 'Adrian was a journalist. He wrote that article about the resort you said you'd read. He was very talented.' She tried to smile. 'We came so he could do some research for it, and also got engaged.' She paused, took a moment to remember. 'He proposed on our last night by the three reindeer ornaments on the hill. You must have seen them?'

'Yes,' he croaked and something dark flashed across his face. 'They're hard to miss.'

'We used to joke that we'd take them to Cambridge so they could be witnesses at our wedding ceremony.' She smiled and squeezed her hands into fists – usually she tried not to think about that. Sometimes when she was out walking she'd stumble on that spot, as if something had guided her there, and she'd let herself have a quiet moment, let herself think about Adrian again. Then she'd force away those memories and imagine him living in their house in Cambridge and she'd feel better.

'This place is filled with so many memories.' She put a hand on her chest and rubbed where her heart was supposed to be – although sometimes it felt so numb she wondered if it had leaked out. 'But they're not just my memories. We've got people who come back year after year – people like Barney and the rest of the Bennetts. This place has given families the kind of Christmases you only see in Hallmark movies. Stress-free and filled with love, laughter and good times.' She cocked her head. 'Did you know Innes and Leo got married here?'

Damon jerked his chin, looking unhappy. 'He told me.'

'I know you probably haven't seen how much we do for the local community, and I know Barney's not exactly been broadcasting how much this place means to him' – she pursed her lips – 'but it saved me when Adrian died. I was a living zombie, existing from day to day until something led me here. It's where I feel at home. It's a place where I get to live Christmas Day over and over. I become part of other families, even if it's just for a week. But it's more than that...' She leaned forwards and put her hands on her knees, desperate to make Damon understand. It wasn't just that she wanted to save the resort, she wanted him to recognise how special this place was. How vital it was that he didn't change anything. 'People make important memories here – it makes them happy, helps them to connect with one another. There aren't many places in the world you can say that about.'

Damon frowned. 'Not everyone feels that way,' he said softly and there was something in his voice and expression that made Holliday sit straighter.

'What do you mean?' she asked.

'I just mean...' He shook his head, avoiding her eyes. 'Not everyone who comes will leave feeling the same,' he said, obviously choosing his words carefully. 'Perhaps for them it'll be the opposite.' His cheeks flushed.

Holliday wondered what Damon wasn't telling her. Had he been to Christmas Resort before and had a terrible time? Bonnibell and Kenzy thought they'd recognised him. Was that why he wanted to build a new hotel? If so – what had happened? Her mind buzzed with a million scenarios and her insides flooded with sympathy, but she tried not to show it.

'I'm just saying you can't make assumptions.' He sat back abruptly, leaning away from Holliday again. His voice had changed, grown more business-like – almost cold.

She watched his body stiffen and his broad shoulders widen, as if he'd erected a barrier around himself. A wall she'd have to work extra hard to get beyond. Was it odd that suddenly she wanted to?

'Did something happen to you here?' she probed gently, staring into his eyes as they dilated. She watched his Adam's apple bob and leaned even closer, attempting to read his expression. He was doing his best to show no emotion but she could see flashes of something in the movement of the muscles across his cheeks. Knew he was considering whether he could tell her. Her whole body froze when his shoulders sagged, signalling a break in his defences.

'I...' he began and her stomach skipped because for the first time since they'd met, she suspected he was going to tell her something real. Perhaps he'd even explain the reason he was here, confide about the hotel and his plans. She was surprised by how much she wanted him to open up, to be truthful.

'Holliday!' Bonnibell suddenly boomed from the doorway. 'Barney's just reminded me that we promised to run a dance class for him this afternoon. I'm sorry, hen,' she added when Holliday twisted around. 'He's very insistent. Isn't interested in cake decorating at all.'

If she'd had just a few more moments Damon might have told her everything. She'd just have to get him alone again later.

'It's okay,' Holliday said regretfully, starting to rise. 'It used to be his and Mabel's favourite activity.' Holliday darted a meaningful look at Damon; this illustrated her point. 'I don't think you should join in, but you could stay and watch?'

She might not have got to the bottom of his story yet, but now Holliday was doubly determined to make sure Damon fell in love with Christmas Resort. Hopefully in the meantime she'd learn about his past too...

Holliday heaved the sofa away from the fire so she could clear a space ready for Barney and the Bennetts' arrival. She frowned at the empty chair where Damon had been sitting a moment before, wishing he'd agreed to stay for the dancing lesson too. Instead he'd disappeared to his bedroom, intent on shutting himself away. Though she was sure he was sore after his fall, Holliday suspected he'd left because he was worried about how much he'd almost shared. Perhaps he was scared that spending more time with her would mean he'd open up even more. But what was he so afraid of telling her?

'The room's a little cold,' Barney grumbled as he wandered into the sitting room and then stood at the edge of the rug, leaning on his cane, examining the space with a critical expression. 'I hope you've got Mabel's favourite music ready,' he said. 'I did make a special request.'

'Of course,' Holliday soothed.

'Oh, Dad, I'm sure Holliday will make sure everything's perfect,' Kate comforted, striding into the room with her husband Robert, who was a few steps behind. 'The kids will be here in a minute, they're just changing into more festive clothes.' She sighed, glancing around. 'I remember the last time we had one of these lessons. The music was loud and Mum giggled so much.' She exhaled and her husband patted her shoulder. 'It's alright,' she said faintly. 'Being here means so much. I know she's looking down on us now, probably wishing she could join in with the dance.' She glanced at her father who was still frowning. 'Is it just us this afternoon?'

Holliday nodded. 'I think so. We've got new guests arriving tonight, perhaps we can do another lesson with more people later in the week?'

Barney sniffed and opened his mouth just as Damon appeared at the doorway, making Holliday's stomach perform a series of mini pirouettes. He'd changed into jeans and a long-sleeved navy shirt and looked very handsome. It might have been the slight flush on his cheeks from sitting by the fire, or maybe it was just because she was getting to know the angles and planes of his face which made her appreciate his good looks even more.

'Your cat's in my room again,' he complained, looking around. 'Bonnibell tried to get him to move but he found a gap in the floorboards beside the shower and he's disappeared under them and won't come out. She said she'll get Leo and Connell onto it later. I can't stay there so...' He sighed, his shoulders sagging. 'She's hidden my coat and boots and insisted I join you. She said someone should keep an eye on me anyway because I hit my head. Also apparently this is going to be *fun*.'

'How's your head?' Holliday asked.

'It's fine.' Damon folded his arms deliberately as Lucie and Arthur came racing into the room wearing jeans and Christmas jumpers, the teenager's on the small side for him. Arthur angled his arms in front of the pattern as if he were trying to hide it.

'Can I dance with you, Dad?' Lucie asked in a high-pitched squeal, skidding to a halt so she could grab her father's leg.

Arthur groaned and rolled his eyes. 'This is *so* lame.'

'And yet, if you can endure it for just half an hour, I'll let you have your iPad back for the rest of the afternoon,' Kate said, smiling. 'You can dance with me.' She caught his elbow and scooped the lanky teen closer. 'This was one of your favourite things to do when you were younger.'

'Mabel always said the boy had her genes,' Barney said, taking another step into the room. 'The numbers are off,' he pointed out, counting all the people on his fingers. 'We've got one extra person, that's not going to work,' he moaned.

'I'm really very happy to sit this out.' Damon looked longingly at the chairs. 'I'm sure I can learn everything I need to from over there.'

'Nonsense,' Bonnibell said, breezing in to join them with Claus trotting at her heels. 'Connell's just got back from running his errands – and said he'd take over the cooking so I can come to your class. Barney.' She placed her hands on her curvy hips, swishing her red velvet skirt. 'Are you ready to partner up?'

'Grandad and Grandma were the best dancers,' Lucie gushed, her pretty young face lighting up as she beamed at her grandfather.

His frown instantly melted away. 'We were, weren't we?' he said, his voice husky and his eyes glistened as his chest expanded. 'I'd almost forgotten. Okay – I'll dance with you, but you'd better keep up,' he said to Bonnibell. He turned to Damon and narrowed his eyes. 'So long as you dance with Holliday.' He wriggled an eyebrow in her direction and for the first time since he'd arrived, she saw a spark of humour there, as if the old Barney – the one Mabel used to be able to tease out – was poking through the black clouds.

Holliday looked at Damon – a myriad of emotions were roving across his face but she couldn't tell if he was happy or sad. 'You don't have to. You had that fall...'

'Ach, don't be a coward.' Barney sounded annoyed. 'In all the years we came here I never let my girl down, once I recall I'd broken my leg and I *still* danced.'

Damon's lips squeezed and he finally nodded. Holliday wished she knew what was going through his mind. Was he thinking he'd never offer classes like this in the new hotel?

'Can we start with "Rockin' around the Christmas Tree"?' Arthur asked gruffly. 'That was Grandma's favourite.'

Barney nodded. 'It's the one I asked Holliday to put on.'

Robert squeezed Arthur's arm. 'It's a comfort doing the same things, isn't it? Remembering her.' He smiled as Holliday went to the small desk in the corner of the room and plugged in her phone. Then she connected it to the main speaker and chose the right version of the song; the one she remembered Mabel had preferred.

'Okay, start by facing each other,' Holliday said, indicating to Damon that he should stand opposite her too. Then she pressed 'play'. 'So, begin by pushing your bottom out and wriggling your hips and wave your arms back and forth like this.' She demonstrated, trying not to look at Damon in case he was frowning again. Or worse, laughing at her.

Lucie giggled. 'Grandma hated the word bottom – she liked to call it a jacksy.' She chuckled again and flushed when everyone turned to look at her.

'You're right,' Barney said, nodding. Then he raised an eyebrow at Holliday. 'So can we wriggle our jacksys instead?' He walked to the Christmas tree and unwound a piece of silver tinsel from one of the branches so he could dangle it around his neck.

Holliday laughed. 'No problem!' She waggled a hand at Damon, who was still watching them. If she'd had to guess, she'd have said he rarely danced, and had probably never been asked to wriggle anything in front of a bunch of strangers. When he didn't move she went to stand closer to him. 'There are more moves so you're going to want to follow my lead,' she said quietly. 'Just give it a try, you might enjoy it.'

She smiled when he pulled a face. Then Damon's eyes skimmed the family before he inched closer to her.

'I don't understand why they'd want to do something that reminds them about...' He leaned in further until his breath was stroking Holliday's ear, setting off a wave of tingles that swept to her feet, warming every cell in between, some of which had been dormant for years. She swallowed, overwhelmed by her reaction and a little stunned. 'The woman – Mabel – passing away,' Damon whispered before taking a step away. The look on his face and the fact that his eyes were at least three shades darker suggested he'd been affected by their closeness too.

Holliday jerked a shoulder. 'I suppose... I don't know.' She frowned until she realised everyone was watching and they'd all stopped wriggling despite the music playing in the background.

'Sorry,' she chirped as her cheeks flamed, spinning around so she could stop the music and take her place at the front again. 'Okay.' She cleared her throat. 'So I've got a few more moves to show you. I'll go through them one by one and then we can turn up the song until our ears hurt and boogie beside the tree. Maybe we can even do a conga?'

Both of the children cheered and even Barney joined in. Then he rested his cane against the wall and grasped both of Bonnibell's hands. 'Can we add this move?' he asked, creating a dome with their arms and stepping forwards and then back.

'Oh, I remember that,' Kate chuckled. 'Mum used to call it your "gothic arch".'

'She told me it was because you were both old enough to remember when gothic architecture came in.' Arthur belly laughed and then shook his head, looking guilty. 'I'm sorry – it's not funny.'

'Oh, it is,' Barney said, stepping forwards into the group. 'It's good to remember her. She was a witty woman.' His smile was reflective and sad. 'I suppose in a way it's why we worked. I was her darkness and she was my dawn, we complemented each other.' He swallowed, taking a moment before turning and nodding at Holliday. 'So are we going to stand around all day talking or are we going to dance?' he snapped, proving his point.

'I choose dance!' Lucie cheered, hopping up and down.

Holliday nodded. 'Okay – so the three moves are the "jacksy wiggle" followed by the "gothic arch" – which you know.' She grinned at Barney who actually beamed back. 'The next move is stepping from side to side and circling both your arms around like a windmill, keep your elbows bent and make sure you follow the beat of the music.' She demonstrated and saw Damon's mouth twitch when all the members of the family and Bonnibell mirrored her movements.

'What about you, boy?' Barney asked, as they stopped, obviously noticing he hadn't joined in. 'This is not a spectator sport. We're not continuing until you've tried it.' The older man folded his arms and the children did the same until they were all staring at him solemnly. 'Mabel would never let any of us sit out, which means you can't.'

Damon looked pained. 'Okay, fine,' he said shortly, before twirling his arms a lot less enthusiastically and shifting an inch from left to right.

'You need to practise *a lot* – but let's call that one "the windmill",' Arthur said once Damon had finished.

'What's the last move going to be?' Damon asked, looking worried.

'You put one arm out, then the other, then you raise them to the sky and make a Christmas tree-shaped hat,' Holliday said, demonstrating again, feeling a little ridiculous, although she was having fun. This was why she loved her job.

'Ah...' Damon shut his eyes and when he opened them again Holliday could tell he was trying hard to contain a laugh. 'What's that called?'

'Why don't we call it "the spruce"?' Bonnibell suggested.

'That's perfect,' Barney gushed. 'Now we have all our moves, why don't you start the music again?'

'And don't forget to make it really loud,' Lucie shouted.

Holliday went to her phone and started it up, and when she turned back the family were all facing their partners and even Damon was waiting by one of the chairs she'd pushed back, watching as she walked up to join him. 'You start with the "jacksy wiggle", remember,' she yelled above the music, pointing to Bonnibell and Barney, who were going for it, their clothes and bodies flying from side to side.

'I can't believe I'm doing this,' Damon yelled, shifting his body, making a face that suggested moving might be painful.

'Are you okay?' Holliday shouted back, taking a step forwards and resting a palm on his shoulder, feeling her body go rigid with worry. 'You're wincing. If it hurts you know you can stop?'

Damon kept dancing but shifted closer so she could hear – and the tingles she'd felt before spread downwards from her ear. 'Nothing's hurting, aside from my pride,' he admitted. 'If you'd told me a few days ago that I'd be doing this – dancing with a crowd of strangers, I mean – I'd have said you were mad.' Holliday saw his brow wrinkle in confusion, felt her heart soften more. 'But they're enjoying it, aren't they?' He pulled away so he could nod at the others, looking baffled.

The family were flinging themselves around the room now, snorting and giggling. Arthur belted out the song at the top of his voice while Lucie squealed as tears spilled from the corners of Kate's eyes. But Holliday knew they were happy tears, knew they all needed this. They had come to Christmas Resort to remember Mabel; they had wanted to celebrate her. To acknowledge how much she'd given them, and that somehow she was still in their lives. Her heart filled and she felt tears prick the corners of her eyes too.

Damon cleared his throat. 'Okay,' he said, looking mortified as he demonstrated a particularly non-bushy spruce. 'I get it.' He gulped and glanced around, his eyes shining, and she could see he was moved by the emotion filling the room. 'This place *is* special.' His tone spelled surprise.

'It is,' Holliday said, feeling a wave of relief. For the first time since Damon had arrived he was beginning to understand.

15

HOLLIDAY

'The Bavestocks have arrived!' Connell came running into the sitting room and stood at the edge by the door, waiting for the song to end. As soon as it had, Holliday switched off her phone and they all gathered as an attractive couple trotted in from the hallway to join them. The man and woman were obviously in their mid-twenties and both had matching shoulder-length wavy brown hair.

'I'm Alison,' the woman said, stepping forwards to shake everyone's hands. 'This is Dave. We got married a year ago today.' She turned and enthusiastically grabbed hold of the man's hand.

'The Bavestocks are staying in Plum Pud Inn,' Connell told them. 'They were asking if we could take one of the snowmobiles out later this evening.'

'Dave's very experienced,' Alison jumped in, squeezing her body against her husband and beaming up at him with adoring eyes. 'And I hear it's very romantic,' she enthused.

'Can we come too?' Lucie hopped up and down on the rug, her blonde pigtails flying. 'We usually go out on the sleigh and put carrots and seeds out for Santa's reindeer when we come,' she shared. 'If we do it tonight, perhaps we could still do it on Christmas Eve too? I'll bet they're really hungry with all the snow hiding their food.'

'I love that idea!' Alison said.

'No reason why not, hen.' Bonnibell stroked the young girl's hair. 'It might be something Damon would enjoy trying.' She winked at Holliday. 'You could take the other snowmobile out for a whirl around the grounds?'

Holliday glanced over at Damon. After the dancing, she felt sure he was starting to come around to the idea of keeping the resort. It made sense to follow up their lesson with a beautiful evening jaunt in the snow. She was sure he'd love seeing the lights in the woods, taking a speedy ride up and down the valley. 'Good idea,' she said. 'If you're up for it?' she asked him.

Damon frowned and Holliday wondered if he was going to back out, but instead he nodded. 'I'd like to see more of the resort; I haven't managed to venture very far,' he said. 'I've not been on a snowmobile in a while but it sounds like fun.'

'All you have to do is hang on,' Connell joked.

'Then that's settled. We're all set for an early dinner.' Bonnibell clapped her hands. 'If you want to relax and change then let's all meet back here at half past five, we can eat and be ready to go out again at seven?'

Connell nodded. 'After I've got Frosty out of your room.' He nodded to Damon. 'Then Leo and I will get the sledge and snowmobiles ready for a spin.'

'Don't forget to wrap up!' Bonnibell exclaimed as she headed back into the hallway.

Snow was falling again when everyone tramped outside after dinner. Holliday took a moment to enjoy the fresh air and looked up at the stars, blinking as a flake of snow settled on her nose. It was powdery and the wind, which had been blustering earlier that afternoon, had settled into a gentle breeze.

'Are you happy for me to drive?' she asked Damon as they followed Connell and the Bavestocks, Barney and the Bennetts along the pathway towards Christmas Maze. The snowmobiles were kept in the same barn as the sleigh, although Holliday suspected they would all be out and ready to go by now. She wore navy salopettes, a thick coat with a lucky pom-pom in one of the pockets, a hat and gloves, and had borrowed the same gear for Damon. The knitted gloves and scarf she'd given him earlier weren't warm enough to use so she'd had to find him something bulkier.

'You probably should,' Damon admitted. 'I've not driven one for a long time. Promise me you won't try to lose me in the woods.' The edge of his mouth kicked up so she knew he was teasing.

'I'll think about it,' Holliday joked, keeping pace with his long strides, realising how much things had changed. Just a few days ago she'd been tramping this same pathway trying to work out how to get rid of him. Now she wanted to make him fall in love with being here. Perhaps even liked the idea of him staying. She knew she was attracted to him, although she wasn't ready to do anything about that.

'I'm looking forward to seeing how big the resort is,' Damon shared. 'There are probably lots of places I don't know about.'

Holliday stopped herself from asking why. The plans for the new hotel had included much of the grounds – almost all of it had been repurposed. Was Damon coming around and changing his mind, or just looking for new nooks and crannies to alter and build over?

'This is yours,' Connell said to Holliday, pointing at a red snowmobile as they approached the large shed where the outdoor equipment was stored. 'Dave.' He pointed to the young man. 'I hear you've driven one of these before?'

'I have,' Dave said, tramping up to stand by the blue snow-mobile. 'A few times.'

'If you all climb into the sleigh.' Connell nodded to Barney and the Bennett family. 'Get yourselves comfortable. There are blankets and hot water bottles inside to keep you warm.' He watched as they all clambered in, chattering and laughing – even Barney looked excited, clearly caught up in the joyous atmosphere. Although when Holliday looked over and he spotted her, his smile dimmed.

'I'm going to pull you along, and I want you to keep pace with us, Dave, please, until I know you've got the lay of the land and are comfortable with driving. Holliday' – Connell tossed some keys in the air and she caught them – 'you go ahead. Follow the usual trail. We'll meet you just outside the clearing where we leave food for the reindeer. Leo checked the lights down in the woods already so you shouldn't have any trouble finding your way. Be careful,' he added sternly before winking at Damon. 'And make sure you hold on tight.' He grinned.

'Oh and' – Connell's lips pursed –'I heard from Edina earlier that Bob might be on the loose so keep an eye out for stray donkeys. Also, Tavish says there are a number of tourists straying around the village looking for whoever's making the Secret Cider that everyone's talking about.' He sighed. 'If you spot anyone hiking the trails, please make sure you don't squash them. Which means don't drive too fast and please keep your eyes peeled!' He jabbed a finger at Holliday before waving Dave and Alison over.

'So we're going ahead on our own?' Damon asked, as Holliday trotted up the small incline towards the red snowmobile.

'We can go faster if we make our own way and if no one else is around we'll have an uninterrupted view. It really is quite beautiful, especially since most of the places we're going to pass have never been built on.' Holliday hoped Damon might pick up on the hint. She grabbed a helmet from the top of the machine and handed it to him. 'Please make sure it's secured and tight enough so it doesn't move,' she advised as she put hers on.

'You're going to sit here.' She patted the back of the long leather seat. 'And put your feet here and here.' She indicated to the stirrups on the sides. 'And use these handles to grip onto, or if it's more comfortable hold onto me. I'll try not to lose you,' she joked. 'I think you've had enough excitement for today.'

'You might be right,' Damon said dryly as he checked the helmet and swung his long legs over the bike. He waited as Holliday did the same and then he shifted around until he was comfortable. 'I'm going to hold onto you,' he said, easing forwards until he was touching her back, setting off prickles of awareness across the surface of her skin. 'That way it'll be more difficult for you to throw me off.'

'No promises,' Holliday teased. She twisted a little so he would hear her clearly – once they were moving he might not be able to hear her speak: 'I need you to lean into the turns – it's a balance thing. I'll take it slowly to start with until I know you've got the hang of how to move.'

'You do this a lot?' He sounded surprised.

Holliday nodded. 'When it snows I love escaping into the fields, just driving through the night so I can take in the scenery.' She sighed. 'It gives me time to think.'

'About Adrian?' he asked with a strange hitch to his voice.

'No, not really.' She cleared her throat. 'I try not to think about him when I'm here.' Unless she was imagining him sitting in the house in Cambridge, she tried to block him completely out of her mind. Sometimes now she could go days without thinking about him at all.

'Why?' he asked gently.

But Holliday pretended she hadn't heard. She fired up the engine and patted the hard muscle on Damon's knee to let him know she was about to move. Then they were heading down the hill and into the fields, shooting past trees layered with sparkling and knitted Christmas ornaments. Holliday spotted one of the large barns in the far distance and noticed a light inside. She sped up as they drew closer just in case it was where Connell had hidden Damon's car. If he asked to stop so they could check out why the light was on and realised they'd been lying to him, she knew he'd be angry and hated the idea. She was enjoying their strange truce – enjoying his company.

'I'm going to head for the trees,' Holliday shouted, but wasn't sure if Damon heard. She could feel warmth running along the outside of her thighs and across her back from where his body was pressing against hers and tried to stop herself from leaning into him. It had been so long since she'd been touched by anyone. Innes had once told her she was probably touch-starved. Holliday hadn't thought she'd miss the sensation of someone else's skin against hers, or find herself craving it until this moment. But she liked the feel of Damon's hard body, liked the heat she could feel penetrating through her clothes. Couldn't help imagining how it might feel if they didn't have so many layers between them. She shook herself, trying to throw off the thought – it was a betrayal of Adrian. At least that's how she would have felt until today...

Holliday took a sharp right to avoid getting closer to the barn, and felt Damon lean heavily into her back as she steered the bike right and skirted the top edge of the field, slicing through the powdery snow. She kept her eyes fixed ahead. The lights on the front of the machine picked out random shrubs and bushes peppered with ice and she avoided them, staying vigilant in case any animals decided to dart in front of them. Holliday inhaled through the scarf she'd wrapped around her nose and smelled pine needles, but was there a hint of Damon in there too? She hadn't been this close to him until today, but when she'd been looking into his eyes after the accident earlier she'd caught the scent of linen again. She'd never thought a smell could be sexy before, but there was something about this one she responded to.

Did that mean she was falling for him? Holliday frowned, wondering how she could stop, knowing even as they tore down the hill that it was probably already too late.

16

HOLLIDAY

The snowmobile jolted as it went over a bump and Holliday's stomach pitched at the movement. She heard Damon's delighted laugh and felt it vibrate across her shoulders and back and it made her want to giggle too. A few more metres down she skidded to a stop at the edge of the woods and cut the engine, climbing off the machine. She unhooked her helmet and glanced back the way they'd just come.

She sighed as Damon got off too. 'These rides always end too quickly.'

Bells rang in the distance and Damon looked back up the hill to where a set of headlights wove back and forth to the left of the loch. Behind those, the sleigh – lit with sparkly silver and red Christmas lights – glided towards the bottom of the valley and she imagined Connell chugging along at the front in his compact red tractor, roaring with laughter or yelling *ho ho ho!* at the top of his voice.

'That looks like fun,' Damon remarked after a beat.

'It's very popular with our visitors,' Holliday confided. 'But slow. It'll take them about five more minutes to get here.' She turned to look at Damon; he was watching the machines navigate the inclines and seemed... enchanted. This was what she'd been hoping to get him to feel since he'd arrived. She pressed her lips together as she studied the hard planes of his jaw and realised he wasn't frowning. 'Do you like it?' she asked huskily as the other snowmobile drew closer.

He wrapped his arms around himself, contemplating her question, and then jerked his chin. 'I've never seen anything quite like it,' he said, sounding awed. 'It's magical, isn't it? I had no idea you offered this kind of thing. I'm half expecting one of Santa's elves to pop out from behind a tree.'

'They only do that on Christmas Eve,' Holliday joked, smiling again when Damon chuckled. He seemed so much more relaxed – it was like the accident today had loosened something inside of him. Or perhaps it had been that knock on the head? He seemed more human somehow – perhaps even vulnerable. She wanted to ask what he was feeling, but then Dave and Alison slid up beside them, took off their helmets and beamed, and Connell pulled the tractor to a stop beside them too.

'I hope you all had fun? It's just a few metres walk through there,' the older man boomed, pointing to a gap in the trees. Lights were twinkling along the narrow pathway, making it easier for them to find their way. 'If you're really quiet, you might see a reindeer,' Connell whispered to Lucie.

She squeaked and hopped up and down, grabbing Barney's hand. 'Can we go first?' She tugged her grandad forwards but the older man didn't complain. 'Do you think Grandma is watching us from somewhere?' Lucie asked, glancing up at the sky.

'Who knows,' Barney said gruffly. 'Even if she's not, I think she'd be really happy we've come. She loved feeding the reindeer.' He shrugged. 'I've no idea why.'

'Because it's fun,' Lucie gushed, her eyes twinkling. 'Oh, what's that? Looks like reindeer footprints!' She sprinted away, still holding her grandfather's hand.

The rest of them followed, walking deeper into the sparkling trees, but Damon held back. 'I don't get it,' he whispered to Holliday. 'It's like the dancing – they want to remember all the things that should make them sad. Surely it would be better to just move on? If it were me I'd never come here again.'

Holliday watched the family as they started to sprinkle the seeds Bonnibell had handed out earlier. The Bavestocks joined in, skipping around the space, peering into the trees as something jingled in the undergrowth.

'I'll bet that's a reindeer,' Arthur told his sister, urgently searching the darkness.

Holliday folded her arms. 'I think being here makes them sad, but also happy,' she said to Damon in a low voice. 'Remembering Mabel, thinking about and celebrating all the things they most loved doing with her. It's not a quick fix, but every minute they're here it seems to me they're feeling a tiny bit lighter. Even Barney's starting to mellow.'

She watched the older man as he flung seeds around the clearing with his granddaughter. He didn't have his cane now and was walking normally and she wondered if he'd been using it to get himself out of joining in.

'It's like he's finding himself again and mixing a little of Mabel into his temperament. He's not one hundred per cent sour anymore – doing things they used to do together is adding in some of her sweetness. It's like he's becoming a little of them both. He seems happier.' She screwed up her nose. 'Am I talking nonsense?'

'Maybe, but I get it,' Damon said. 'Is that what you're doing?' he asked, earnestly. 'I mean, is that why you're living here at the resort?' He took in their surroundings. 'Are you trying to remember your fiancé – does that make you happier too?' He took a step closer until he could look into her eyes.

Holliday looked away, embarrassed. 'I... not exactly,' she said, swallowing a bubble of confusion because she hadn't thought about that before. Mostly, she'd avoided her feelings. Tried to pretend nothing had changed. But it had, hadn't it? So was she being fair to Adrian's memory? Or to herself?

'So you don't feel close to him here?' Damon asked.

Holliday glanced at the Bennetts, who were pacing around the clearing, miming binoculars with their hands, trying to spot animals and elves in the trees. Something made a honking sound in the darkness and she wondered if Bob was on a walka-bout in the woods, perhaps joining forces with the reindeer. Either that or her imaginary wildcat was about to put in an appearance.

'Holliday?' Damon repeated.

'I don't know.' Holliday sighed, reaching into her pocket and squeezing a pom-pom. It usually calmed her, but hadn't been working that well since Damon had arrived. 'I...' She ground her teeth, trying to find the right words, wondering why she was suddenly sharing so much with him. 'When I'm here, it's like Adrian's still alive somewhere. I like to imagine him out in the world, still reading, writing his articles...'

'So you're hiding?'

A tear trickled down her cheek and she swiped at the sudden spill of emotion. 'I know it sounds stupid.' She hadn't seen what she'd been doing through someone else's eyes before. Hadn't wanted to. Innes and Bonnibell knew a little about what had happened, but she hadn't ever mentioned the house. She knew Mr Hornbuckle didn't get it. She wasn't sure if she did now. She heard the Bennetts laugh in the distance and turned to watch them. She could tell that even in these few days, they'd begun to heal. Whereas she'd been stuck in the same emotional vacuum for two years. Still grieving, wishing nothing had changed.

When she looked back Damon was staring at her. 'It's not stupid,' he said gently. 'My sister, Scarlett, would probably say the same thing to you as she does to me.' He searched her face, his expression intense. Holliday couldn't bring herself to look away. She'd thought Damon was cold, but there was nothing cold about the way he was looking at her now.

'What does your sister say?' Damon started to step away and Holliday reached out and touched his arm. 'Don't,' she said. 'Please. Tell me.'

He hesitated. 'Scarlett would say you have to move on, accept what's happened and build on what's left.' His voice was gruff and his chest shuddered. 'I don't know...' He lifted a shoulder. 'She doesn't think it's a good idea to ignore things that have happened. She believes in dealing with them.' He pulled a face.

Holliday nodded. 'Is Scarlett always right?'

A tiny smiled curled the edge of Damon's mouth. 'She'd say she was. But...' His forehead scrunched. 'Maybe not always.'

Connell appeared behind Damon's shoulder. 'You two ready to go? You didn't feed the reindeer, lass.' He shoved a small bag into Holliday's hands. 'Why don't you do it now, while I load up the others? It's getting colder and we should probably head back to the lodge. Bonnibell's planned mulled wine and Christmas carols.' He winked at Damon. 'You'll love it.' He chortled as he passed, then he frowned as he looked up the hill. 'Did I just see lights up there?' He craned his neck as Damon and Holliday tried to look too.

'I can't see anything,' Holliday said. 'Are you sure it wasn't just the Christmas decorations?'

'Ach, lass, must be. Bonnibell's always accusing me of seeing things that aren't there.' He chuckled again before leading

Barney, the Bennetts and Bavestocks down the snowy pathway out of the trees.

The sleigh was only a few metres ahead when Holliday started up the snowmobile. Damon wasn't sitting as close to her now and she wondered if their conversation had spooked him. It had surprised her. She had an odd burning feeling in the pit of her stomach but didn't know what it meant. Pieces of the carefully constructed world she'd built were beginning to crumble away and she wasn't sure if she was ready to face what was underneath. Then again, would she ever be?

She slid the snowmobile away from the woods and saw Dave and Alison fire up the hill, faster than before. They bumped over a couple of slopes before zigzagging at speed along the edge of the loch. If Dave wasn't careful, he and his young wife were going to go for an evening swim. Then he accelerated and took a hard right, shooting up the hill.

Holliday sped up too. Connell wouldn't be able to catch up with the snowmobile on the tractor, especially not when he was towing the sleigh. She saw him point ahead as she passed, and nodded her understanding. If she could catch up with the younger couple, she'd be able to advise them to slow down. She heard a braying sound through the whistling in her ears and prayed it wasn't Bob. The donkey had been known to roam the hills in the dark and she didn't want anyone crashing into him. So she accelerated and took a hard right too, hurtling faster up the hill, widening her eyes when she saw lights glowing in the distance, guessing they were the same ones Connell had spotted a few minutes ago. They were too low to the ground to be Christmas lights and Holliday suspected they were torch beams. It seemed the Secret Cider hunters were out in force searching the grounds.

She raced Dave up the steep ridge, hoping he'd spotted their visitors, but then realised he was heading straight for them. Perhaps the snow was obscuring his view, or maybe he was too caught up in the scenery and excitement of the ride. She tried to shout, knowing it was pointless. Felt Damon squeeze her waist as if signalling the danger too.

'I know,' she shouted into the night and felt him press her knee. She took a hard right, almost skidding in the powdery snow, and felt Damon heavy against her back as he leaned closer, mirroring her movements. They were almost at the top of the hill and she could see the three reindeer ornaments in the far distance. The lights were bobbing to the side of them and the snowmobile was heading straight for them. If it didn't stop, someone was going to get hurt.

Holliday felt her breath catch as the snowmobile continued to race towards the torch lights. If Dave didn't spot them soon, he'd plough straight into the walkers. She shouted again, then watched the blue snowmobile take a hard right, skidding as it hit a bump, thankful he was finally taking action to avoid a collision. Then everything seemed to slow as the snowmobile continued to shoot forwards, heading straight for the three reindeer ornaments where Adrian had proposed. Holliday froze as she saw the walkers sprinting away, the light from their torches disappearing into the darkness. When she glanced back again she saw the snowmobile skid as Dave tried to stop. But it was too late. He was driving much too fast.

Holliday's breath, heartbeat, even the pump of her blood, everything slowed as the snowmobile skidded and then she stopped moving altogether as she watched it crash into the three metal reindeer. Saw the lights pop off one by one and watched the three sparkly shapes soar unceremoniously in the air before disappearing into the inky blackness with a crash, just as Dave's snowmobile skidded to a stop.

Holliday pulled to a standstill too, her heart icy in her chest. She felt sick and knew tears were rolling unchecked down her cheeks, pooling at the bottom of the goggles. She pulled them off, along with the helmet and scarf.

'It's okay, Holliday,' Damon soothed, tugging her frozen hand off the handlebars and reaching around to cut the engine. 'The Bavestocks don't look like they've been injured.' Then he squeezed her shoulder and climbed off before striding to check on Dave and Alison, looking back as he was talking to check she was okay. She watched him chat with the couple before giving her a thumbs up.

All the while Holliday sat frozen, clutching onto the helmet, her mind racing with a million memories of Adrian, reliving the moment he'd proposed over and over. She tried to imagine him in Cambridge, tried to conjure him sitting by the fire in their house reading one of his books, but couldn't. The illusion had been broken and she wasn't sure if she'd ever be able to believe in it again.

Feeling nauseous, she climbed off the snowmobile as Connell reached them. Watched as he slowly shone his torch beam across the ground, picking out each of the three reindeer lying battered in the snow. They were so misshapen Holliday barely recognised what they'd been. The Christmas lights lay in tatters around them and she could see where the force of the impact had ripped the strings into shreds. Damon wandered to the smallest reindeer ornament and knelt so he could set it on its feet, but it toppled over. He glanced towards Holliday and she could see sympathy in his expression, guessed he was about to offer some comforting words – but she gulped and shook her head as waves of emotions crashed through her.

'I can't,' she said roughly as she leapt off the snowmobile and took off, still clutching the helmet, running and sliding towards the pathway she knew would lead her back to the lodge and the privacy of her bedroom.

'Wait!' she heard Connell and Damon shout, but she didn't stop. Not until she'd navigated the path and swept through the unlocked entrance of Christmas Lodge. She heard Bonnibell yell as she sprinted up the stairs and charged down the hallway. Then when she was finally in her bedroom, still wearing her snow boots, thick coat, hat and gloves, Holliday locked the door, slid to the ground and began to sob.

17

DAMON

Damon forced himself not to follow because he guessed Holliday needed to be alone. He shouldn't have cared; she was supposed to mean nothing to him, just a member of staff in a business he wanted to fold. But something had changed and no matter how hard Damon wanted to fight it, he knew it was too late.

'I know, lad,' Connell growled, wandering up to the largest reindeer and trying to pull it to its feet. It immediately fell to one side because one of the legs had been flattened and from the state of it, Damon wondered if it would ever stand again.

'I'm so sorry,' Dave babbled, coming to study the carnage. 'Those people came out of nowhere.' He gulped. 'I wasn't expecting... I know I was going too fast...' He faltered, his voice loaded with guilt. 'I'll pay for any damage.'

'That won't be necessary, lad. The main thing is nobody got hurt,' Connell said. 'Could you get your snowmobile back to the barn where we started our journey?' The younger man considered the request and nodded before Connell continued, 'I'll drive the sleigh there too so Barney and the Bennetts can make their way back to the resort before they get cold. It'll be a faster walk and easier to find in the dark.'

'We could help?' Barney suggested, wincing at a misshapen reindeer that appeared to have lost part of its head.

Connell patted the older man on the back. 'No reason for you to get hypothermia. I'll find Leo and we'll see what we can do. The lad mentioned he was going to be working on something in the barn we passed on our drive to the woods. I noticed a light on inside so he's probably there now.'

'I'll find Leo if you take everyone to the lodge and get them settled,' Damon offered, nodding at the others. 'We can meet back here later.' What the hell was he doing? He was supposed to be knocking the resort down, not fixing it up. Then he remembered the look on Holliday's face when she'd been gazing at the broken reindeer – he hadn't witnessed that kind of devastation before, aside from when his marriage had imploded and he'd looked in the mirror and stared into his own eyes. He turned to Connell. 'We can fix this,' he said firmly.

'Ach, lad, I hope you're right,' Connell said, sounding unconvinced. 'The wee lass looked very unhappy. I had no idea she was so attached to these.' He sighed and took one last look at the mess. 'Do you know how to drive that thing?' he asked, pointing to the red snowmobile.

'I've ridden one before and I watched Holliday, I'll be able to work it out,' Damon assured him.

Connell nodded before he hopped back onto the tractor and followed Dave as he drove off in the direction of the lodge.

It was quieter on the journey down into the valley, but the light was still on in the big barn so Damon knew which direction he should head in. He took the journey slowly because the snowfall had thickened, and kept his eyes peeled for stray donkeys or people with torches wandering the grounds. He drew up beside the large barn and parked up, then opened the main door that led inside. As soon as Damon stood in the threshold he spotted Leo in the corner surrounded by a collection of myriad equipment he seemed to be packing away. There were bottles stacked on counters, what looked like scales, a bucket, some paperwork, a keg, thermometer and some gas bulbs. The younger man flinched, clearly startled, when Damon entered and the wind caught the door and it slammed.

'Why are you here?' Leo demanded, looking guilty.

'I could ask you the same thing,' Damon said, drawing closer until he could see each of the empty bottles on the counter had a label attached. He picked one up and read the label. 'Secret Cider...' He turned to stare into the younger man's face. 'So you're the mystery brewer?'

'Fermenter, actually.' Leo flushed and slumped onto the stool set to the edge of the counter. 'But not anymore. I was just packing everything away.' He swiped a hand across his forehead, smearing dirt over it. He looked tired and a little stressed.

'Why?' Damon asked.

Leo shrugged. 'I can't risk getting caught. I don't have a licence to make and sell cider, I was just doing it on the side to earn a bit of extra cash.'

'Which is why you called it Secret Cider,' Damon guessed.

Leo's chest heaved. 'Now that TikTok video's gone viral people are searching the village – and it's only a matter of time before someone finds out it's me. Then I'll be in trouble; I might get prosecuted, have to pay fines – who knows. Worse, Connell and Bonnibell might be implicated, even though no one knows what I've been doing in the barn.'

His face paled. 'I told Innes today that we weren't as close to moving out from my mam's as I'd hoped. She was *so* angry.' His eyes widened. 'I've never seen her like that. I'm not sure how much longer we can stay where we are before she's had too much. It was just Mam and me for such a long time, she's not ready to let someone new into the family.' He gulped. 'It's why I wanted to talk to you about how to set this up properly.' He pointed to the equipment.

'How long have you been making cider?' Damon asked, grabbing another stool so he could sit and face the younger man.

'About six months. It was just a small thing at first. Local. I went to school with Matt, who part-owns The Corner Shop, and I convinced him to let me sell some of the bottles there.' He shut his eyes momentarily. 'We both knew it wasn't okay, but it was only supposed to be temporary. I started looking into licences, but it was expensive and complicated and I wasn't looking to expand. I like working at the resort. I just need extra cash so we can get our own place. I figure people sell home-made cakes at school fetes, it's almost the same thing.' He winced when Damon gave him a disbelieving look. 'Okay, I know that's not true...'

'Who knows about this?' Damon asked.

'No one aside from Matt and he's sworn to secrecy. Tavish probably suspects but he hasn't asked directly,' Leo said gravely. 'That's it. Innes doesn't know. I couldn't risk it. I know she wouldn't approve.' He leaned forwards and put his elbows on his knees, rested his forehead in his palms and his shoulders heaved. 'That TikTok video has spoiled everything. I'm going to have to lay low until everyone's forgotten about the cider. I reckon a couple of months and then perhaps I can start making it again. It'll take us longer to move out of my mam's, but...' He shrugged. 'At least I won't get myself or the resort into trouble.'

He looked up, his face filled with misery. 'Innes is furious,' he hissed. 'I'm afraid she's going to leave me. She thinks I don't want to move out and only live with her – I don't know what to do.'

He perused the half-packed boxes which were piled against one edge of the bar. He'd obviously started sorting the bottles and equipment but there was still a lot to do. Then his face dropped and he straightened on the stool. 'Oh God, what are you doing here?' He looked worried. 'I thought you'd gone to scatter reindeer food. Has someone guessed this is where I've been making the cider? Are the police coming? Are you here to keep me busy until they arrive?' His voice shook.

'No.' Damon rose and scratched his head, considering the mess. 'No one knows anything. But we need to talk about this later. It isn't my field but I might be able to help. Keep everything hidden but don't pack it away. Do you have your toolbox handy?'

Leo nodded, visibly relaxing. 'Sure, why?'

'Because something important has been damaged and I'm going to need your help to fix it,' Damon said.

'What is it?' Leo asked, growing concerned. 'Is everyone okay?' He swiped his hands on his overalls as if they'd suddenly grown sweaty. 'Is Innes alright?' he asked urgently. 'Last time I saw her she'd just slammed out of my mam's house...'

'As far as I know she's absolutely fine.' Damon wagged a hand. 'You're obviously aware of the three reindeer on the hill?'

'Of course,' Leo said and his face fell when Damon explained what had happened with the snowmobile.

'It's all my fault,' he rasped. 'If I hadn't been selling the cider, no one would have been walking around the grounds.'

'Accidents happen,' Damon said. 'Something you'll learn in business is you can't control everything. But you can help to fix it.'

'Just give me a moment.' Leo nodded and then rose before heading behind one of the large shelving units at the far edge of the room. 'I walked here earlier, so I might need a ride up the hill.' He turned to peruse the mess on the floor. 'I'll come back later and make sure the rest of this is concealed.'

Damon nodded. 'I'll give you a lift on the snowmobile,' he promised. Then he stayed where he was, taking in his surroundings while Leo gathered his tools.

What was happening to him? He was supposed to be

focusing on all the things he was going to do when the resort no longer existed. When Willow had been erased from his memories. Damon shut his eyes, trying to imagine the new hotel. If he was right, he'd be sitting at the ninth hole of the golf course now, but no matter how hard he tried to imagine it, to feel the warmth of the sun on his face as he prepared to take a shot, he could only see Holliday and her expression when the reindeer had been destroyed.

'Right, I'm ready,' Leo suddenly barked.

Damon shot to his feet and headed for the door. Hoping once they'd fixed the reindeer, he'd start to feel normal again.

18

DAMON

'Hold on while I try to get this nose back into shape,' Leo commanded as they tackled the final twisted reindeer.

They'd been working for almost two hours straight and Damon wanted to blow onto his hands to warm them because they were so numb, but it wouldn't do much good through the thick gloves he was wearing. He'd definitely been outside for too long now, but neither he nor Leo had wanted to give up. Somehow getting the reindeers back to the way they'd been had been more important than anything, including getting cold. Damon held on tight as the younger man used a wrench to yank the warped metal into a nose, then he set it on its feet and took a step away.

'It's not perfect,' Leo said critically, surveying the three reindeer. 'But at least they're all standing and you can tell what type of animal they're supposed to be.' He scowled. 'Almost. It's the best I can do while they're here – if I can get them to a workshop I'll be able to improve on this a lot.'

Damon stood back too. The reindeer looked a little worse for wear but they were upright and in the same positions. He

was filled with an odd feeling of contentment as he studied
them. He'd spent the last four years dismantling things,
changing them or knocking them down – it was oddly satisfying
to fix something instead. To repair what was broken. He pursed
his lips as his sister's voice filled his head, informing him in her
most superior tone that she'd been right all along. *But had she?*
Was this quest to transform everywhere he'd been with Willow
as shallow and petty as Scarlett thought?

'Sorry I was so long. How are you getting on?' Connell
shouted, suddenly appearing on the pathway carrying a flask
and cups. He poured steaming hot chocolate and handed the
mugs to Leo and Damon, then set the flask into the snow so he
could pace around the ornaments, bending and angling his head
so he could get a better look.

'What do you think?' Damon asked when the older man
didn't comment.

'If you saw them from somewhere down there' – Connell
pointed towards the bottom of the valley – 'you'd never know
they'd been in an accident.'

'And if you were closer?' Leo asked, nodding his agreement
when the older man pulled a face.

Would Holliday care about the flaws and odd angles?
Damon wasn't sure why it mattered – but it did. The look on
her face when she'd taken in the ruins of what had once been an
important memory for her was etched into his brain and for
some reason he wanted to repair it.

'I'm just glad you had another set of lights, even if they are
red and green.' Leo sighed. He hadn't been able to do anything
with the white ones, but these sparkled in all the right places
and were only a temporary fix. 'Is Bonnibell bringing Holliday
here soon?' the younger man asked Connell, patting his arms
and shivering a little. His work gear was padded but he wasn't
properly dressed for the type of cold they were working in and

since they'd stopped, Damon could see Leo had started to get
cold.

'Ach, lad, you should get yourself back to the lodge. I didn't
realise you weren't wearing enough,' Connell said, noticing too.
'I believe Innes might be in the kitchen. She was talking with
Bonnibell earlier, and things don't look too good for you.' He
cringed before turning to Damon. 'Do you want to get back to
the warm too? I heard you fell off a ladder earlier, are you in
pain? I'm happy to wait until Holliday comes out. I'm not sure
how long it's going to be.' He lifted the bottom of his thick red
sleeve and checked his watch. 'When I left, Bonnibell was
talking to her...'

Damon cleared his throat. 'I'm fine, nothing hurts.' He wriggled a little, proving it. 'I'd rather wait.' He patted his clothes,
trying not to shudder. 'I'm warm – perhaps if *you* went and
talked to Holliday too, you'd be able to persuade her to come?'

Connell looked thoughtful. 'If you're sure?' he said eventually. When Damon nodded the older man called for Claus and
looped an arm around Leo's shoulders before the two of them
headed back towards the lodge.

Damon stood at the top of the hill and looked down into the
valley. He could see the glimmer of lights in the woods where
they'd been earlier, scattering seeds for the reindeer he wasn't
convinced existed. But he'd had fun – more than he'd had in a
long while. It was strange how this place got under your skin; he
hadn't expected it to happen at all, let alone so fast.

He heard a crunch of footsteps and when he turned he saw
Holliday walking up the path. He watched and waited until she
noticed the three reindeer ornaments. When she did she froze,
stumbled, then hesitated, folding her arms, studying each of
them in turn, before walking up to join him.

'Connell told me you were waiting for me. He wanted to
come too but I told him to stay in the warm,' she said, her voice

croaky with emotion. 'He told me this was your idea.' Her eyes were red and Damon could see she'd been weeping. It shouldn't have bothered him – he'd hardened himself to tears when he'd learned of Willow's affairs and she'd sobbed for days, begging him to forgive her – but knowing that Holliday had been crying affected him more than he wanted to admit. 'Thank you,' she said, hesitantly.

Damon folded his arms too, embarrassed. 'Well.' He scratched the back of his neck and looked down at the snow. 'I know the visitors like seeing the reindeer and they're good for business. Besides, you really should be thanking Leo. He did all the work.'

'I caught up with him at the lodge.' Holliday touched Damon's arm. 'He told me you were in the snow alongside him, stretching all the reindeer limbs back into shape. He also told me you were very insistent they were mended this evening...' He glanced up: she looked stunned. '... in the dark, when it was snowing – in minus degrees.' She quivered.

Damon studied the ground again, feeling something building in his chest. It had been a long time since he'd felt anything resembling emotions there – he didn't know what to do. He only knew they unsettled him, made him feel as if he was losing control. 'You were upset.' His mouth twisted and he schooled his face until it was blank. 'I know why they matter.' He glanced back at the reindeer, feeling a twist of jealousy, and fought hard to tamp it down. 'They remind you of your fiancé.'

Holliday considered Damon before turning so she could look at the reindeer too. 'When they were destroyed tonight it brought back a lot of feelings for me.' She rubbed a palm where her heart would be. 'Painful feelings.' She winced.

Damon wanted to tell her to stop. He didn't want to make her sad and he really didn't want to hear how much she was missing Adrian. 'You don't need to explain,' he said, taking a step away. He stopped when she turned and lifted her face until their eyes met. Hers were dark and filled with emotion.

'The thing is, I spent a long time sitting in my room, feeling upset. But then I realised something I've not considered.' Holliday's gaze was intense.

'Which is?' Damon asked.

The skin around her eyes wrinkled. 'I've spent two years pretending Adrian was still alive.' She pressed a palm over her mouth and then let it fall away. 'The way I dealt with my grief was to bottle it up, to pretend nothing had happened to him. But that wasn't true.' Her voice wobbled and Damon saw Holliday clench her hands inside her gloves. He trembled with the need to take hold of them, to soothe. 'When the reindeer were destroyed, I think I was so upset at first because I was finally forced to face it. I couldn't pretend anymore and I wanted to.'

'Really, you don't need to explain,' Damon said again, almost desperate now. He could feel something inside of him cracking wide open and wanted to stop it, to find some way of sealing it shut. Wanted to go back to the way things were – to when Holliday was angry at him, and her eyes shot fireballs of pure hatred every time she looked his way, when he wasn't so attracted to her, when he didn't give a damn about what she felt...

'I want to,' she said simply, stepping closer, her face earnest and so open it scared him. 'I've been bottling this up for too long. I realised that when I was crying in my bedroom. Then Bonnibell came to see me and we talked it through.' She glanced back at the damaged reindeer. 'This has all been a mirage, hasn't it? A way for me not to feel.'

She gulped. 'But I've just been keeping all those emotions locked inside. Instead of processing them, I've let them fester. I love Christmas Resort but I've not been living my life in the way I should. Not really. I've been doing an amazing job of staying frozen in time. I adored Adrian and in some ways I always will, but he's gone and I have to accept that and move on.' She sighed. 'Does that make any sense at all?' Holliday looked at Damon with such desperation he knew he had to tell the truth.

'Yes,' he said hoarsely. He might even recognise a few things from his experiences. Not that it was the same.

'But I want to thank you anyway.' She looked back at the reindeer just as one of them creaked and tumbled onto its side.

'Leo said he'll be able to fix them properly once he gets them to a workshop,' Damon promised, worried Holliday was going to start sobbing again.

'It's okay,' she said thoughtfully. 'I mean, I hope he can mend them, but...' She shook her head. 'Even if they never look the same, even if... someone' – her mouth twisted – 'decides to put something else in their place, I'm still going to have my memories.' She patted a gloved hand on her forehead. 'I... I really hope they don't, but no one can take them from us, can they? I've realised I should take comfort from that.'

'Can't they?' Damon asked. Eradicating the places and things where he'd formed memories had worked for him – or had it?

Before he could figure it out, Holliday stepped closer. She put a gloved palm under his jaw and stood on her tiptoes so she could press a soft kiss against his cheek. 'I want to say thank you,' she whispered, moving so her mouth was beside Damon's ear.

He felt the shock of her closeness reverberate through him. Felt something shift inside him again. Damon stood immobile as Holliday moved until he was staring into her face, then suddenly he was reaching for her, pulling her into his chest so he could rest his head against the top of her head because if he didn't hide her face, he knew he'd kiss her. Then Holliday wrapped her arms around him too, and squeezed.

'Are you okay?' she asked softly, looking up again until her blue eyes bored into his.

Damon thought about gently moving her away, considered stepping back and apologising so he could return to his room. But he was rooted to the spot, unable to form a sentence, let alone a coherent thought. He wasn't strong enough to do it. He swallowed as the blood thundered inside his head, filling his ears, drowning out every one of his warnings. Including the voice screaming that he was an idiot for even considering kissing her. She wasn't ready for that and neither was he – and he wouldn't be until Christmas Lodge, the maze, all the cabins and the whole damn resort was gone.

Then Holliday went up onto her tiptoes again and this time she slid her lips against his. They were soft and Damon could almost taste her through the barely there brush. 'I want to kiss you, is that weird?' she asked softly, lowering her heels to the ground, putting some distance between them. 'I think it is.' She looked confused.

Damon swallowed. 'I don't understand,' he murmured, glancing back at the reindeer.

'Neither do I,' Holliday said as she noticed where his gaze had landed. 'You have the oddest effect on me. Then again, this has been a very strange night. It's like I've just woken after a long sleep.' The breath whooshed from Holliday's throat, then she lifted her face to Damon's and their eyes met. She went up onto her tiptoes again and this time the kiss that flickered across his lips was loaded with intent.

Damon guessed reacting to it was a mistake; knew with every inch of his being that he should pull away, chalk this up to too much emotion and the remnants of grief. But then Holliday curled her arms around his neck and pressed her body closer and he couldn't seem to help himself.

They were both wearing snowsuits so Damon couldn't feel the warmth of Holliday's skin but he could imagine it. Imagine how it might feel to have her pressing against him for real. It had been a long time since he'd been with anyone he cared for, so the wave of lust that sped through his body was a shock. He swallowed and wound his arms around Holliday's waist, leaned down so he could deepen the kiss.

He hadn't been looking for this and it went against all his rules. The ones that told him not to get involved, not to mix business with pleasure, especially not when it involved a woman who worked for the business he was planning to destroy. It wasn't just complicated: it was wrong. But the slow slide of Holliday's tongue against his had Damon groaning with surprise and he couldn't seem to curb his reactions. Couldn't control the fierce rush of heat.

Holliday must have felt the same because suddenly she surged forwards, almost knocking Damon off his feet. Her arms unwound from his neck and she grabbed his hair and pulled until it throbbed, tugged him closer as the kiss heated and intensified.

Damon was glad they were outside and in the open because he wasn't sure what would have happened if they were in the lodge. He suspected if he looked down, the seven inches of packed snow beneath them would have evaporated, proving the chemistry that had been building between them had finally reached boiling point. Had it ever been like this with Willow? He couldn't recall and he couldn't fathom why he was thinking about his ex in the same moment he was pulling Holliday closer, as if trying to climb inside her skin.

He only knew he was more confused than ever. Which was why when Holliday pulled away and put some distance between them Damon was torn between celebrating and wanting to protest.

'Well that was more than I expected,' Holliday said hoarsely, tracing a glove across her mouth which was now puffy and pink. 'I'm sorry, I didn't mean to throw myself at you.' She looked dazed. Before Damon could respond she shook her head and took a step away. 'I need to think about this.'

He had to hold his arms to his sides to stop himself from reaching for her. Instead he watched her shake her head and turn before power walking along the snow-spattered path in the direction of Christmas Lodge. He wondered what had just happened and if he'd ever be the same again.

19

DAMON

Damon paced his bedroom and stopped so he could stare into the crackling fire. Then he paced again, ignoring the clock on the mantlepiece as it chimed midnight. He couldn't sleep. Not after the kiss. Hadn't been able to settle at all since getting back to the lodge. He wandered to his bed and stared down at the plans for the new hotel which he'd spread across the festive duvet.

He'd spent the last few hours trying to reaffirm his commitment to the project – looking at where he intended to build the restaurant and bedrooms, rethinking the golf course before deciding he definitely needed one. But something had changed. No matter how hard he tried he couldn't visualise the new decor, buildings or pool; couldn't conjure the guests. In fact, all he could see when he closed his eyes were misshapen reindeer, mince pies, snowmobiles and cats...

He pulled what Scarlett liked to call his 'lemon face' as he shook his head and circled the room, stopping momentarily beside the oak dresser where he'd dumped Holliday's pompoms, glue and the note he'd rescued from the bathroom floor.

He grabbed the letter and unfolded it, wondering what it meant.

He picked up his mobile and reluctantly dialled, knowing he needed to talk to someone. And since the last few years had mainly been devoted to work and his desire to eradicate Willow from his world, there really was only one person he could wake.

'Well, well, I thought you'd forgotten this number or wiped it from your phone,' Scarlett murmured. 'You're lucky I'm up. The twins are asleep and I'm alone for the evening. It's the only reason I'm still awake. Full control of the TV remote,' she said, appreciatively. 'One day, little brother, you'll understand.' She sighed as the programme that had been blaring in the background suddenly muted. 'What's up? Did you see a post box Willow used once that you're looking to bulldoze?'

'Funny,' Damon said dryly.

'Spill,' she demanded. 'I'm missing my programme and I have a short attention span.'

'I'm confused,' he admitted, putting down Holliday's letter and pacing again. He couldn't sit, but his legs were tired. He knew he should sleep, but the minute he lay down and closed his eyes his head would probably fill with Holliday again.

'Well, hurrah,' Scarlett cheered. 'Because that means you're finally allowing something other than Willow and revenge to penetrate that clever brain. Are you rethinking your life choices?' she asked sweetly.

'I'm wondering why someone hasn't told me something,' he admitted, glancing at the letter again. 'Although, honestly, I don't know why it matters.'

'Ohhh, a new dilemma, just what you need.' She hesitated. 'Perhaps it's because you like this person. Can I ask who it is?' Scarlett sounded perkier now. 'Make it good. As I mentioned before, I'm missing my programme – it's very romantic, and the main characters are about to snog.'

Damon thought about the kiss he'd shared with Holliday

and decided not to tell his sister about that. 'I don't know. There's this... person. She's keeping secrets, and I'm not sure why.'

His sister sighed. 'Well that's not a lot to go on. Firstly, are you sure she's keeping something secret, could it be she hasn't told you because: A. It's none of your business. B. She's embarrassed. C. Are you sure this isn't Willow transference? D. Refer back to C?' She paused. 'I'm guessing you're going to have to think about that, so let me pose a new question while you are. Have you decided what to do with Christmas Resort, and if you have or haven't – have you told your mystery woman about that?'

'I choose A,' he muttered. 'And no, I don't know what I'm going to do.' He sighed as he slumped onto the edge of the bed, crinkling the hotel plans. 'Being here is making me see things in a' – he winced – 'entirely different light.'

'Then hurrah for Christmas Resort. I'm going to read between the lines and guess you're having a change of heart. I'm definitely booking us all in for a week in the new year,' Scarlett declared, sounding entirely too satisfied. 'I knew you'd come to your senses.'

'Hang on,' Damon grumbled, 'I never said that.' He looked down at the crumpled plans and frowned. 'I'm just thinking, that's all...'

'Okay,' Scarlett muttered, 'well give me a call again when you're all thought out. In the meantime, I've got a kiss to watch.' With that his sister hung up.

Damon had just finished folding up the hotel plans when he heard a gentle knock on his bedroom door. He considered not answering, but since there was a light on in his room, he guessed whoever was calling would know he was awake. His heart leapt into his throat when he found Holliday standing in the hallway.

'Um.' She flushed. 'Can I come in?'

He nodded and stepped back, making sure he gave her plenty of space. 'Sure, I was just...' He frowned and rolled his shoulders. 'I couldn't sleep.'

'That's going around.' She nodded. 'I finished your hat. I meant to give it to you before, but...' She looked embarrassed as she whipped a red woolly beanie from behind her back. It matched the gloves and scarf she'd given him already and was covered in pom-poms too. 'This felt like the right moment.'

'Because I'm really going to need it tonight?' Damon joked, taking it from her and pulling it on. 'How does it look?' he asked, feeling his lips curve when she started to laugh.

'Very you,' she giggled, making his heart thump hard. 'Look, we both know the hat was just an excuse.' Holliday's eyes dropped to the floor. Then she wrapped her arms around herself and wriggled from side to side. 'I've been thinking, which is why I can't sleep either. That happens occasionally – when it does I bake biscuits which means I've now got a glut of them in the kitchen.' Her eyes rose to meet his. 'It's an emergency, really, because I can't possibly decorate them all by myself.'

'Ah.' Damon grinned. He liked that Holliday was seeking him out, that she obviously wanted to spend time with him and wasn't regretting what had happened earlier. 'Sounds like a total disaster, do you need some help?'

Holliday's eyes twinkled. 'Unless you'd rather go back to doing' – she wafted a hand at his room – 'whatever you were doing.'

'I'm in,' Damon said. He didn't want to continue pacing and he did want to be around Holliday. Perhaps so he could learn more about her, or maybe because he'd enjoyed their kiss and was guessing – since she was here – Holliday had too. Kissing her again would be a mistake, but he wasn't going to think about that. For the first time

in four years he was just going to see what happened
next.

'We need to be quiet.' She slid a finger over her lips as she
stepped into the hallway. 'Innes is staying in the room opposite
mine. She had a fight with Leo. Long story but we don't want to
wake her.' She tiptoed past the room and down the stairs and
Damon followed, fascinated by her as she took a left at the
bottom and made a beeline for the kitchen. The lights were on
and everything twinkled and he took a moment to look around.
He hadn't appreciated how pretty the kitchen looked before, or
how much trouble Bonnibell and the team had gone to in order
to make everything so welcoming. Would his new hotel be able
to offer this kind of warmth?

The counter was tidy, so Holliday had obviously cleared up
most of the cooking equipment, but there were trays and trays
of biscuits. Damon stood on the other side of the breakfast bar
so he could study the reindeer, Christmas tree, snowflake,
present and snowman shapes.

'I love baking,' Holliday said shyly when he didn't
comment. 'But I enjoy decorating even more.' She went to grab
her apron from a hook to the side of the cooker and did it up,
searching in the pockets and pulling out pots of edible glitter,
silver baubles and icing tubes along with a couple of pom-poms
that she immediately shoved back.

'What's the significance of the pom-poms?' Damon asked,
pulling up a chair as Holliday slid some of the decorating equipment towards him. There was a lot he didn't know about Holliday because he'd been so absorbed in what would be
happening with the resort, but now he wanted to know more. 'Is
it something to do with Adrian?'

Holliday undid the top of a tube of green icing without
looking at him. 'I've always loved them so I used to sew them
onto his jumpers, but that's the only connection.' She half
smiled and looked up, her eyes shining. 'This is the first day I

can talk about him and it feels okay, I feel okay. I still think that's weird,' she said huskily.

Her forehead bunched and she reached into her pocket and pulled out a green pom-pom and held it up. 'Actually, my granny used to make them. I lived with her after my parents died,' she said. 'Gran's gone now, but' – she shook her head, half-smiling – 'she was obsessed.' She twisted the pom-pom between her fingertips. 'I used to get them when I did well in school; she'd make them to put in the bottom of my Christmas stocking. When I lost my baby teeth the fairies left pom-poms under my pillow instead of coins. Granny would sew them onto my clothes too, which was a bit embarrassing when I was a teenager.'

She chuckled, her expression brightening, and tucked the pom-pom back into her apron. 'It was a big joke, but I loved them. Granny used to say they were pieces of her. That's why I make them I suppose – they help me to remember her, but also, maybe I like the idea that I'm giving people pieces of me. I know that probably sounds stupid.'

Damon could see colour rising from Holliday's neck to her cheeks and thought about the pom-poms she'd sewn on the pieces she'd knitted for him. He should have thought she was ridiculous and oversentimental, but he liked the story, knew whenever he saw a pom-pom from now on he'd think of her, and it would be a good memory. He'd held onto so few of those. Why was that?

He cleared his throat. 'That's actually...' He had to force the words out of his suddenly dry throat. 'Really nice.' He winced because he knew it was inadequate but he couldn't seem to put how he felt into words.

She looked up. 'Do you think making my pom-poms is the same as when I tried to hold onto Adrian by pretending nothing had changed?' She looked worried.

Damon shook his head. 'You're celebrating your gran – like

the Bennetts have been doing with Mabel. It's a lovely way to remember her and it's very different. I suppose in a way we're all just pieces of our memories, aren't we?' He mulled the words on his tongue, wondering why he'd never considered that before.

Holliday jerked her chin. 'What about you? What do you do with your memories?' Her eyes grew rounder and Damon felt like a kilo of pennies had just been dropped into the pit of his stomach.

What did he do with his memories? *Ignore them, demolish them, change them so he could pretend they'd never happened at all.* He felt a bit sick. 'Um, I...'

Holliday's brows lowered as she read his expression. 'I'm sorry. This is far too serious a conversation to have so early in the morning,' she said lightly, pointing to the clock. 'And these biscuits aren't going to decorate themselves.' She picked up the tube of green icing and squeezed a large blob onto one of the Christmas trees, then got a brush from her apron so she could spread it around.

Relieved he didn't have to respond, Damon grabbed a tube of white icing and squeezed some onto one of the snowman's stomachs before layering silver baubles on top.

'Nice,' Holliday said, obviously intent on lightening the mood. She brushed her hair out of her face, leaving a trail of green glitter along her cheek. Then she used another paintbrush to dab black icing onto one of the reindeer, brushing colour on the antlers and adding a set of eyes, inadvertently transferring some to her nose at the same time.

Damon selected some red icing and spent a few quiet moments squidging and brushing until he'd finished three of the snowflakes. Decorating was oddly meditative and when he looked up he realised they'd been silent for almost half an hour.

'Granny got me into craft,' Holliday said, suddenly looking

up. 'Just in case you were wondering why a grown woman would spend her days doing things like this.'

'I'm not wondering that,' he said honestly, dabbing glitter onto a Santa biscuit. 'I was just thinking what a wonderful job this is...' He took in the kitchen again. 'The resort is an amazing place,' he said slowly. 'I know you all told me it was special, but I'm just realising how unique it is.'

Holliday gave him a slow smile, which hit Damon somewhere mid-chest and he momentarily forgot to breathe. 'I've been hoping to hear you say that since you got here. I'd almost given up until today,' she said, her eyes glittering. 'I'd like to think it was me who persuaded you, but I think I might owe it to the biscuits and Bonnibell's mince pies.'

'It was you,' Damon shot back, his voice gruff, and he stared until she met his eyes.

Holliday was obviously surprised because she didn't respond, and they continued to stare at each other until she took in a shaky breath and brushed stray hair out of her face – this time smearing red icing on the corner of her mouth.

'You're...' He waved a hand.

'What?' Holliday asked, obviously confused.

Damon got up and tracked around the breakfast bar until he was standing in front of her. His heartbeat had quickened on the short walk and he knew it had everything to do with her. Knew he'd not felt this excited – or nervous – in years. It terrified him. 'You've got icing on your face,' he said gruffly, holding up a palm, asking for permission to touch her.

Holliday looked puzzled, but then realisation dawned and she jerked her chin. He swiped his thumb over the soft skin on her cheek, lifting off the green glitter before placing it in his mouth.

She cocked her head and took a step closer. 'How does it taste?' Her voice wobbled a little.

'Like you,' he said, roughly. 'Only not as sweet.'

That must have been the right answer, because she nodded once, then went up onto her tiptoes and circled her arms around his neck. 'How about we try again then?' And she pressed her mouth to his, tracing her tongue along the seam of his mouth, making everything inside Damon go up in flames.

20

HOLLIDAY

Holliday leaned into Damon and gulped as his hands snaked from her face and slid down her body, until he tugged her into his chest. She could feel him through his clothes, that perfect muscular body she'd seen in the shower. All those hard lines she'd dreamed of during the last few sleepless nights. She pushed a hand into his thick hair and skated her fingertips across his scalp as the kiss deepened and he pulled her onto her tiptoes until she was barely touching the ground. Holliday knew this was crazy. Things like this didn't happen.

Less than a day ago she'd been bound up in grief, held back by the lie she'd been telling herself for two years. Then in just a few hours, the illusion had shattered and she'd understood in that instant that things had changed. That somehow over the last few months she'd begun to heal. She just hadn't realised. It had taken the threat to the resort, the arrival of this man, to see it. She knew it was too soon, knew there were still far too many things she didn't know about Damon, but she couldn't seem to stop herself.

Holliday slid her fingers from Damon's hair and clutched his hand, pulled away and twisted so she could skirt around the breakfast bar, leaving the half-decorated biscuits and scatter of equipment behind.

Damon hesitated – perhaps he wasn't sure? And Holliday wondered if he was going to suggest they wait. But when she turned and looked into his face, he must have read the question in her expression because he nodded.

They stopped three times on the stairs to explore one other, and each time the kiss grew hotter and deeper. So by the time they reached the landing, just a few metres from Holliday's bedroom door, her apron was untied, her dress was bunched up around her hips and her heart was racing so fast it would probably win gold in an Olympic sprint. She pushed her hands into Damon's jeans and tugged out his T-shirt, pressed her fingertips to the flat of his stomach and slid them upwards, felt him shudder. His reaction made her smile and she did the same again, stopping only when he caught her hands and nodded to her bedroom door.

'Where's Frosty?' he asked as they reached the threshold.

'He decided to sleep over with Innes,' Holliday admitted, pressing a fingertip to the cleft in his chin so she could guide his mouth downwards. 'No talking, remember, you don't want to wake her.'

He smiled and kissed her again, then opened the door to her bedroom, pushing her backwards before shutting it slowly.

Holliday saw Damon glance at the mantlepiece and was relieved she'd put the photo of Adrian away earlier. She'd said goodbye, had taken time to think about him again before deciding to go to the kitchen to bake. Because she knew a few quiet moments alone would centre her, give her time to think and decide what to do next. Then she'd picked up the hat she'd knitted and knocked on Damon's door. Had she known what would happen when she did? Of course she had. It was just another step she'd been ready to take, another acknowledgement that Adrian was gone and it was finally time to move on.

Damon eased back and pushed the apron off Holliday's head, making another handful of pom-poms scatter across the floor. Then he reached down and lifted the bottom of her dress. She'd changed after coming in from outside, put on one of her jumper dresses because she'd been cold, and also because she'd wanted to look pretty. He pulled her dress over her head and then tugged his T-shirt over his before dropping them both on the floor. Then he guided Holliday backwards. 'Are you sure this is a good idea?' he asked, as they reached the edge of the bed. 'Because I don't want to rush you.'

'I'm not sure about anything right now,' Holliday admitted, grabbing Damon's hand when he tensed. 'I do know I want to do this. Is it enough just to know that?'

She didn't want to tell Damon that she liked him. It hadn't started out that way, but he'd carried her to the house when she'd fallen in the maze, knitted, danced even when it was obvious he hadn't wanted to. He'd helped Leo fix a roof, taken a ride on the snowmobile in the dark and decorated biscuits. None of which seemed in character with the man who'd arrived. But the thing that had made Holliday begin to fall for Damon was that he'd insisted on fixing the broken reindeer. He'd come to build a new hotel here, but was a good enough man to repair something that mattered to her. Something it would have been far easier for him to discard. It gave her an insight into the person he was – the man he might have forgotten existed. He had wounds, that was clear; perhaps in time he'd share them with her. She'd give him the time and space to do it.

'I don't want you to regret it,' he said seriously and she suspected he was about to change his mind.

'I won't,' she whispered, softly. 'I suppose I've manipulated the truth for so long, I'm just looking for something I know is real.' She traced a finger across Damon's cheek, felt the rough ends of his stubble. 'You feel very real,' she said hoarsely.

Damon sucked in a breath then let it out before cupping Holliday's cheek. 'You feel real,' he whispered. 'I've been so wrapped up in the past, I think I've forgotten what that looks like too.' He hesitated and then bent to kiss her.

This time when their lips met Holliday knew she wasn't going to pull away, knew she was doing the right thing. She eased Damon around so she could push him onto the bed and wriggled out of her tights and bra, then tugged off her pants. Then she took her time staring at him. Damon didn't move – perhaps he understood she needed to take things slowly? He just watched until Holliday bent so she could unlatch his belt, then she took her time slowly undressing him too.

The jeans came off first, exposing long, athletic legs, then she pushed her fingertips under the black boxers that clung to his hips and pulled. She took a moment to admire what was underneath before dispensing with his socks. Now they were both naked Holliday paused, because she wanted to make this count. Didn't want to rush it. Needed to acknowledge every moment because it mattered. It was the first time in two years that she'd allowed herself to experience the present, permitted herself to see a life beyond Adrian.

In the end, it was Damon who reached out and took her hand so he could link their fingers. Then he tugged them to his lips and kissed the top. It was a sweet gesture, one that had her insides fizzing and her heart doing a little spin.

'You still sure?' he asked huskily and waited until she nodded. He smiled and tugged her forward so she was standing in between his legs. Then he took one of her nipples into his mouth and Holliday trembled. She made herself stand completely still as he scattered kisses across her skin, making every inch of her tingle. All the while, his hands stroked her hips, before they dipped to the globes of her bottom and he began to explore and learn each curve, driving her crazy as her body flooded with heat. Holliday had to clutch Damon's shoulders because her knees were wobbling so much she was afraid she was going to lose her balance. He must have realised because suddenly he tugged her down until she was straddling him and he was looking into her face.

'You're beautiful,' he said huskily as he began to kiss her again and Holliday wrapped her arms around his neck, pressed her body into his chest. She loved the feel of him, loved how it felt to learn the angles and planes of his body. His chest was broad and muscular and she traced a fingertip between their bodies, stroking his nipples and stomach until he shuddered too. Then suddenly she was on her back and he was looking down at her; those grey eyes so dark they were almost black.

'I wasn't expecting this when I came here,' he said, his voice a little rough.

Holliday leaned up so she could kiss him again. She could taste coffee and mince pies now and she wondered if Christmas Resort was changing Damon from the inside out?

'What were you expecting?' she asked, kissing him again, the meeting of their lips slow, sexy and hot. She nibbled at the edge of his mouth and felt him quake above her.

Then he pulled away and gazed at her face. 'I don't know, not this.' He kissed her again and Holliday let herself get lost, let her body relax as she melted into him – let them become one.

When they joined they moved slowly. It was like neither of them wanted it to end. Perhaps it was because it had been so long, or maybe it was because they were still so new to one another? There was still so much to explore and learn... secrets that had to be revealed and admitted. The end built steadily and when Holliday eventually tipped over the edge, Damon was right with her – and she hoped this was only the beginning.

. . .

Holliday woke and opened one eye. The bed was warm beside her and for a moment she thought Frosty had somehow sneaked into her bedroom overnight. Then she twisted onto one side and saw Damon. He was sleeping – those long dark lashes tickling his cheekbones. The dusting of stubble across his angular chin had grown longer and coarser and Holliday had to fight the desire to reach out and stroke a fingertip across it like she had last night because she didn't want to wake him.

He was even more attractive in sleep. There was no guarded expression now; it was like he'd finally allowed himself to relax. If she asked, would Damon tell her anything she wanted to know? Holliday's stomach clenched. He still hadn't mentioned his plans for the resort. Was that because he'd changed his mind and decided to keep everything as it was? After he'd fixed the reindeer and the things he had said in the kitchen, Holliday hoped he might be having second thoughts – but it was strange that he still hadn't told her anything about his life, aside from that he lived in London and had a sister called Scarlett. There was obviously a lot he hadn't shared.

Damon eased open an eye and studied her through his long lashes, gave her one of the sexy, slow smiles Holliday had seen for the first time last night. 'Good morning,' he yawned, stretching and turning onto his back, the sheet sliding down to his waist, revealing the lightly tanned six pack and toned stomach she'd been stroking her fingertips over just a few hours ago. 'How did you sleep?' He propped himself onto an elbow and glanced around the bedroom.

'Better than I expected,' Holliday said, as her eyes skimmed lower and a part of her wished she could ease the sheet further down. 'I had a nightmare about undecorated biscuits though,' she joked.

'Ah,' Damon chuckled, before his eyebrow twitched. 'We didn't clear them away. Could Frosty have got to them?'

'Innes messaged at about three o'clock to say she'd gone to

get some hot milk from the kitchen and tidied everything up,' Holliday said. She didn't add that her friend had guessed exactly what had happened and had sent her three high-five emojis along with a couple of hearts.

Damon nodded and Holliday inched closer. He tangled his feet together with hers and she inhaled slowly, smelled linen and mince pies. 'Where do you live in London?' she asked, hoping the intimacy of the moment, what had happened between them, might encourage Damon to open up.

'I've got a flat close to the centre of Notting Hill.' He traced a fingertip down her cheek, avoiding her eyes. 'What about you?'

'I live here,' she said, and saw a tiny flicker of something flitter across his eyes. 'And... I have a house in Cambridge, but I haven't been there for two years.'

Damon stared at her for a beat before nodding. It was almost imperceptible but he seemed to relax a little. 'I have a confession to make,' he said, and Holliday's stomach thumped. 'I found a letter on the floor amongst your tubes of glue and pom-poms, after we...' His cheeks flushed endearingly and she eased closer still. 'Bumped into each other in the bathroom the other day. I'm sorry. I should have returned everything.'

'Ahhhhh,' Holliday said, hiding her disappointment. 'I wondered where that had gone. Do you still have it somewhere?'

He nodded. 'It's still in my room with everything else, I'll find it for you later.' Damon gazed at Holliday as if he were waiting for more.

'The house was Adrian's,' she explained. She didn't need to hide it, she'd stopped lying to herself. 'He left it to me, but when he died I couldn't bear being there. Too many memories.' She winced. 'I came to live at Christmas Resort and left the house empty.' She swallowed. 'It was easier for me to pretend Adrian was still living there. It meant I didn't have to face up to what had happened.'

He stroked the edge of her face again, his eyes inky black. 'And now?' Damon asked.

Holliday shrugged. 'I don't know. Things are... a little different after last night. But I need time to think about it.' She wasn't sure she knew what was in her future anymore, although she was happy here. 'What about you?' she asked when he remained silent. 'Are you still going to buy the resort?' She waited for him to respond, saw something flash across his face she couldn't read and wondered what it meant.

'Yes,' Damon said eventually and Holliday had to bite her lip to stop from asking what his plans for it were.

'So you love it now?' She swallowed, trying not to look anxious.

'Let's say it's grown on me,' he said, giving Holliday another of those slow smiles. 'I wasn't expecting that. I wasn't expecting you...'

Holliday nodded as all the tension she'd been holding in her body seemed to dissolve and disappear. 'Are you planning to stay longer?' she asked, hoping he'd say yes.

'I can't go anywhere at the moment because of my car, but...' Damon stared at her for a beat. 'Once I get it back I think I might hang around for a few more days. I'm going to take some time to look around properly. Perhaps I'll talk to Bonnibell about her ideas for expansion. Leo said he'd talk me through what needs repairing and replacing too.' His eyes twinkled. 'Besides, don't we need to finish decorating those biscuits?'

Holliday barked out a laugh and nodded. Damon may not have told her everything – but now she knew the resort was safe and he planned to stick around for a while, perhaps he'd tell her about himself. At least she'd have time to get to know him and see where this thing between them might lead.

21

HOLLIDAY

'I need to talk to you,' Innes whispered to Holliday gravely later that morning as the housekeeper walked into the kitchen clutching something close to her chest.

Bonnibell, who was kneeling beside the Aga after placing a tray of biscuits inside to bake, rose to her feet and opened the emergency biscuit tin. 'That doesn't sound good, hen. Why don't we all have one of these before you explain?' She grabbed a chocolate biscuit for herself and offered Holliday and Innes the tin. Then the older woman bit into a snowflake which Holliday remembered Damon decorating the night before. 'Okay, you can tell us now,' Bonnibell sighed, pulling up a chair as she finished the biscuit.

Innes carefully placed one of the resort's photo albums onto the breakfast bar. 'You need to see this,' she said gravely, her forehead creasing in concern. 'I found the picture last night when I was looking through some of the albums trying to take my mind off what's been happening with Leo. I don't know what it means though.' She opened the book in the centre and slid it across the table so Bonnibell and Holliday could see.

Holliday leaned down so she could get a closer look and her stomach went into freefall. 'It's Damon.' Tears bubbled into the corners of her eyes and she eased in a slow mouthful of air. If she hadn't seen the photo for herself, she wouldn't have believed it was him. His hair was longer but there was that angular jaw with the tiny cleft in the centre, those intense grey eyes.

'Who's the woman?' Bonnibell cleared her throat.

'I don't know,' Holliday said vaguely. Whoever she was, she was beautiful, with long dark hair, huge brown eyes and a predatory expression that signalled 'hands off, he's mine' to whoever was admiring the picture. She wore a black sequinned dress with a split up the front and was wrapped around Damon like a limpet. Holliday fought the jealousy as it battered her from all sides. Who was the woman and what did the photo mean? Why hadn't Damon told them that he'd been to the resort before? Did it have something to do with the plans for the hotel?

'I looked on the back,' Innes admitted, slowly drawing the picture from the plastic sleeve and turning it over. 'It says Mr and Mrs MacAndrew and it was taken four years ago.'

'Ah.' Bonnibell sounded distressed. She grabbed another biscuit from the tin and popped it in her mouth, barely chewing. 'Okay.' She swallowed, nodding. 'I remember now. That's Damon's wife – or at least it was.' She frowned at the picture and squinted and Holliday guessed she was trying to remember more.

'Wife,' Holliday repeated hoarsely, trying not to jump to conclusions even as her body seemed to freeze. He couldn't still be married, he'd told her he was alone. Or had something happened to her? Her mind swirled with a million scenarios but none of them put Damon in a good light.

'I believe they stayed in one of the cabins.' Bonnibell winced. 'It might even have been Reindeer Retreat. I remember now it had just been redecorated because on the day they moved in we realised some of the paint in the bathroom wasn't properly dry. It was at least four years ago. I *knew* I'd met him.' She pursed her lips. 'I don't remember a lot about their visit except...' Her brow knitted. 'His wife was very shy with the other guests and they mostly kept themselves to themselves. You weren't here then, Holliday, so we didn't run as many craft classes and we didn't offer dancing or singing either. They never ate in the dining room which I thought was odd. Then again, I did wonder if it was because his wife was a little insecure.'

'Why didn't Damon tell us he'd been here before? Why keep it a secret?' Holliday asked, pulling the album closer so she could look again. Damon looked sad and thinner around the jaw. Had he been unhappy? What had happened with his wife? The fact that he'd been married and had chosen not to tell her made her feel ill.

Bonnibell let out a sigh. 'There could be all sorts of reasons, hen. Maybe being at the resort brings back bad memories. Sometimes it's easier to ignore or forget the things that bother or hurt us.' She looked sympathetic.

Holliday slumped onto a breakfast stool and nodded. She'd been guilty of doing exactly that, hadn't she? Pretending Adrian was still alive and living in Cambridge. Getting Mr Hornbuckle to put up the Christmas decorations and to keep an eye on the house as if nothing had changed. She hadn't talked about her fiancé either, not since he'd died. She scratched the back of her neck, trying to process the new information.

'I suppose I do understand.' Hope shot through her, layering over the hurt. Because she did get it. She just wished Damon had told her everything. Then again, perhaps he would – they were only just starting to get to know each other, after all. There was still time.

'Do you think that's the reason he wanted to build a hotel here?' Innes asked, frowning.

'Perhaps,' Bonnibell said. 'It also might explain why he didn't look very happy when he arrived, why all the decorations might have upset him. Perhaps they brought back memories he'd rather forget...' She lowered her voice. 'I wish I'd remembered him. I'd never have put the boy back in Reindeer Retreat. If he has bad memories from his marriage, it would have been awful for him.'

'I suppose, it depends on how he feels now?' Innes said, her eyes darting to Holliday.

'He told me the resort is starting to grow on him,' Holliday told them, hanging onto a thread of hope.

'But the real question is, does that mean he's going to leave things exactly as they are?' Innes' pretty face darkened in confusion.

'Who knows, hen.' Bonnibell's eyes swivelled to Holliday too.

She shrugged. 'I wish I knew.' Despite everything that had happened last night, she still had no idea what Damon was thinking. She hoped, but that wasn't the same as knowing.

The front door opened and closed and a scatter of footsteps pre-empted Claus bounding into the kitchen. Connell followed closely behind and Leo brought up the rear. 'We've got the cabin ready for our new honeymooners arriving today,' Connell boomed. 'The heating wasn't working properly again, but Leo managed to sort it.'

'Well done, lad.' Bonnibell grinned.

The younger man didn't reply because his attention was now fixed on Innes. 'I missed you last night,' he said roughly, walking slowly across the kitchen to greet her. He opened his arms but she sidestepped them and Leo's face fell.

'I decided to give Damon his car back,' Connell told them before Leo could say anything more to his wife. He stopped and grabbed a biscuit from the tin as Bonnibell put the kettle on the Aga. 'We've done everything we can. Given him plenty of time to get to know us and learn about the resort.' He patted his stomach thoughtfully. 'I think it's time for us to let him decide what he wants to do next.'

'I think you're right,' Holliday said, swallowing. 'We can't force Damon to love it here or to keep it as it is.' She blinked. 'I think he will, I think he's begun to fall in love with Christmas Resort.' She shrugged. 'But ultimately, what he decides to do is up to him.' Same as if he decided to confide in her about his past.

'Don't worry, lass.' Bonnibell squeezed Holliday's shoulder. 'Have faith. After what Damon did for those wee reindeer ornaments, I think the resort's magic has started to rub off.'

'Aye, well he's been in touch to book a meeting with me, Leo and Ross,' Connell confided, grabbing another biscuit and swallowing it in one, ignoring Bonnibell's loud tuts when he immediately picked up two more.

'He has?' Holliday asked hopefully.

'Aye, first thing this morning.' Connell eyed Leo as if he were taking in his dejected expression for the first time. 'You two need to sort this out,' he said gently, nodding at the younger couple.

Leo turned and gave his wife an imploring look.

'I'm not moving back.' Innes's eyes flashed and she folded her arms. 'I've lived with your mam for five months now and she's made me feel unwelcome for every single second of it.' Her bottom lip wobbled.

Leo held up a palm and stepped closer. 'She's my mam,' he said as if that explained everything.

For the first time Holliday had an inkling of what Innes had been dealing with. Felt sympathy for her.

'And I'm your *wife*,' Innes said, her bourbon-coloured eyes filling. 'I've never tried to come between you, but in the entire time I've been living in your mam's house, you've never once stood up for me, or taken my side.'

She narrowed her eyes as Leo opened his mouth to protest. 'No!' Innes said, shaking her head. 'You haven't. I don't care if we don't have enough money to move out. I understand it's not easy. I'm not spoiled, Leo, I'm a grown woman. I know how hard you work because I do the same. I know we might not have the resources to have our own place for a long time. I've accepted that.' Her lips narrowed. 'But what I won't accept, what I refuse to put up with anymore, is being put down and made to feel small by a woman who has no reason to dislike me. All I've ever wanted is for her to accept me, but I don't think that's ever going to happen.'

She blinked and Holliday saw her eyes sparkle, guessed soon those tears would spill over her cheeks. 'I know I should have said all this before.' She swallowed as the rest of them stared, too afraid to interrupt because it was obvious this was important.

'I'm so sorry,' Leo said huskily, taking a step towards Innes, frowning when she took another step away.

'I'm sorry too. Because I'm not moving into that house again until something changes,' Innes said firmly. 'And if it doesn't, I'll be staying at Christmas Resort until we can finally move out and get our own place. If we're almost retired before that happens, then...' She shrugged and her mouth twisted.

'Innes...' Leo gulped. 'You know I can't leave Mam, she'd never forgive me if I moved into the resort. Please, I want you to come home.'

'It's not *my* home, Leo,' Innes said sadly. 'And it won't be until I feel welcome there.' Then she nodded to Connell, Holliday and Bonnibell, and bolted from the kitchen.

Holliday finished setting up the large, bright room at the back of Christmas Lodge where she ran her craft workshops. It had bright lights for close-up work, white-wipe clean counters,

plenty of shelving and drawers filled with various art equipment. It was perfect if classes got messy or the guests needed
room to spread out. Today she'd planned to run a pom-pom-
making class. The Bennetts had already signed up and the
Bavestocks had promised to attend too, so she put out plenty of
wool, card and scissors.

'Hi,' Damon said, wandering in through the door, making
Holliday's stomach turn over. She hadn't seen him since this
morning when they'd been in her bed but now she'd seen the
photo album, realised just how much he hadn't told her, everything felt different.

'Hi yourself – where have you been?' she asked, deliberately
keeping her voice even. 'I heard Connell got your car back from
the garage.' She put her hands in her apron and squeezed a
pom-pom but it didn't really help. 'I was worried you might
decide to leave.' She felt her cheeks warm.

Damon gave her a thoughtful look. 'I wouldn't do that
without talking to you first. I went for a drive. I wanted to make
sure everything worked okay. I told you this morning, I'm not
going anywhere.' He took in Holliday's expression. 'Is everything okay?'

'Sure,' she said calmly, grabbing some scissors and card and
busying herself rearranging them on the counter before he
asked more. She was being insecure because he hadn't told her
about his wife – and the twist in her gut told her his lack of
honesty hurt. There was still so much she didn't know about
Damon. So much she needed him to share. But she wanted the
information to come from him, wanted him to willingly explain,
so she wasn't going to ask.

'Are you here to join in with the class?' She gave him a
tentative smile as he leaned in to kiss her and she smelled linen
again, felt the warmth from his touch flow down her body all
the way to her toes. She was falling for Damon, despite his
secrets, and knew she couldn't stop the feelings from growing.

'Of course.' He gave her a slow smile and his eyes sparkled. 'No way was I going to miss out on learning how to make one of your granny's pom-poms.'

There was a flurry of noise outside the door and it opened, then a crowd of people walked into the room. The Bennetts and Bavestocks were chatting and laughing together as they assembled around the table.

'Sorry, are we late?' Kate asked. 'I had to do my hair.' She patted her bouncy curls.

'We're just grateful you made it before it was time for bed,' Barney muttered as he joined everyone at the table.

'You're not late at all, and your hair looks beautiful so it was worth the wait. You're just in time,' Holliday said, smiling at the family, who were all wearing their Christmas jumpers. Even Arthur, although he'd folded his arms as though he were trying to hide it again. They all leaned over the craft table, eagerly studying the wool and equipment.

'I've never made a pom-pom before,' Alison said, her eyes widening. 'Is it difficult?'

'It's very easy,' Holliday said, picking up some card that she'd already cut into circles. 'We'll start by making ourselves pom-pom templates just like these.' She waggled the card. 'It's up to you to choose how large you want them to be but please be mindful the bigger they are the larger your pom-pom will be. You don't want to make something that won't fit in your car when you leave.' The group chuckled. 'After you've made the template I'll take you through the rest of the process step by step. Once we have our pom-poms we can turn them into whatever we like.'

'Can I make a snowman?' Lucie asked, exuberantly.

'Of course!' Holliday said. 'Snowmen, reindeer, snowflakes – even bunting. There are lots of craft pieces here you can use to decorate them with.'

'Can I join in too?' Everyone looked up as Leo's mother, Mairi, slowly wandered into the room and gave the rest of the guests wary looks. 'I know how to make a pom-pom already, any bampot can do that,' she added airily. 'But I came to see Bonnibell and she told me she couldn't talk for twenty minutes because she's too busy.' She rolled her eyes. 'She suggested I come and take part in your lesson while I'm waiting.' Her mouth pinched as her eyes hopped across the mass of wool and then she frowned. 'A messy worktop is a sign of a messy mind, you really should tidy as you work,' she grumbled, putting her handbag on the floor and taking a seat around the table.

Holliday wondered if this was the kind of reproof the older woman had been levelling at Innes. She could understand why her friend had decided to move out.

'I like mess, especially in my bedroom, but Arthur's even worse,' Lucie blurted, ignoring her big brother when he pulled a face. Mairi pursed her lips as Lucie grabbed a ball of wool. 'I want to make a green pom-pom,' she told Holliday. 'It's my favourite colour. Is that okay?'

'You can use whichever colour you like – why don't you all choose the wool you'd like to use?' Holliday suggested, watching as Damon picked out a pretty shade of blue. She kept expecting him to say something critical, or frown his disapproval. But instead he looked interested and engaged. She knew he'd moved on over the last few days, but her trust in him was wavering since she'd seen the photo album.

'I'm going for white.' Mairi plucked up a ball of wool just as Kate reached for it too.

'Oh.' The younger woman's face fell as she scanned the rest of the collection. 'It was Mam's favourite colour.' Her forehead crumpled. 'But that's okay.'

'It's fine, I've got plenty more wool.' Holliday searched under the counter and found another white ball.

'That's a proper Christmas colour and it's lucky,' Mairi said smugly, starting to unwind hers. 'At least for me. My Leo had this exact colour hair when he was born and there was so much of it,' she sighed. 'I'll be making a snowman for our Christmas tree.'

'I'm going to make a polar bear.' Kate grinned, unwinding some of the wool from the ball. 'It was Mum's favourite animal. She used to sponsor one every year.'

'She did love a polar bear.' Barney grinned, looking at the purple wool he'd selected. 'Perhaps I'll make one too. The colour doesn't really matter.'

Lucie shook her head. 'Not when it's Christmas,' she agreed.

'True,' Holliday said as the rest of them grabbed various balls of wool and then waited quietly. 'Now we need to make our templates. I've put some card and some round objects on the table already, which you can use to cut around, and there are compasses in case you want a different size.' She pointed to a stack of plates, mugs, place mats and glasses. 'First decide how big you want your pom-pom to be. You'll need two circles in your template, one will form the outside of your pom-pom and the other will be cut out to be the centre – make sure that circle is large enough to fit enough wool inside if you want your pom-pom fluffy. If you want to make more than one, I'd advise you to cut all your templates in advance.'

She demonstrated, creating a couple, and then waited while the group used pencils and scissors to make theirs. The room fell silent as they worked, although Arthur and Lucie kept nudging each other and giggling, drawing more stern looks from Mairi. Did the woman disapprove of everything?

Damon eased closer so he could whisper in Holliday's ear. 'I thought I might go for a drive later. I've not seen much of the area and I'd really like to explore.' He held her eyes. 'Will you come with me?'

The request surprised Holliday and she took a moment to

respond. 'Um... yes,' she said, trying not to get excited. When she looked up Mairi was staring at them.

'Are you still teaching this lesson?' the older woman asked, holding up her templates. 'You remind me of Innes,' she muttered. 'The girl's always got her head in the clouds, I never know what she's thinking. If it wasn't for Leo I've no idea where she'd be.' She glanced around the assembled group as if expecting one of them to agree, but everyone avoided her eyes. Even Barney studied his ball of purple wool and didn't nod which surprised Holliday because usually he was the first to criticise.

Holliday turned back to the group. 'Now your templates are ready, just take the end of your wool and wind it around the circle, like this. Make sure you leave a longish end.' She demonstrated using the brown wool she'd chosen earlier. 'I know it sounds simple, but take your time. Every one of the threads is important, and you want to get it right.'

'Gran used to say you can't rush perfection,' Arthur said, smiling a little. Then he flushed when his eye caught on Mairi, who sniffed.

'Aye.' Barney nodded, sighing. 'I'd forgotten that, lad. She was right too.' He began to wind his wool again, deliberately taking his time.

'That's really good,' Holliday commented, watching him. 'You want to keep the wool tight and tidy just like that.'

Mairi snorted as she wound her white wool quickly around her circle. 'At the rate you're working you won't finish one pompom before this lesson ends.' She glanced at her watch. 'I'm meeting Bonnibell in fifteen minutes, do you think we can speed things up?'

She continued to wind the wool at speed, making a mess of the template. Holliday opened her mouth to comment but one look from the older woman and she shut it again. She was surprised: Mairi was a competent knitter, she clearly understood accuracy – was the fact that she was going too quickly a sign that something wasn't right?

'When you've got your ball to the right thickness,' Holliday continued when the room fell silent again, 'let me know because I'll show you how to finish it off.' She glanced at Damon who was clearly concentrating intently as he carefully wound the blue wool. He seemed like a different man to the one she'd first met. Less distracted, more relaxed. Would he stay if he decided to keep the resort as it was? And if he did would he finally tell her about his wife and the plans for the hotel?

'I know what I'm doing,' Mairi said, winding the last piece before twisting the end of the wool around the centre to secure it, then tying it off. 'I don't need any help and...' She checked her watch again. 'I really need to be going soon. I have to speak to Bonnibell about that... girl staying here.' Her lips thinned. 'It's not right for a wife to live away from her husband. Leo's very upset.'

Barney frowned at the older woman, his face pinching. 'Perhaps your daughter-in-law will return if you ask her?' he suggested thoughtfully.

Holliday was surprised by the older man's insight. Perhaps there was more of his wife in him than she'd thought?

'I'm not going to do that!' Mairi snapped, snipping the ends of the wool, now way ahead of the class. The wool sprang open and she pulled the template off, tutting.

'Even if your son is unhappy?' Barney asked quietly.

Mairi's brows knitted, as if the thought had never occurred to her. 'He's fine,' she said, frowning again, picking at the pom-pom with a worried expression. 'He's perfectly okay. It's just Innes, she's stubborn and...' She huffed and shook her head. 'This equipment's no good,' she snapped, plucking at the stray pieces and rearranging them again. 'This pom-pom isn't as good as the ones I make at home.'

'I think you might have made it too quickly,' Lucie said

bravely, staring at her creation, which was only half finished but looked perfect.

Holliday waited for Mairi to say something unkind. Instead she huffed. Then she placed the pom-pom she'd just made onto the table. 'I can't wait for Bonnibell any longer, I'm going to go and find her now, this has to get sorted. It's not my fault,' she said under her breath, although there was a catch in her voice now. Then she picked up her handbag and headed out the door, leaving the pom-pom behind in her rush.

It was silent for a few moments after the door shut. Then Barney let out a long sigh that ended in a chuckle. 'If I ever get as grumpy as that I hope one of you will mention it to me...' He shook his head.

The family turned to gaze at each other with wide eyes, then Kate put her pom-pom on the table and cleared her throat. 'I don't want to fall out with you dad but—'

'You are *really, really* grumpy,' Lucie said loudly. The little girls face flushed and she glanced at her brother.

'I'm...' Barney stumbled, his face flooding with colour too as he slowly took in each of their expressions.

Arthur straightened his bony shoulders and his skinny chest inflated. 'You mustn't be angry with Lucie – she's telling the truth,' he said, twisting the half-finished pom-pom between his fingers.

Kate nodded. 'We've all been afraid to tell you,' she said carefully. 'Mum used to know exactly the right thing to say.' She sighed and her husband pulled her in for a quick squeeze. 'She'd make you laugh or say you were being silly and you'd listen to her. She always knew how to coax you out of a bad mood.' She winced. 'But you have been grumpy, Dad,' she said. 'I know you're sad – I am too – but sometimes you take it out on the people around you, the ones who love you most...'

'I'm...' Barney looked around, clearly aghast. Holliday thought he might get angry, but his face suddenly sagged. 'I'm sorry,' he croaked. 'I got so used to Mabel being around. I could say anything I wanted, be any way I wanted because I knew she'd know just how to put things right.' He stared down at his pom-pom. 'Now she's not here it's like I've lost the best part of me, the bit everyone loved. The piece who never upset anybody, or who made everything okay.'

He cleared his throat as Kate walked up to put an arm around him. 'I'm always saying the wrong thing. I didn't care at first.' He looked up, his eyes watery. 'But I don't want to hurt or upset people. I want to be more like her.'

'It's okay, Grandad,' Lucie said, wandering up to hug him too, wrapping her arms around his waist and squeezing. 'Every-one's allowed to make mistakes.'

Barney chuckled. 'And I know those wise words came from my Mabel too,' he muttered, pressing a gentle kiss into his granddaughters hair. 'I'm glad we came back here.' He glanced around, his eyes misty. 'I know I didn't want to at first but it was the right thing to do. It's made me remember... so many things. Good times, sad times, but mostly it's made me think about who I want to be now.'

'Looks like Christmas Resort has worked it's magic again,' Damon murmured as he finished off the blue pom-pom he'd been working on and held it up for Holliday to see.

'It does change people,' she said, smiling at him. 'I never thought I'd see you make one of those,' she murmured.

'Neither did I,' Damon choked, glancing around. The Bennetts were all now hugging and the Bavestocks were locked in a passionate embrace. He held up his pom-pom and swung it from side to side. 'Am I supposed to hang this on a tree?' he asked.

'Why don't you take it back to London with you?' Holliday said, thinking perhaps if he did it would remind him of being here. 'Put it in your pocket.' She watched as he shoved it into his jeans. 'Then we can make another one for the tree.'

Holliday watched Damon as he reached out and grabbed another ball of wool and winked. She had no idea what he was thinking, but hoped since he was staying longer, the resort would continue to work its magic until he finally told her everything.

22

DAMON

Damon stared at the blue pom-pom which he'd taken from his jeans pocket and left on the bed. It reminded him of something but he couldn't work out what it was. If someone had said to him just a few weeks ago that he'd be staying in Christmas Resort making festive decorations he'd have told them they were crazy.

He pulled the hotel plans from his wardrobe and unfolded them before laying them on the bed. After the last few days he knew there was no chance he'd be building anything in place of Christmas Resort – Scarlett was right, it was too special to change. It had taken his visit here to see that. He strode to the window and looked out – could just see the three reindeer on the hill which reminded him of Holliday now. When he looked around the room, he thought of Bonnibell and the mince pies she'd baked, of dancing around the Christmas tree. Even Frosty was creeping into his memories now. Willow had almost completely disappeared from his mind and he knew the only place she existed was in one of the photo albums. Even when he tried to remember her he realised he didn't care. Somehow the

power of those bad memories, all the hurt he'd felt, had disappeared. Or perhaps he was just finally ready to deal with it?

Later today he'd tell Holliday about his ex-wife. There was
no reason to keep his marriage a secret anymore. Perhaps he'd
even tell her about his plans for the hotel. Whatever happened,
the resort was safe – he just had to decide how involved he
wanted to be. And whether he was ready to get entangled with
these people permanently and allow himself to be vulnerable
again. He frowned, thinking of Holliday. He cared for her, but
was he honestly ready to step into a new relationship? Then
again, he couldn't imagine walking away for good. Perhaps she'd
consider seeing him when he got back to London, then they
could take things slowly and learn about each other properly.
That might be for the best. Scarlett would probably tell him he
was afraid – perhaps she was right?

Damon's mobile buzzed, signalling he'd received a text.
He'd messaged a business contact the evening before asking for
information on setting up a licence for a cider business – and it
looked like the man knew what he was talking about. At least
his visit here might result in an opportunity to partner with Leo.
It was clear the younger man was onto a good thing – and
Damon was oddly excited about helping him turn his hobby
into a thriving business. He remembered fixing the reindeer
with Leo the evening before – how good it had felt to build
rather than destroy. The world stretched before him and for the
first time in four years he was excited about it. He wasn't
focused on revenge or on how to rid himself of Willow's memories. He felt strangely at peace.

He plucked the pom-pom from the bed and put it into the
pocket of his coat. He might go outside for a walk, see if he
could find Leo, or maybe Holliday would be interested in taking
a stroll in the maze? They were going to go for that drive later
and perhaps he could persuade her to spend the night with him
again? He picked up Holliday's letter from the sideboard – he'd

slide it under her door on his way out. The time for secrets was over – he needed to move on with his life.

As Damon made his way onto the landing he heard voices at the front door. Had the new honeymooners Bonnibell mentioned just arrived? He smiled, thinking about the stunning entrance, glittering decorations around the hallway, the warm welcome they'd receive. Would they smell Bonnibell's biscuits baking, the cinnamon Innes put in the fire and instantly fall in love? Claus barked and Damon heard the dog sprint from the kitchen as he walked down the stairs – guessed the dog would be dressed in his red and white cape and would be part of the welcoming committee.

'This place is so pretty! I can't believe nothing's changed since I was last here,' a woman enthused, and Damon stopped on the stairs, felt nausea rise in his throat as his heart started to pound so violently he thought it might fly from his chest.

Because he recognised that voice, knew the exact pitch and timbre – had spent the last few years attempting to wipe it from his past, to cleanse everything about it from his world. He took another step, hoping he was wrong. But when he reached the bottom of the stairs, Damon saw Willow standing by the door and suddenly every memory he'd worked to forget, eliminate or destroy came flooding back.

His ex-wife looked good. She was just as beautiful, with that long dark hair that flowed around her shoulders and the same curvaceous body that drew attention wherever she went. Her brown eyes softened when she spotted Damon and he wondered in that moment if she'd expected to find him here. Had perhaps made a point of tracking him down.

'Damon,' she gushed, infusing his name with more emotion than he remembered hearing throughout their marriage. She'd always been just a little aloof with him, never comfortable with making him feel like he mattered. The man standing beside her looked surprised and he glanced between them, his brow knitting. He was the same height as Damon, with dark hair in an identical shade. His face was similar to Damon's too – in fact if he'd traced the angle of his own jawline he'd guess this man's would be an exact match. Had Willow somehow cloned him when they were married?

'It's so good to see you again,' Willow said, sliding her hand out of her companion's and stalking across the hallway.

Damon stood rooted to the spot as his stomach churned. He'd never expected to see his ex-wife again. Had expended so much time and energy eliminating her from his life. Now he realised it had just been a stupid dream. As she walked towards him every memory about her came flooding back. The way she moved as if music were playing in her head, the way she flicked her hair over her shoulder, that slight twitch at the edge of her mouth when she knew she was being watched.

Damon knew he should leave, but he was rooted to the spot, unable to move, imbued with all those same feelings of hurt, loneliness and hopelessness. Then Willow stopped in front of him, smiled and leaned over so she could kiss him on both cheeks. Placed a hand on his shoulder until the man standing beside Bonnibell cleared his throat. Damon remembered that, remembered how it had felt to be ignored by his wife while she'd lavished her attention on another man.

'I'm sorry,' Willow muttered hoarsely, spinning around so she could hold out her arms. 'Damon, I'd like you to meet my new husband, Scott Garcia. We're here for our honeymoon.' She turned back to gaze at Damon and her eyes were warm. In that moment he wondered if Willow had done this deliberately, had somehow connived to bring them together again. She hadn't got over him ending the relationship and had tried to get in touch with him over and over. But this was the first time she'd had any success.

Scott made a grunting sound as he came over to join them. He swung an arm protectively around his new wife's shoulders and squeezed. Willow grinned up at him, her face filled with admiration, and Damon felt annoyed. Perhaps his ex had hoped to draw out that response – she'd always enjoyed making Damon jealous, triggering his emotions whenever she got the chance. And he'd always given her exactly what she wanted because he'd been so blinded by love.

'It's nice to meet you,' Scott said gruffly. 'We really should check in, darling.' He kissed Willow's cheek and gave her a half smile. 'Bonnibell said they've got a big dinner planned tonight and a craft lesson later this afternoon if we fancy joining in.'

Willow looked conflicted. 'I'm not sure I'm up for the craft – I was never any good at making things, but I hope we'll see you at dinner later?' she asked Damon hopefully, giving him a small wave as she turned and walked back to the entrance, holding tightly onto Scott's hand. Then they both followed Connell as he carried the couple's luggage out of the door.

'Everything okay, hen?' Bonnibell whispered as soon as the couple had left.

Damon didn't respond, instead he stood rooted to the spot until all three of them were out of sight. He didn't know how he felt. He wasn't jealous and that meant his feelings for Willow had definitely gone. He wasn't angry with her either, but he definitely wasn't over what had happened. He did know he didn't want to stay at the resort to get tangled in whatever emotional web she was trying to weave. He didn't know for sure if this was a coincidence or if Willow had planned the meeting all along – and he wasn't going to play her games.

'I'm sorry, but I'm afraid I'm going to head back to London now,' Damon said to Bonnibell, his voice wooden. 'Something important just came up.'

Bonnibell glanced back to the entrance and jerked her chin. 'I see,' she said gruffly, reaching out to rub his shoulder. 'I know what just happened, hen; I know who that woman is. Innes found the picture of you both in one of the photo albums in the sitting room.' She looked at him sadly as he jerked his head, surprised. Had everyone seen it? Had Holliday? If she had, why hadn't she mentioned it? 'I remember you now,' Bonnibell continued. 'I remember when you came to stay before. I don't know what happened but I will say, please don't let anyone spoil Christmas Resort for you.' Her voice was low and Damon could tell she was feeling emotional because her eyes sparkled.

'It was a long time ago,' he deflected. 'But it's still a time I'd rather forget.' He glanced around the hallway at all the decorations and frowned. Somehow everything had dulled. In his mind, he could still see Willow standing by the door, and when he looked back at the kitchen and sitting room he could remember her in there too. Like all those bad memories had just been unburied and revived. Even the smells he'd started to love had turned fetid and he felt a little sick. 'I have to pack,' he said, his voice hoarse.

'If that's what you think is best.' Bonnibell looked sad, even the fur on the collar of her dress seemed lifeless now. 'I hope you'll come back?' she asked, looking deep into his eyes.

Damon cleared his throat. 'I don't know if I can,' he said quietly – probably the most truthful thing he had said since he'd arrived.

The older woman's eyes glittered. 'Then could you speak to Holliday before you leave? That girl's had enough heartache in her life. Make sure you let her down gently, please.' Then she turned and headed back towards the kitchen.

Damon was left staring at the stairs, wondering if he was doing the right thing, knowing he couldn't bring himself to do anything else.

23

DAMON

Damon stomped into his bedroom and immediately began to pack his things. He grabbed the hotel plans from the bed and quickly folded them, pulled all his clothes out of the wardrobe and stuffed them into his suitcase, jamming in everything he could. He didn't care if everything got creased, he just knew he had to get away. He wasn't ready to deal with the flood of memories – the ones of Willow cheating on him, of the way she'd made him feel. He'd been such an idiot – he thought he'd moved on, hoped in time he'd be ready to open his heart again. But he'd been wrong. One visit from his ex-wife and all those bad memories had come crashing back, which just went to prove you could never outrun your past. The only thing you could do was burn it to the ground.

He winced and threw his toiletries into his bag before turning around and checking the room to see if he'd forgotten anything. He thought about Holliday and pushed her from his mind. In a few hours he'd be back in London and this whole visit would be a bad dream. He'd forget all about Christmas Resort, just like he had before.

He picked up his coat and bag and opened the door, almost tripping over Frosty, who was waiting for him on the threshold. He held his breath as his nose began to itch and sidestepped the cat before marching towards the stairs, ignoring Holliday's door as he passed despite the ache in the pit of his stomach and yearning to see if she was there.

Bonnibell must have heard Damon on the stairs because she appeared from the kitchen as he marched to the front door.

'Leaving already, hen?' she asked, taking in his suitcase and laptop bag and shaking her head. 'Wait a minute,' she begged, then she dashed into the kitchen before returning with the emergency biscuit tin and offering it to him. 'You'll need this for your trip. I've filled it up. If you can wait a little longer, I'll make you a flask of coffee to take too?' She frowned and looked meaningfully at the window when Damon shook his head. 'It's snowing,' she warned. 'Maybe you should wait.'

He swallowed. 'I'm sorry but I really need to go.' He took the tin from her hands, wondering if he'd ever be able to taste mince pies without thinking of Bonnibell, hoping once he was back in London the memory would fizzle and disappear along with his heart.

The older woman blinked. 'It's been good to have you here, Damon – I really hope you'll come back. I realise the resort has mixed memories for you... but even if you decide not to invest, we'd love to see you again. You're part of our family now.' She gazed at him intently.

Damon stood rooted to the spot because the words touched him, even as he tried to freeze the ache in his chest.

'We've enjoyed having you here,' she said warmly.

'I don't know if I'll ever return,' Damon admitted as emotion clogged his throat. He knew he had to leave, it would be easier all round. But the tug in his heart was almost painful. 'I'll...' He waved the tin and shrugged when he ran out of words. He wasn't ready to express how he felt – wasn't sure if he'd know what to say. 'Thank you, for everything,' he said hoarsely.

As soon as he stepped onto the porch of Christmas Lodge he saw Holliday standing by his car. It was still parked beside Reindeer Retreat and he heaved his bags down the steps and steeled himself because he knew they had to talk. Knew he had to tell her he was leaving for London and had no intention of coming back. That he wasn't ready to have a relationship – might not ever be ready.

'Damon.' Willow suddenly appeared from the side of the lodge, blocking his path. It was as if she'd been waiting there, ready to ambush him.

What did she want? Damon considered walking around her, but instead put his suitcase in the snow. Perhaps it was finally time to have it out.

'Can we talk?' she asked, her beautiful face flushing.

'I don't think we have anything to say,' he said coldly.

'I do.' Willow looked at the ground, then flicked her hair over her shoulder before her chin rose again. But her expression was tinged with enough vulnerability to affect Damon and he swallowed.

'You need to be quick. I'm leaving,' he said. Out of the corner of his eye he saw Holliday still waiting beside his car a few metres ahead. She wouldn't be able to hear their conversation from where she was standing, but it must have bothered her because suddenly she unzipped her coat and plunged her hands into the pocket of her apron. Damon knew Holliday didn't know about his ex, so had no reason to feel insecure. But the suitcase by his feet had probably given away the fact that he planned to leave.

Willow sighed. 'It's good to see you,' she said, stepping closer, her dark eyes fixed on his. 'I hated how things ended between us and I've been wanting to explain...'

'By how things ended, you mean I found out you'd been cheating on me throughout our marriage?' he asked, bluntly.

Willow winced. 'I'm sorry.' She looked embarrassed. 'You have to know it had nothing to do with you.' She winced. 'I know I hurt you. But Scott's made me realise it was all about my own insecurities.'

'What does that even mean?' Damon asked, glancing at Holliday again. He tried to pick up his suitcase, realising he wasn't interested in explanations, but Willow put out a palm, encouraging him to stay.

'Please let me explain.' She swallowed. 'I've always been under confident.' She pulled a face. 'You know I didn't get on with my parents and I've never had many friends, I only cared about work.' She gulped as she looked up, her eyes glittering. 'When we got married I was so young. Completely obsessed with being needed.' She cleared her throat. 'You always knew exactly what you wanted. You were so much better at everything than me.'

Damon folded his arms. He'd once loved this woman with all his heart, she'd been everything to him. But he felt almost nothing now.

Willow sighed. 'I was so insecure I had affairs – maybe at first it was to get back at you because I didn't think you needed me, or maybe it was because it made me feel wanted.' She blinked. 'Only it didn't work.'

'Hang on.' Damon waved a hand as his brain caught up with her words. 'Are you telling me your affairs were *my* fault because I somehow made you feel like you weren't enough?'

'No!' She put her palms together and winced. 'I'm trying to tell you I'm sorry. I'm trying to make up for my mistakes. My relationship with Scott is so different.' She blinked. 'I'm a better person with him. I've had to come to terms with my need for attention. I've had to move past it. I just wanted to tell you that and to say I'm truly sorry for what I did.'

Damon narrowed his eyes. He knew he couldn't trust Willow. Was this just some weird way of getting his attention? 'And you're doing that on your honeymoon?' he asked incredulously. 'In the same place we stayed just before I found out you'd been cheating on me?' He cocked his head. 'Do you know how wrong that sounds?'

Willow winced, her pretty face bunching. 'I do. But I'm trying to have a different experience – a do-over, if you like,' she said earnestly. 'I've tried to go back to a lot of the places we used to go to see if I can rewrite the past, but none of them are around anymore. You know the restaurant you proposed to me in is a deli now?' She looked upset.

'Yes,' Damon snapped.

'This is the only place I found that hasn't changed.' Willow glanced around. Snow was still falling, and the thick flakes settled on her eyelashes so she had to swipe them off. 'I booked it months ago and when I heard recently that you were staying here too, I decided it was a kind of serendipity. Like it was meant to be.' Her eyes welled. 'I'm trying to redo the past, to see if I can do better. I know I can't make up for what I did to you, but I'm hoping my marriage to Scott will be different, that maybe I can be different too.'

Damon shook his head. This wasn't what he'd expected. 'If that's true then I wish you luck,' he said. 'I don't think I can forgive you if that's what you're asking and I hope we never see each other again.' He hesitated. 'But I will wish you a good life and I hope your marriage works out this time.' His eyes flickered left, towards the lodge where Scott was probably waiting for her now. 'I need to get back to London.' He picked up his bags, sidestepped Willow and started walking towards Holliday and his car.

His head was spinning. What had just happened? How had the woman he'd spent years hating changed so much? He couldn't process it. He only knew he had to get away or all the memories would become too much. He saw Holliday zip up her coat. Knew if he could get to the car, explain and then make it to the bottom of the driveway he'd be able to put Christmas Resort behind him and Holliday too. If the memories followed him home, he'd have to deal with that. He marched past her and opened the boot.

'You're leaving?' Holliday asked flatly, watching as Damon piled the laptop bag and suitcase inside and slammed the door. 'What happened to our drive?'

'I got an urgent call from work,' he lied without looking at her.

'Did it have something to do with your ex-wife?' Her voice was toneless and when Damon looked up, Holliday was staring at him.

'So Bonnibell told you about Willow?' he asked, his voice flat.

She shrugged. 'Not entirely. Innes found a photo of you both in one of the resort albums. It had your names on the back and Bonnibell remembered you.' She frowned. 'She said you both stayed at Christmas Resort before I started working here.' She swiped a hand across her cheek and Damon wondered if she was wiping away tears. Had to force himself not to comfort her. 'I told you about Adrian, why didn't you tell me about her?'

'Because Willow is in the past,' he bit back, feeling a stab of guilt when Holliday's face fell and she undid her coat and dipped her hands into the apron again.

'Then why are you leaving?' She stared pointedly at the car. 'Is it because you still have feelings for her?'

'Of course not!' Damon growled. 'I just don't want to be here now. There's so much I remember.' He frowned, glancing towards Reindeer Retreat. 'A lot of hurt.'

'A lot of things you haven't let go of?' Holliday asked bluntly, staring at him. Then her shoulders sagged. 'I understand that and I can't really blame you when I did exactly the same thing. Is Willow the reason why you wanted to build a hotel here?'

Damon stopped breathing. 'You knew about that? I don't understand.'

She sighed. 'Innes found the plans in your room soon after you arrived.'

'What?' Damon choked, stunned. 'How?'

Holliday winced. 'It was an accident, she wasn't looking, but they fell out of your wardrobe when she was cleaning your room.' She took a step closer and Damon wanted to step away but couldn't seem to move. 'She told Bonnibell and me and we decided to persuade you not to go ahead.'

'But how? You didn't talk to me.' His voice cracked.

'We thought it would be better if we showed you how wonderful the resort was. We hoped you'd fall in love with it and change your mind by yourself.' Holliday looked at the ground. 'I realise you might be upset...'

'But...' Damon hesitated, as he tried to unpick his jumbled thoughts. 'When did Innes find the plans, because as I recall, she didn't clean my cabin until the day Leo was working on the heating?' He was trying to unscramble the timeline because something wasn't adding up.

Holliday nodded. 'That's right, that's when she found them.'

'But...' Damon frowned. 'That was the day before I was supposed to be leaving for home... How did you know I'd still be here?' He put his hands on his hips. 'If the car had started I'd have left for London that morning, and I'd already put every-thing in motion to replace the resort. You wouldn't have had a chance to persuade me.'

Damon guessed what Holliday was going to say before she opened her mouth. It was in her eyes – the guilt, the knowledge that she'd done something wrong.

'Well...' She winced.

'There was nothing wrong with the car?' he said, fighting the waves of hurt, the sense of betrayal. If Holliday had lied about the car, then so had Bonnibell, Innes, Connell and Leo. Even the man from the garage who'd called him had lied.

'I'm sorry,' Holliday said, her cheeks colouring. 'Connell did something to the starter motor and Bonnibell talked to the garage, asked them to stall you for a while.'

'So where was the car?' he asked, scraping at the snow that had settled on his hair while they'd been talking.

'In a barn on the grounds.' Holliday cringed. 'It was only supposed to be for a few days, just to give you a chance to see what we really did. I know it was wrong but we wanted you to change your mind.'

Damon straightened, steeling his heart as everything fell into place. 'That means all that time we were together, all the things you said and did...' He breathed in, almost choking as the hurt slammed into him. If he thought Willow had turned him inside out with her lies, it was nothing compared to how he felt now. 'The knitting club, dancing, even when we were on the snowmobile.' He blinked. 'When we decorated the biscuits. When we...' His voice cracked. 'You were lying the whole time.'

'It wasn't like that.' Holliday reached out a hand but this time Damon stepped back. 'I was waiting for you to tell me about the hotel. When you didn't, I suppose I thought you must have changed your mind.' She pulled a face. 'I honestly didn't know about your wife until this morning.' She tried to reach for him again but Damon shook his head.

'You lied. I don't know what I'm supposed to think about that, how I'm supposed to react.' He looked at his surroundings and now instead of Willow, all he could think about was Holliday's betrayal. 'I don't want to be here.' Never would again. If his heart had been broken here once, it had been annihilated today.

Holliday blinked. 'But you were lying too,' she said, her

voice low. 'I'm not trying to excuse what I did but you didn't tell me about your plans for the resort, and you didn't tell me about your wife either – isn't that the same?'

Damon frowned. 'I didn't lie, I omitted,' he muttered, opening the car door. 'You didn't need to know about Willow and you didn't need to know about the hotel because I started to have second thoughts.'

'You did?' Holliday said, as the tension left her face. 'Please stay so we can talk,' she begged, pressing a hand against the car door, trying to close it again, but Damon shook his head.

'I want to leave,' he said coldly. 'Before you find some other way of keeping me here.'

'I wouldn't do that, Damon,' Holliday said, her eyes prickling.

'I don't know what you'd do,' Damon said, looking around. 'It's like nothing matters to you but the resort.' He slid into the driver's seat and put the biscuit tin Bonnibell had given him on the passenger side, feeling ill.

'That's not true. I know I hurt you,' Holliday said, her voice hushed as she leaned closer. 'I'm not trying to excuse what I did, and I'm sorry. But please don't go. If you spend your whole life avoiding your feelings you're going to spend it being unhappy. Look at me...' she said huskily, blinking away tears. 'It's been two years since Adrian died and it's only since you arrived, since the reindeer were damaged, that I've acknowledged what happened to him.' She took her hands out of her apron and rubbed them over her arms. 'I've been clinging onto the past – just like you – but that's over now. Please don't walk away from me because you're afraid. You matter to me.'

Damon shook his head and tried to shut the door again.

'You're running away.' Holliday looked around. 'We're all here for you, you're always going to be welcome – and I'll be waiting if you decide to return.'

Damon glanced around. Tried to remember how he'd felt

just a few hours before. He'd been falling in love with the resort, allowing himself to have feelings for Holliday. But he'd been hurt once and he wasn't ready to risk that again.

'I've made a mistake,' he said as he shut the door and started the car.

24

HOLLIDAY

The pain inside Holliday's stomach was climbing up her throat, threatening to choke her. She'd watched Damon's car disappear down the driveway, feeling like he was taking a piece of her too. But she knew she couldn't wait to see if he'd forgive her, knew it was up to her to save the resort.

'Where's Damon?' Bonnibell asked as soon as Holliday made her way into the kitchen. 'I saw you two talking a moment ago, I hoped you might persuade him not to leave.' She took in the snowstorm raging outside the kitchen window and pulled a face.

Tears pricked the edges of Holliday's eyes and she drew the letter from the pocket of her apron, the one Damon had pushed under her door. 'He's gone.' She forced the bubbles of emotion from her throat. 'I mentioned his wife and the hotel and he guessed we'd been lying to him about the car. He was really upset. But he was planning on leaving anyway.' She shut her eyes, trying to block out the memory, then opened them again, forcing herself to stay in control.

'I thought he'd understand we kept him here for the right reasons, but all he cared about was that we hadn't told him the truth.' A heavy tear rolled down Holliday's cheek. The relationship they'd started might be over, but she couldn't think about that now. If she did, she might break.

'Oh, hen.' Bonnibell moved around the breakfast bar so she could pull Holliday in for a tight hug. 'I'm sure when Damon's had a chance to think about things he'll realise it was done with the best of intentions. I'm sure he'll come around. Surely he'll be back – he's supposed to be buying the resort.' She looked worried.

'I don't know what he plans to do with it now.' Holliday swallowed.

'But there must be hope for the two of you?' Bonnibell looked upset.

Holliday shook her head. 'I think I've lost him. Then again, can you lose what you never really had? There was so much he didn't tell me, so much of himself he held back.' She looked up when Barney wandered into the kitchen.

The older man watched as Bonnibell drew away and Holliday wiped her cheeks as he moved closer to the breakfast bar. 'Everything okay?' He glanced between them.

'Mostly.' Bonnibell sighed.

The older man's bushy grey eyebrows wobbled. 'Mabel used to accuse me of being tone deaf, but even I'm not that hard of hearing. I know that's not true.' Barney pulled out a stool and carefully climbed on. 'The rest of my family are on a snowy adventure in the woods with Connell and Ross; I thought I'd stay inside and keep warm.' He faked a shiver then studied the two women when they didn't laugh. 'Are you going to tell me what's wrong?' he grumbled. 'Because I'm not leaving until you do.'

'You're going to want to have some sugar before we tell you.' Bonnibell slid a plate of mince pies towards Barney and he took one and bit into it without complaint. 'I think we need a new buyer for the resort, because it's possible someone might want to put a hotel here instead – which means nothing from the original would survive,' Bonnibell explained. She didn't mention Damon, perhaps because she was hoping he'd come to his senses, although every minute that passed made that less likely. Holliday knew he'd probably travelled a couple of miles outside of Christmas Village already. One look out of the window at the dark driveway told her he hadn't had a change of heart and turned around.

'That wouldn't be good,' Barney huffed, glancing around the kitchen. 'We can't let that happen. Where would all our memories go?' he asked anxiously. 'What are you going to do about it?'

Holliday sighed, then unfolded the letter and placed it on the table so she could study it. There was only one way to secure the future of the resort and her future too. If Damon was walking away, someone was going to have to step up. She was going to have to be brave – move on properly before it was too late.

'I'm going to buy it,' she said firmly.

She earned a sharp look from Bonnibell.

Barney looked surprised. 'But how could you possibly afford it?'

Holliday shrugged. 'I have a house in Cambridge and there are some people interested in owning it. They wrote me this.' She tapped a finger on the letter.

The older man pulled it towards him and started to read. 'That's a lot of money,' he murmured.

'It is, and they've promised a quick sale,' Holliday said.

'Oh, hen,' Bonnibell gasped. 'You shouldn't have to do that. I know how much that house means to you. I'm sure we can find another way...'

Holliday shook her head. 'The house in Cambridge means a lot but Adrian's not there anymore and it's time for me to let it go...' She looked around the kitchen, her eyes filling as she remembered decorating the biscuits with Damon last night. 'This is my home now. I'm finally ready to accept that and move on.' She blinked. 'Selling the house in Cambridge is the only way to ensure the resort is safe.'

'What about Damon?' Bonnibell asked as a new tear tracked down Holliday's cheek.

She shook her head. 'I don't know what he's going to do,' she whispered, looking around. 'I thought... after the last few days he'd started to love it here. I hoped this place meant something to him.' Hoped she had too.

'I'm sure it does,' Barney said, leaning over to grab another mince pie. 'But in my experience people can be stupid and they don't always realise what they've got until it's gone.' He pressed a hand to his chest. 'Just look at me. I needed a break here to remind me of a lot of things.'

Holliday nodded. 'I don't know if Damon's ready to realise anything. It's time for me to take control, to secure my own future. Even if I'm going to be alone.' She hesitated as a dark flood of emotions threatened to overwhelm her. 'I have to *do* something.' She looked at Bonnibell. 'What if Damon decides to get rid of the resort because of some bad memory or because of the way I've made him feel? I have to make sure he can't.'

The tension eased from her shoulders even as her heart felt like it was splitting in two. 'Do you think Mr Gray would be prepared to wait until the sale of my house goes through to get his money?' she asked Bonnibell. 'Will he let me buy the resort instead of Damon?'

The older woman shrugged. 'I don't know, but I'm happy to ask. If I tell him what would happen to the resort he might wait.' She hesitated. 'Hen, are you sure Damon is going to walk away? From what I've seen he's grown attached to Christmas Resort – and I think he's definitely started to fall for you.'

Holliday shook her head. 'I can't risk it.' But the idea of losing him had her insides crumbling.

Barney looked closely at the letter. 'That's a lot of money, as I said.' He sucked in a mouthful of air. 'But is it enough to buy the resort?'

Bonnibell skirted around the breakfast bar so she could peer over his shoulder. 'It's a sizeable chunk. It will buy most of the place outright and Connell and I can invest all our savings too. Between us we could secure it.' She winced. 'But, hen, the resort needs a lot of updating and repair – there's a lot that needs looking at if we're going to flourish and grow. Even if we both put all our money in, it won't be enough.'

Holliday's legs wobbled and she pulled up a bar stool. She'd just lost the man she'd started to care deeply for and now she was going to lose the resort too. She slowly crumpled the letter in her hands. It was hopeless.

Barney cleared his throat. 'You know Mabel and I put money away every month for a rainy day. But we never spent it.' He frowned. 'I never wanted to. I always thought we'd have so much time – and perhaps I was just too grumpy to admit doing something new would be fun.' His mouth pinched, the lines deepening at the edges. 'We loved taking our holidays here. It's a special place. I've realised just how special since I came back.'

He paused and sat straighter, his attention skirting the kitchen – then his face lit in a very un-Barney-like way. 'I want to put in the rest of the money.' He nodded as if he'd decided. 'I think it's what Mabel would have wanted.' His eyes sparkled as Holliday's eyes widened and she glanced at Bonnibell, who looked equally surprised.

'But I thought you didn't like it here,' Holliday said. 'I know you've started to enjoy some of the activities, but you've complained so much since you arrived. You always acted like you hated it.'

'No, that was just me being me.' Barney tugged at the sleeves of his shirt, looking embarrassed. 'Being here has brought back a lot of good memories. But it's held a mirror up to the way I've been dealing with things.' His shoulders heaved. 'I feel like I've got a bit of my wife back, the part I need to be a better version of me.' He gave them an apologetic smile. 'What Mabel would have called the nicer side.' He looked thoughtful. 'If I hadn't come to Christmas Resort, if it didn't exist anymore, I'm not sure I'd have been able to find that piece again. I'd hate the thought of anyone missing out on the same chance. But I suppose the real question is, are you happy for me to become a partner too?' He gazed at the two women, his expression anxious.

'We'd love it, hen.' Bonnibell reached over and rubbed the older man's shoulder and glanced across at Holliday who nodded too. 'So long as you're sure?'

'Of course I am,' Barney growled as his grin widened. 'It'll mean the family can have even more holidays here.'

Holliday and Bonnibell laughed.

'One of you get a pen and some paper, let's start making notes about what we need to do.' His face glowed. 'I vote we offer dancing lessons every day, fill the whole resort with pom-poms and offer gingerbread biscuits with every meal!'

'I think we can do that, hen,' Bonnibell giggled, grabbing a pad and pen from one of the kitchen drawers and sliding it across the breakfast bar to Barney.

Then the three of them put their heads together. Despite this new plan, Holliday glanced out the window, feeling sad. Because the driveway was still dark, and that meant Damon hadn't decided to return…

25

DAMON

Damon could hardly see. The roads were awful. Snow had been falling heavily since he'd left Christmas Village, almost like the weather was coming out in sympathy with his emotional state. The traffic on the motorway was crawling and at this speed he wouldn't be back in London for at least another seven hours. He slowed again as the car in front pulled to a stop and Damon saw a queue of headlights trailing into the distance and cut the engine. He was tired, upset and all he wanted to do was flop into one of the velvet chairs in Christmas Resort and eat a plateful of Bonnibell's mince pies. His stomach growled; he hadn't eaten since breakfast and was hungry.

Damon glanced at the gingerbread-man tin on the passenger seat. Maybe he should see what was inside. He'd been too devastated before by Holliday's confession and the news that she'd been lying to him. He thought about how she'd looked when he'd left, how upset she'd been, and his stomach churned. But he was doing the right thing. Seeing Willow and being blindsided by all those memories had made him realise he had to leave. But then finding out about the car, how everyone had conspired to make him stay, had made him certain he wasn't ready for a relationship, and he definitely wasn't ready to trust anyone again.

The traffic began to move and he started the engine, then frowned when his Jeep let out a pop and a loud bang before starting to shudder.

'Seriously?' Damon cursed as it began to whine too. 'Is this part of some cunning plan to get me back to Christmas Resort?' he complained, knowing he was being ridiculous. The steering wheel was wobbling now and he switched on the hazard lights, checking Google Maps on his phone, which told him he was just a few miles short of a service station. If he could get to it, he'd have a quick check of the car and hopefully find someone to tell him what was wrong and fix it. If no one could help he'd call a rescue service. If he'd done the same when he was at Christmas Resort, he'd have been home days ago. Then he'd never have fallen in love with the resort, never got close to Holliday. He winced, pushing the memories of her away.

Damon sighed and slowed as the car in front put on its brakes and then continued to stop and start for the next few miles. He felt like cheering when he finally pulled off the motorway into the service station and crept across the car park.

He spotted a space outside the hotel at the far end of the parking area and limped the Jeep to the small area in front. At least he'd made it this far. Hopefully the more miles he put between himself and Holliday, the better he'd start to feel. Shaking off the uncomfortable sense that he wouldn't, Damon got out and had a quick walk around to see if he could spot a garage or somewhere he might find a mechanic, but aside from a petrol station and large domed rest area where you could shop or get food, there was nothing.

Irritated, he called the car rescue service and discovered it could take up to five hours before anyone got to him. He wasn't the only person having a nightmare today, it seemed. On impulse, Damon wandered into the reception of the hotel and booked himself a room, then grabbed his laptop bag and the gingerbread-man-shaped tin from the car.

'Is there anywhere here I can buy food?' he asked the man working at the hotel counter because he couldn't face the walk to the rest area. He was directed to a couple of vending machines where he purchased coffee and a sandwich, before making his way to the double room. It was spacious with a king-sized bed, table, TV area and small bathroom and looked clean. The furniture was dark which made the room appear gloomy and Damon found himself imagining what it would look like with Christmas lights draped around the headboard and ceiling before he quickly shut down the thought.

The room was cold so he whacked up the heating. Then he gazed out of the window. Had the snow gotten worse? There was a thin layer in the car park now and at least a few inches on the roof of his car. He put his laptop bag on the table and set it up, then sipped his coffee and winced. It tasted bitter, like it had been made hours before and reheated. He ignored the sandwich, which he didn't fancy now, and opened the tin Bonnibell had given him. The smell wafted into the room, making his stomach grumble, and he let out a long contented sigh because it was filled with biscuits and mince pies.

'I'm going to miss these,' Damon muttered as he bit into a mince pie and hummed. The taste immediately reminded him of the resort, and his mind filled with Holliday and he almost smiled. Then he remembered she'd been lying to him. Everyone had.

'I'll get through this,' he promised, searching for his suitcase because suddenly he fancied a shower – then he realised he'd left it in the car. He shut his eyes and his head instantly filled with Holliday's face. Her expression when she'd caught him in the shower. When would he stop thinking about her? It had been so much easier to forget Willow. As soon as he'd discovered she'd been cheating, he'd focused on wiping her from existence. But he couldn't seem to do that with Holliday. Perhaps because he didn't want to imagine a world without her in it.

Damon slumped into the chair beside the window so he could watch the weather. He could see the edge of the motorway and all the cars creeping past. 'It's going to take hours to get out of here,' he muttered. 'Hours before I get home.' But what was waiting for him there?

Damon closed his eyes again, remembering his pretty bedroom at the resort, and his eyes shot open. He still felt cold, so put his hand on the radiator. It was pumping out heat so he'd have to be patient. He stuck his hands into the pockets of his coat, trying to warm them. That was when his fingers curled around something soft. Curious, Damon pulled out the gloves Holliday had knitted, and then the blue pom-pom he'd made in her craft class. He stared at it and swallowed. That colour was familiar and he squeezed it between his fingertips, trying to work out why. When he couldn't, Damon placed the pom-pom on the table, picked up his mobile, and called Scarlett.

'Have you come to a decision?' she asked immediately.

'About what?' Damon could still see the pom-pom from the corner of his eye so he shifted his chair until he was facing the opposite direction.

'Christmas Resort,' Scarlett said, in the tone Damon recognised. The one that said *you're an idiot*.

Damon thought back to this morning. To Willow's arrival and Holliday's revelations. If he razed the resort, would that mean he'd eradicate Holliday too? 'I had, but now I don't really know...' he murmured as his insides went cold.

'You don't sound sure, which is progress I suppose,' Scarlett said gently.

Damon moved his chair back again, drawn to the siren's call of the pom-pom. 'I don't know anything anymore,' he said as a car let off its horn in the car park.

'What's that noise?' Scarlett asked. 'It doesn't sound very Christmassy.'

'I'm in a hotel at a service station, part-way between Christmas Resort and London,' he admitted, peering out the window. 'My car's broken down; I'm waiting for a rescue service.'

'You've left the resort?' Scarlett asked slowly.

'Willow arrived,' he admitted.

'What?' she yelled.

'She was with her new husband. She apologised for the way she'd treated me but...'

'She's there on her honeymoon and she decided to talk to you?' Scarlett squeaked. 'She hasn't changed. Was it difficult to see her? It's no wonder you wanted to leave, but you can't blame that on the resort.'

'I didn't feel anything, but...' He stopped. He wasn't going to explain what had happened with Holliday. Wasn't sure he was ready to face it himself. 'It made me realise a few things.' He paused.

'What, that she was wrong for you all along?' Scarlett asked, dryly. 'That she cheated on you because she didn't feel like she was good enough?'

'You never told me you thought that,' Damon spluttered.

'I told you a thousand times.' His sister sighed. 'You just weren't ready to listen. I hope you're ready now?'

'For what?' Damon asked, frowning.

'To live your life,' Scarlett said, sounding frustrated. 'To let go of the past, and forget what happened with your ex who was never good enough for you anyway.' She cleared her throat. 'You're a grown man, Damon, a man who doesn't know how to let go. You're letting your past control you rather than the other way around. I've told you to walk away from what happened, I've told you you're an idiot.' She sighed. 'I thought you'd finally started to listen. You sounded confused but happier the last time we last spoke.'

Damon thought about Holliday, Leo, Bonnibell and Connell. 'I was,' he said, realising that was true. 'Only something happened when I was there.'

'What?' she asked gently. 'And are you sure you're not just using it as an excuse to walk away?'

Damon didn't want to explain. Perhaps because now there was distance between them he was starting to wonder if his sister was right. Sure, Holliday had conspired with the others to keep him at the resort, but had they been so wrong? Hadn't he lied about why he was there and wasn't that worse? His stomach pitched uncomfortably. 'Perhaps,' he admitted.

'You know I was googling Christmas Village last night and there's this large plot of land up for sale about five miles from the high street,' Scarlett said lightly. 'It's ripe for a building project and there are some amazing views of the valley in the photos. But do you want to hear the best news?'

'Tell me,' Damon said, picking up the pom-pom.

She laughed. 'No one's bought it yet.'

'So?' Damon asked, his lips curving because he could guess what she was going to say.

'It might make a good location for a new hotel.'

'You think?' He couldn't stop the smile from spreading.

'I thought I might drive up to Scotland to take a look,' she said gently. 'I've got this brother, you see.' Her voice was soft. 'He's a good man but he's a little lost.'

'He is?' Damon squeezed the pom-pom, feeling himself relax.

'He's spent the last four years trying to run from his feelings. He's an idiot of course but I don't hold it against him because his heart's in the right place. At least it could be if he'd just let himself feel something again.'

'What does he want to do, this brother of yours?' Damon

asked, getting up and pressing his nose against the window so he could stare outside. It was difficult to see through the blizzard but he could just detect some lights in the distance and if he squinted he could imagine it was the three reindeer perched on the hill, waiting to welcome visitors. Would Holliday welcome him if he went back now?

'He wants to build a hotel,' Scarlett continued, with a smile in her voice. 'The best and most amazing hotel in the whole of Scotland. He's had plans drawn up already, all the investors he could need – only I think he's gone a little off course. So I'd like to help him find his way to the right spot. I want him to find the perfect place to put it. A place with no memories attached, a clean slate, somewhere for him to start afresh.'

Damon felt himself deflate as he squeezed the pom-pom again, then as he held it up his body froze. Because suddenly he knew what it reminded him of. It was the same blue as Holliday's eyes.

'You can't live in the past forever, Damon. You're going to have to move on sometime.' Scarlett hesitated. 'Willow is either a chapter that has ended, or she's going to be the theme of your entire life. It's your choice. Are you going to let her define it?'

Damon looked at the pom-pom before putting it back in his pocket. 'I need to go,' he said firmly. 'I've got some shopping to do.'

'Why?' Scarlett sounded surprised.

'It's going to sound ridiculous, but I need some wool, scissors and a piece of card,' he murmured. 'Thank you.' He hesitated. 'For being the sister I need. Let me know when you're driving to Christmas Village because I'd like to take a look at that land too...'

As he hung up, he heard Scarlett cheer.

26

HOLLIDAY

Holliday wandered into the kitchen in search of coffee. She'd hardly slept, too caught up in thoughts of Damon and the fight they'd had. She'd considered calling him in the early hours, but a stiff pep talk with herself and a couple of Bonnibell's biscuits had made her put the mobile down. She wanted to see him again, but the decision had to be his.

'Morning, hen,' Bonnibell sang brightly as soon as she entered the kitchen, then she frowned as she studied Holliday's face. 'Didn't sleep?' She swept to the Aga and offered her a big mug of coffee and a cinnamon bun without waiting to find out. 'Why don't you take a walk after you've eaten?' she suggested softly. 'I'm sure things will look different after some fresh air.'

'Aren't we supposed to be making the guests their Christmas dinner today?' Holliday asked wearily – they always made a special festive feast on a Sunday but for the first time in two years she wished she could skip it.

'We've got all morning and you need to take care of yourself first.' Bonnibell stepped closer so she could give Holliday a quick hug. 'I almost forgot, I talked to Mr Gray first thing,' she said, pulling back. 'He was horrified when he heard about the plans for the hotel and he's happy to wait for the money to ensure the resort's safe. Connell's going to contact the bank about our savings tomorrow and Barney's already emailed me asking where to deposit his share – if we're lucky the sale will move quickly and we'll all be partners before the end of the month. If that's not a Christmas gift, I don't know what is.'

Holliday forced a smile. It was good news, but she knew it wouldn't fill the new gaping hole in her heart. It was one she'd learn to live with though – she was past avoiding her feelings and pretending everything was okay.

'I messaged the couple who want to buy The Ambles last night, too,' she said, folding her arms. It had been late, but they'd immediately texted back and the subsequent phone call with the delighted couple meant the wheels were already in motion for a quick sale. Holliday had spoken to Mr Hornbuckle this morning and he'd congratulated her on her decision, although there had been sadness there too – but she'd promised to visit him in Cambridge as soon as she could. There were things to sort at the house, things that were way overdue. But for the first time in two years, Holliday was ready to face them.

The door into the kitchen swung open and Leo and Mairi wandered inside. They were both wearing coats and the young man held a huge bouquet of red roses in his hand. 'Is Innes around?' Leo asked, eagerly searching the kitchen before his face fell.

'She's cleaning the sitting room, hen,' Bonnibell advised, fixing Mairi with a quizzical look.

'We have some things to say,' the older woman muttered, looking embarrassed.

'Apologies to make,' Leo added, looking at his mother and holding her eyes until her shoulders hunched.

'Then why don't you both take a seat? Holliday, could you pour three hot chocolates and serve some slices of Christmas cake, please?' She smiled, before heading from the room. Leo gulped and pulled out a chair at the breakfast bar. He put the flowers on the table and sat, fiddling with the buttons on his coat. He'd dressed up and looked nervous and unhappy, but when Bonnibell led Innes into the room his face lit up.

'It's so good to see you,' he gushed the moment his wife caught his eye. He jumped down from the chair and thrust the flowers into her arms. 'We're here to apologise.' He glanced at his mam who hadn't said a word.

'Are you?' Innes asked, her eyes scanning the older woman before they rested back on Leo. She looked tired too and Holliday suspected her friend hadn't slept much. She'd asked if Frosty could sleep with her again last night because she didn't want to be alone and the cat hadn't appeared until this morning.

Mairi frowned as her eyes tracked to her son and then back to Innes. She pulled a face and Holliday stopped breathing. Afraid whatever the older woman was about to say, she was going to make things worse. Instead Mairi's chest heaved and she nodded.

'I didn't sleep last night,' she said, her voice raspy. 'I've always believed a mam's job was to protect her child and make sure he's happy.' Her attention shifted to Leo who was watching her, his face pale. 'And for the first time since I became one, I recognised I've failed.'

'Why?' Innes asked Mairi as the rest of them looked on in shocked silence.

Mairi frowned. 'Because since you moved into the resort, he's been more miserable than I've ever seen him.' She sagged as if the admission had made her body melt into the chair. 'I know my son loves you.' She gulped, placing a hand to her neck as if she needed help easing out the words. 'It's all I ever wanted for him. To have someone who made him happy, to have a good life. I think I forgot that.' She squeezed her eyes shut and then opened them again. 'But when you came along and I saw how he felt, I was scared.' She paused, looking vulnerable. 'I wanted him to reject you. I wanted things to go back to the way they were.'

'Because?' Innes asked, drawing closer to Leo.

'I didn't want to be left behind,' Mairi admitted, looking up when Barney wandered into the kitchen too.

The older man took in everyone's serious expressions before he raised a bushy eyebrow and tracked to the Aga so he could pour himself a hot chocolate too. 'What's going on?' he asked after sipping from his mug.

'We're making up,' Innes said thoughtfully, her eyes fixed on Mairi.

'Because you may have had a small point, but don't let it go to your head,' the older woman grumbled at Barney.

Innes glanced between them both before shaking her head. 'I never wanted to take Leo from you.'

'I know,' Mairi whispered. 'And even if you had, I had no right to get between a man and his wife.' Her eyes shifted to her son and she frowned. 'He's a good lad.'

'Because of you,' Innes said firmly. 'I see you in him sometimes.'

'Aye?' Mairi looked at her, surprised, but there was hope in her expression now. Something Holliday hadn't seen before. 'When?'

'In his laugh,' Innes muttered.

'And isn't that ironic?' Beside the Aga, Barney cackled loudly.

'When he's kind to me, it reminds me of how you are with him.'

'You must hate me,' she said, her voice raw. 'I've been so awful to you.'

Innes sighed. 'If I did, it would be like rejecting a part of him.' She looked at Leo, her eyes full of love. 'I don't want to do that.'

'You're going to move into your own place,' Mairi said sadly.

'One day,' Leo admitted. 'I'm sorry, Mam, but it's going to happen eventually. I'm hoping to be able to get back to making that happen soon. Mr MacAndrew's going to help.'

At the mention of Damon, Holliday's insides shrank.

'Chicks fly the nest,' Bonnibell said gently. 'They're supposed to – it means you did everything right.'

Mairi hesitated before nodding. 'But where does that leave us now?'

'I'd say you need to apologise to the girl and start again,' Barney said and his cheeks went rosy when everyone turned to stare at him. 'I mean, that's something my Mabel would have said.'

'She was a wise woman,' Bonnibell admitted. 'You're starting to remind me of her.'

Barney's cheeks flushed and he gave her a delighted smile.

Then everyone turned to Mairi and for a moment Holliday wasn't sure what she'd do. They watched silently as she rose from the chair and walked until she was facing Innes.

'I'm sorry, lass,' she rasped. 'I didn't give you a chance and that wasn't fair. I picked at you because I was afraid of being lonely. You're a good woman and you make Leo happy. I hope you'll find it in your heart to let me make it up to you.' She swallowed again, visibly shaking.

Innes must have noticed because she handed Leo the flowers. Then she pulled the older woman into her arms. They stood for a moment, rocking silently from side to side, until Innes pulled away and everyone pretended not to notice Mairi wipe her eyes.

'Why don't you go and pack your things?' Bonnibell said kindly. 'I think you've both earned a day off.' The couple beamed at each other before skipping away, holding hands.

Mairi watched them until they disappeared from the kitchen and then she sighed and wandered back to the breakfast bar to sit.

Bonnibell wandered over to rub her shoulder. 'That was brave, hen.'

'I didn't realise I was making them both so unhappy,' the older woman admitted. 'I should have seen.'

'You have now,' Barney said, trying some of his new wisdom on for size again. 'Isn't that enough?'

'I suppose,' Mairi whispered, reaching out for her mug. 'But I'll be lonely when they're gone.'

Bonnibell and Barney exchanged meaningful looks, then the older woman caught Holliday's eye and, realising what she was asking, Holliday nodded.

Bonnibell turned to Mairi. 'We're looking to expand Christmas Resort in the new year and I expect we'll be looking for helpers when we do.'

'No one knits like you,' Holliday said.

Mairi jerked her chin, then gave them all a tentative smile.

It was still snowing when Holliday circled her usual walking route and pulled her coat tighter, looking up at the trees and hoping the fresh air and snow would make her feel better. After Leo, Mairi and Innes had left for home, Bonnibell had insisted Holliday take her morning stroll – encouraging her to take a quick walk around Christmas Maze. Bonnibell had said she wanted Holliday to start thinking about ways they might improve the experience, but she suspected the older woman was just trying to distract her from feeling sad about Damon.

In the distance, Holliday could just make out the three reindeer twinkling on the hill and her heart ached as she remembered Damon mending them with Leo and what had happened later that night. Would Damon be home by now? She checked her watch, realising he would have arrived hours ago. Was he still mad about her lying or would he have forgotten her already? How would he feel when he discovered Christmas Resort was no longer for sale?

A bell jingled ahead and Holliday tried to see through the sparkle of snowflakes, spotting a flash of red by the entrance of Christmas Maze before it disappeared. 'Frosty?' She picked up her pace. Her cat had a habit of sleeping in the branches of the maze, but it was cold and Connell had mentioned the weather might be getting worse so her pet would be better off in the lodge. As she drew closer she heard music playing and stopped in her tracks trying to identify the tune. Had Leo started the entertainment and forgotten to switch it off before leaving with Innes? She tentatively stepped inside the entrance and started to sing along with, 'All I want for Christmas is You'. It was one of her favourite songs, but today the chorus made her feel awful.

'Frosty?' she cooed again, moving further into the maze and spotting a trail of blue pom-poms hanging on the branches of the fir trees that lined the pathway. She gasped, stepping further inside. 'What?' Had the Bennetts or Bavestocks conspired to play a trick on her after the art class yesterday – if so, what did it mean?

She paused, taking a closer look at one of the pom-poms. It reminded her of the one Damon had made in the craft session and she plucked it from the tree and nuzzled it, feeling a little stupid when she realised it smelled like him. Irritated with herself, she shoved it into the pocket of her coat and continued to follow the trail, calling out for Frosty as she padded along the path, past the inflatable snowman, chimney and Father Christmas, remembering how she'd teased Damon about them when he'd arrived. She forced the memories away as she continued to pace. It would be a while before she wanted to enter the maze again. She wasn't going to ignore what had happened between them, but she needed time to come to terms with losing him, with losing what they might have become.

'Frosty?' Holliday called out again, shaking her head when

she turned a corner and saw a dozen more blue pom-poms hanging in the trees. Her cat suddenly popped out from between the branches, startling her. 'There you are,' she soothed, bending and attempting to scoop him up. But as soon as she reached down he scurried off along the trail. 'Frosty, it's cold,' she complained, standing up so she could follow.

The cat broke into a trot before turning another corner and Holliday picked up her pace. She saw the flash of his cape as he rounded the next junction and realised they were almost at the centre of the maze now. There were more blue pom-poms dangling on these trees too and Holliday pulled a face, confused. Would the answer to why they were here be waiting for her in the middle?

She followed the final bend and her heart stopped. Standing at the centre of the clearing, surrounded by a scatter of blue pom-poms, stood Damon.

Holliday gulped, feeling the blood seep from her cheeks. She blinked, afraid she might be imagining things. He was wearing a borrowed coat from the lodge, the snow boots he'd been given, and the hat, scarf and gloves she'd knitted.

'Holliday,' Damon said roughly, carefully avoiding Frosty who was ribboning between his ankles, so he could move closer to her.

'Why aren't you in London?' she asked, her voice hoarse.

He shrugged. 'Because I realised when I was halfway home that there's nothing for me there.'

'So you came back,' she said flatly, still not understanding, although the light in Damon's eyes was making her insides spin. 'Because you still want to buy the resort?'

He shook his head, his attention fixed on her face. 'Because I realised I was wrong.' He glanced around. 'About everything.'

'I'm going to buy Christmas Resort,' Holliday blurted. 'With Bonnibell, Connell and Barney. I'm sorry, I know it has bad memories for you, but I can't let you destroy it.' She paused as her heart thumped, waiting for his reaction. Would he be angry, would he leave?

Damon's lips curved. 'That's good,' he sighed. 'I'm glad.'

'You are?' Holliday said slowly.

He nodded. 'And I'm still going to build the hotel.'

'How?'

Damon took a step closer, dodging the pom-poms and Frosty again, who was now sitting on the ground and staring at him. 'Scarlett's found somewhere new to put it. I haven't been yet, but I've seen it online and it looks perfect.'

Holliday frowned. So he hadn't come back to her. He would still be miles away. 'Where?' she asked, expecting the worst.

'The land is about five miles from Christmas Village.' Holliday blinked, shocked. 'I'm not building it there to compete with the resort, I figure the hotel will complement it,' he explained, his expression serious as he held her gaze. 'The most important thing is I'm planning to stay,' he said. 'Move to Christmas Village. I'm going to give you time to forgive me, if you can.'

Holliday tried not to smile, but couldn't stop herself. 'Forgive you for what?' she asked softly.

He raised an eyebrow. 'For not trusting that you were right. For comparing you to Willow, for being afraid to take a chance – or, in Scarlett's words, for allowing my ex to define my entire life. You were right to keep me here.' He glanced around.

'Why?' Holliday asked softly.

'Because being at Christmas Resort taught me a lot about learning to live with my past and move on from it.' His eyes caught hers again and he tugged a blue pom-pom from his pocket and held it out. 'This is for you,' he said as she took it and crushed it in her palm.

'It was you?' She nodded at the carpet of pom-poms at their feet and the ones dangling from the trees.

He nodded. 'They're pieces of me,' he said, holding her gaze. 'I wanted to do something to prove I've changed – that I understand. I'll never be able to look at a pom-pom again without thinking of you, or this place.' He paused. 'Those are the kinds of memories I want to hold onto, not the bad ones. But if there are bad ones, I'm not going to hide from those either.'

Holliday stared at Damon for a moment, then she unzipped her coat and put a hand into her apron, before drawing out a red pom-pom and handing it to him. Damon took it and clutched it in his glove and she saw relief slide across his face, anticipated the slow smile before it came and felt it light a flame inside her when it did.

'I'd like to have the chance to make new memories with you too,' she said quietly. 'And this time I'll take the bad with the good, because you're right, life is a mixture of them both. It's how we learn what to be grateful for, what to cherish and hold onto – and what to move on from when it's time.'

She took a step closer and went onto her tiptoes so she could slowly press her lips to Damon's.

'Thank god,' she heard him mutter and felt him circle her with his arms as the kiss deepened.

Then he lifted her off her toes as their bodies pressed together and Holliday pushed the hood from his coat and burrowed her fingertips into the thick hair under his hat, smelled the familiar scent of linen again. She'd missed him. More than she'd expected considering it had barely been a day.

There was a sudden burst of activity behind them and a roar of loud applause and shouting. Holliday pulled away from Damon and, clutching him tightly, turned to see Bonnibell, Connell, Barney, Mairi, the Bennetts and the Bavestocks cheering.

'You knew?' Holliday asked as Damon set her on her feet.

'I called Bonnibell on my drive up,' Damon whispered into her ear, setting off a new wave of tingles down her neck. 'She told me she'd find a way to convince you to come to the maze. I was hoping you'd see the pom-poms and follow them.' He nodded at Frosty. 'I wasn't expecting the cat.'

'You're not sneezing,' Holliday marvelled.

Damon shrugged. 'Perhaps I'm getting used to him.'

'Were you waiting for long?' She gazed into his eyes.

He shrugged. 'I would have waited all day.'

'You must be freezing.'

He shook his head. 'I had my new snow boots, scarf, hat and gloves to keep me warm.' He grinned, then leaned down and caught her mouth again as everyone began to applaud.

They didn't even pull apart when Bonnibell shouted, 'There'll be hot chocolate and mince pies in the lodge when you're both ready, we'll see you inside—'

But Holliday could barely hear above the rush of blood in her ears, the loud pound of her heart as she turned to face Damon and felt him hug her closer as their kiss deepened and they lost themselves.

For the first time in two years, Holliday knew she was in exactly the right place, ready to remember and acknowledge her past, and excited to finally face a new future. Best of all, she'd found the perfect partner to share it with.

A LETTER FROM DONNA

I want to say a big thank you for choosing to read *Christmas Secrets in the Scottish Highlands*. If you enjoyed it, and want to keep up to date with all my latest releases, just sign up at the following link. Your email address will never be shared and you can unsubscribe at any time.

www.bookouture.com/donna-ashcroft

Christmas Secrets in the Scottish Highlands transported us back to gorgeous Christmas Village and the wonderfully festive Christmas Resort. I hope you enjoyed meeting all the new characters as well as some familiar faces from previous books.

Christmas Secrets in the Scottish Highlands dealt with the theme of memories and the way we choose to deal with them on a day-to-day basis. For Holliday, who chose to pretend her fiancé was still living in the house they shared after he passed, memories were something to avoid. For Damon, who wanted to eradicate any hint of the wife who'd cheated on him, they were something to destroy. For Barney and the Bennetts, who had recently lost their beloved Mabel, they were something to celebrate and acknowledge. Through the healing power of the resort – from Christmas Maze and moonlight sleigh rides, to festive dancing and pom-pom making – each of the characters learnt something important about themselves. It was an emotional Christmas journey and I hope it made you feel like you'd been given a mug of hot chocolate and one of Bonnibell's mince pies. (In other words, warm, and happy with a little buzz from the sugar.)

If it did and you enjoyed reading, it would be wonderful if you could please leave a short review. Not only do I want to know what you thought, it might encourage a new reader to pick up my book for the first time.

I really love hearing from my readers – so please say hi on my Facebook page, through Twitter, TikTok, Instagram or via my beautiful website.

Thanks,

Donna Ashcroft

www.donna-writes.co.uk

facebook.com/DonnaAshcroftAuthor

twitter.com/Donnashc

instagram.com/donnaashcroftauthor

tiktok.com/@donnashc

ACKNOWLEDGEMENTS

I think I've said this in my acknowledgements for a previous book, but anything important is worth saying at least twice, so... Books are the sum of many parts and the author is only one of them. I have a lot of people to thank, but one who deserves a special cheer is my partner Chris. He's incredibly patient (a must I think when you live with an author), happy to listen while I wax lyrical about my imaginary characters and worlds, he delivers copious mugs of coffee without complaint, and can often be seen building sheds, making dinner and mopping up tears when things aren't going so well. Oh, he also always reads my stories while I hop up and down beside him insisting he tell me EXACTLY which word, paragraph or line made him laugh – despite the fact that it drives him crazy. And he reads the final files looking for typos. So this is a huge thank you to him. For being there, supporting me and helping keep me sane on the journey.

I'm also going to say a special thank you to my best writing buddy Jules Wake who is not only an inspiration but helps me so much when I get stuck with my books, need a head-clearing walk, or someone to celebrate writing milestones with. I'm not really sure how I would do this job without her either. She's my writing rock. And another shout-out to my lovely editor Natasha Harding who has to put up with my regular bouts of self-doubt and proclamations that my book is rubbish – at least until I realise it isn't really. Thanks also to my gorgeous kids Erren and Charlie (just for being you): oh the material... To excellent friends/supporters Cindy L Spear, Jackie Campbell, Julie Anderson, Alison Phillips, Trish Osborne, Caroline Kelly, Amanda Baker, Mel and Rob Harrison, Claire Hornbuckle (yes, that's where Holliday's neighbour's name came from) and Danel Munday. There are of course many more so thank you to you too. I'm writing this in March and if you've supported me and I haven't said, I promise to do it next time.

As always, thanks to the fabulous team at Bookouture, including Natasha Harding, Lauren Morrissette, Melanie Price, Noelle Holten, Kim Nash, Jess Readett, Lauren Finger, Hannah Snetsinger, Natasha Hodgson, Rachel Rowlands, Peta Nightingale, Richard King and Saidah Graham. Thanks also to the other Bookouture authors for your support.

Thanks to all the amazing bloggers who turn up every time I have a cover reveal, need a review, or publication day support. I can't mention everyone (and apologies if I haven't mentioned you), but I will shout-out those who were part of my last Xmas blog tour: Open Book Posts, staceywh_17, iheartbooks1911, Page Turners, Captured on Film, This Hannah Reads, Robin Loves Reading, Sam's Fireside, Stardust Book Reviews and Splashes into Books. A HUGE thank you.

Thanks also to wonderful friends, NetGalley users and readers who buy and read my books, let me know they've enjoyed them, review, blog, share and cheer me on.

Thanks as always to my family: Dad, Mum, John, Peter, Christelle, Lucie, Mathis, Joseph, Lynda, Louis, Auntie Rita, Tina, Auntie Gillian, Tanya, James, Rosie, Ava, Philip, Sonia, Stephanie and Muriel.

Finally, to the readers who have been there with me throughout my journey – I honestly wouldn't be here without you. Xx

Printed in Great Britain
by Amazon